BURN THE SKY

Part 1: Hope

Lee and Amanda Breeze

Printed in Australia

First Printing: July 2021

Shawline Publishing Group Pty Ltd
www.shawlinepublishing.com.au

Paperback ISBN- 9781922594020

Ebook ISBN- 9781922594037

To Lee's Dad, Glyn Breeze. Your encouragement helped us to continue writing this story. You will always be missed, but never forgotten.

We would like to acknowledge Margaret Breeze for being our Number 1 proofreader.

To Vision Writers Group for helping with our early works.
And to fellow author Aiki Flintheart for supporting and encouraging us as burgeoning writers. She will be missed.

CONTENTS

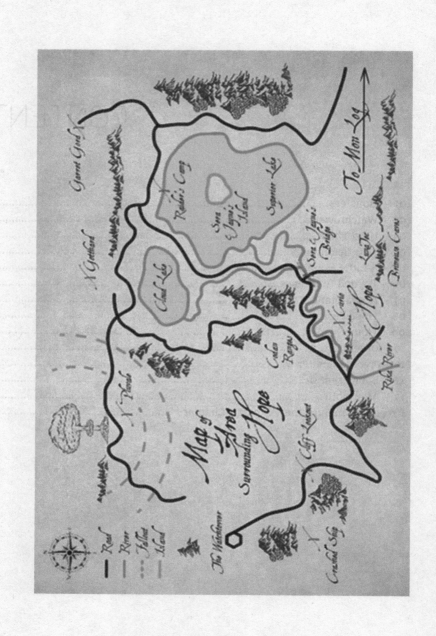

Glossary of Terms

The Decat (decimal) time system
Cycle (330 days with leap year every 6 cycles) : Year
Trey (110 days) : Month
Tendawn (10 days)(singular) or tendaws (plural) : Week
Day : Day (1 day)
Night : Night - nigh is used in conversation
Cendec (1/10 day) : Hour
Dec (1/1000 day) : Minutes
Midec : Seconds

Measurements
Decameta : Kilometre
Meta : Metre
Micrometa : Cm
Nanometa : Mm

Other terms used
Namedawn : the day of naming. can be before or after birth
Kahwah : coffee
Tei : tea

It's hard to believe such a large object as a planet is nothing but a grain of dirt in the galactic scheme of things. Jorth is home; a little green and blue rock, second from Aster, the sun, and one of nine planets in the Astersystem. I think about the people who taught me this and wish I could return to the childhood I can hardly remember.

I didn't know what clandestine operations or an apocalypse were, but within two tendaws of learning the words, I understood the pain of war. Approximately three billion Gaians, our people, lost their lives that day. Exposure and famine from the nuclear winter claimed more in the cycles that followed.

It doesn't matter who you are on the outside; in war, in death, we are all the same.

01 — Monsters

Excerpt from Book of the Progenitors:

Gotthard; the Saint who saved towns from creatures unseen. With his mighty power, he would instil fear into those who challenged him. His call of lightning would create destruction, annihilating all in a blink.

With the forces of evil advancing over the night-land, Gotthard, waking the town, he called on their strength in number to increase his authority. From the vantage of high ground, his arms held high, he focused his might against invisible foes, gathering his will, building the power from the depths of his chest. The sky rumbled and ignited with an intensifying darting light, and night turned to day.

Pointing both arms as a weapon towards the army of the damned, the sky unloaded its electric bolt of death. In the moments after, a plume of deviant energies reached for the heavens, and the world became engulfed in an unnatural shadow as souls of the wicked returned to their realm. Those touched by the unnamed lost their sight; a white shadow covered their eyes.

Our Saint and saviour had us not return there for two nights for fear of our health. Once we returned, the land was dead, burned, and the only sign of the marching enemy stood a crater, slowly filling from a stream.

New Calendar–NC00

My name is Jayne. I'm seven cycles old, and I don't think I'll make it to eight. Right now, I hide where all my nightmares and monsters bury themselves when they aren't tormenting me.

Nothing changes when I open my eyes, although they now burn like I've been rubbing them with grit paper. I would cry if I could, but I have no more tears left to give.

Everything around me is black, and the metal springs of my bed above still press down, squashing my hip in place. My head hurts from all the crying, my throat burns, and I can't smell anything anymore.

All those nights my parents had looked under my bed to scare the monsters away. Now I hide with them. Nothing is scarier than the monsters out there. Intent on eating everything, they rip the house apart, and the noise is so deafening, I have to cover my ears.

There's so much smoke, it's making me cough. I pull my once multicoloured patchwork blanket to the floor, but it doesn't help, so I bury my head in the neck of my dirty t-shirt and try to wish the smoke away.

I'm scared and alone. Maybe it's just a nightmare from one of Dad's stories in that Progenitor book. I just want Mum to tell me off for having a dirty floor, or dad to come in, scoop me up into a warm hug and tell me everything is going to be okay.

The smoke thickens, filling my head, and the world spins...

Dad kneels on the grass and places his hands on my shoulders. 'Now Jayne,' he says, with a sparkle in his eyes, 'you be good for Amity, okay?'
I give a sad nod.

'When your mum and baby brother are fit to leave the hospital, we'll come home.' He scruffs up my ginger hair with his hand as I do the same with his, and he pulls me into a big hug.

'I love you, Jayne,' he adds, kissing me on the forehead. *'Be back soon.'*

'Can't wait to see you.'

'Not if your eyes are closed,' he replies, then stands and heads for the car.

Mum sits in the passenger seat, looking as though she needs to go to the toilet or has eaten something bad. She still leans out the window, her long ash blonde hair flicking in the breeze, and blows me a kiss. 'I love you, Jayne. Hug you soon.'

They both wave from their windows until the large, blue bubble-shaped car disappears around the bend.

Footsteps!

Something's in my room, making the floorboards creak. Afraid the monsters have come to get me, I try to move further to the wall, but I'm still trapped. The pain's gone, and I can't feel anything below my hips. My eyes sting, but I force them open to search for the source of the noise.

Although it's brighter outside my blanket curtain, all I can make out are dancing shadows between the smoke and the grit.

A brick crashes to the floor, then another and another. Gradually, the bedsprings lift away and my legs go fizzy, like someone's pricking me with pins. The pain comes back worse than before and I try to scream, but nothing comes out.

The sound of bricks crashing to the floor stops, and the floorboards creak some more. Whoever or whatever's moving out there, the rug is muffling its sounds, but I know they're looking for me, so I wait with heart pounding in my throat for them to find me.

A big dusty boot appears in a gap of the blanket, followed by a knee.

As though wanting to escape, my heart pounds harder, and I'm afraid whoever is out there will hear it.

'Don't be scared, I'm here to help you,' a muffled woman's voice says as she pulls back my blanket curtain.

All I see is a mask with a big round thing where her nose should be. It should scare me, but I'm too tired and filled with pain to care.

There is something strangely calming about her face peering back at me through the mask. In the world of black and grey, no other colour exists except for her beautiful emerald green eyes, gleaming with a soft look of concern and familiarity.

Reaching out a gloved hand, she says, 'you'll be safe. I promise.'

'Never trust strangers,' I can almost hear mum say, and I retreat inside my dirty top again.

But I can't stay here.

'I know what you're going through,' the stranger says in a gentle voice. 'But it's not safe for you to stay here.'

Eventually, I poke my head out of my blackened top to peer at the stranger, and find my room smashed to pieces. The stranger is right, my safe place isn't safe anymore.

Is she a friend of mum and dads? Do I know her?

Her hands reach for me again, and this time I let her cradle me under my armpits and drag me out.

For the first time since crawling under the bed, I squint through painful eyes at the missing roof and the angry red clouds swirling overhead, where strange bolts of lightning dart between them.

The woman rests me against the remains of my shattered wardrobe.

'Keep your eyes closed,' she says gently. 'I'm just going to wipe your face. This may sting a bit.'

The woman rustles with something, then smothers my face with a wet cloth, making me jerk my head away. 'I did warn you,' she says. Then something soft touches my forehead and chin.

'You can open your eyes now if you like,' she says when she's done.

Stinging pain grinds away at my eyes, making it hard to open them, but when I do, a window covers my face, and I have one of those big round things at my nose.

She packs towels around the edges and pulls the straps tighter.

'Are you ready to go?' she asks, trying to lift me to my feet.

Everything goes white and my head swirls again...

'Amity, watch me, you have to watch me,' I call out.

My next-door neighbour sits in a chair on our front verandah, reading her book and pretending to supervise me while I attempt to do cartwheels. She flicks back her long brown hair. 'What is it, Jayne?' she huffs, peering over her thick-rimmed glasses with disinterest.

'Look what I can do!' I yell, lining up my trick. My feet flail through the air, and I collapse on my head.

Amity chuckles before returning to her book.

Fresh afternoon air creeps up the hill towards the mountains not far away, while shadows from the neighbouring houses continue to grow longer. The sun gets ever closer to the mountain. But I want to keep playing, stretching out the afternoon for as long as I can.

Eventually, the sun goes to its hiding place for the night, taking the light and warmth with it. Amity closes her book. 'Jayne, time to come inside,' she calls.

'Can't I play a little longer?'

In the arms of the stranger, I snatch at the vest of her green, grey and black patched uniform for something to grab hold of.

'Nice to see you again,' she says. 'How are you doing?'

I reply with a cautious nod, cling tight, and she carries me to the door.

When I peek over her shoulder, smashed bricks and splintered timber cover my bedroom floor, and I can't imagine a trey's worth of clothes and toys ever making this much mess.

The hallway walls seem to have held up better, and passing the newly painted room for my brother, then my parents' room, entire sections of the house are missing. Crumbled walls reveal piles of outdoor furniture, trees and play equipment burning in the park beyond, shadowed by the wicked storm above.

More rubbish covers the lounge room floor. Everything is out of place, burnt or smoking.

The green-eyed woman kicks a footstool upright and sits me down. 'Stay here,' she says before walking off toward a pile of bricks and other things heaped where the front door should be.

There, amongst the rubble, a blackened arm unfolds from the pile.

Like a charred branch from one of Dad's bonfires, it reaches out for the stranger.

What appears to be a burnt face with singed hair stares up with white eyes.

At first, I don't recognise the owner of the melted face, but that's where I left Amity.

What happened to her?

The stranger crouches, leaning in close to Amity, and seems to say something to her.

As if by permission, the arm falls, relaxing in the rubble. I can almost hear the woman crying while she pulls a throw rug from the battered green couch and lays it over Amity. Then slowly, she stands. 'I'm sorry,' she says, returning to pick me up. 'I can't do anything for her. We have to go.'

The stranger holds me firmer, squeezing out a tearless whimper as she carries me away from my broken home and into the street.

Out here, there's no sun, only fire raging through the houses downhill, making it look like sunrise.

We scurry through the street, around fallen light poles, trees, and bits of houses.

The neighbourhood seems like another world I no longer recognise. All that's left of the local shops is a hollowed-out shell of a building and a car park littered with burning cars. One building is all that stands of my school, the rest lies flattened over the playground.

What happened to everyone? Where are Mum and Dad? I want my mum and dad.

Without stopping, the stranger carries me up the hill away from the school, past the nature strip where flattened trees burn. As we near the top, the trees thin out, and the roof of a truck emerges. It's painted in the same green, grey and black as the stranger wears. Its tyres are massive, taller than me, and it has a box on the back where passengers sit. I've seen these trucks before, moving soldiers around—I never thought I'd ever ride in one.

The back door opens when we get closer, and a man dressed in a similar uniform and mask as the stranger's stoops in the doorway, stretches his arms out to me and signals for her to lift me to him.

If I hadn't been clinging to her vest like my life depended on it, she would have given me away. My heart pounds as hard as it did under the bed, and I squeal in resistance.

She won't hand me away that easily.

'All right, all right,' she says, positioning me so I can see her eyes. 'I'm coming with you, but I have to put you in the truck first.'

I don't know why, but her words are calming, and I let go, allowing the soldier to pull me up into the box. Bathed in red light, it makes the back of the truck seem like Dad's photo studio. I always found it scary in there. Like a frightened animal, I dart across the wooden bench to the opposite corner and bury my head between my knees.

'Lieutenant, welcome back,' the man says, helping my friend up and closing the door.

So that's her name. Lou Tenant.

Lou Tenant and the other soldier crouch in the low space, talking. 'What's the situation?' she asks the man.

'The fires are burning through the town and up the hill. We should move on.'

'We've got a few decs. Let me look after her first,' Lou says, nodding to me.

He places his right fist to his left shoulder, and she does the same before taking a seat beside me.

'How are you doing there?' Lou asks with a soft voice, pulling a shiny blanket from under the bench and draping it around my shoulders. 'You're so brave. You're doing really well.' She hands me a clear bottle of white liquid, like milk, removes the cap and a straw pops up. The drink has a strange, sweet smell, but it's not milk.

Lou removes my mask so I can drink, and I suck on the straw like I hadn't had anything to drink for days.

'Go easy,' she says, 'this will make you sick, so spit into...'

Too late. Good thing Lou has a bucket.

Not only does it taste disgusting, it comes up like grey sludge, and it burns and scratches all the way from my stomach to my teeth. Throwing up rocks would have been easier.

'I'm sorry about that, darling, but we needed to get that horrible stuff out of you,' she says. 'After all that, you should feel better soon.'

Once I'm done, Lou bangs on the wall, and the truck lurches forward.

To where? I have no idea.

Through the window in the back door, past the two strangers with their masks and lace-up boots, the world I know burns. As we drive away from the monsters and their flames, I clutch hold of the weird shiny blanket, the only thing of comfort I have, and take a last glimpse of the place I called home.

'You've already played longer than you should have,' Amity says, preparing to go inside.

With reluctance, I turn my back on the road and head towards the front steps. Behind me, the evening sky lights up in a bright flash. It's so bright, I see green fairies dance in the corner of my eye.

Amity and I freeze, then turn to face where the light had come from. Above the mountain, fluffy white clouds clear like they've been swept away, only to be replaced by one enormous tree-shaped cloud that looks like a grey tangled ball of lightning and fire. It balloons into the sky, getting bigger and bigger as a dust cloud boils out from its sides and rolls down the mountain towards us. That's when the ground shakes with a terrifying boom that steals the sound from my scream.

'Jayne,' Amity's voice quivers with fear, calling me in closer, 'we have to get inside.'

'Amity, what is that?' I cry, running over to bury my head in her waist. With her clothing muffling my voice, I whimper, 'I'm scared.'

'We've got to get inside... now!' Amity yells, turning and pushing me towards the open front door.

With my head buried and eyes closed, I see blurred light through Amity's body. She screams.

Another blast, more terrifying than the last, comes from the mountain, like a million thunderbolts striking all at once.

It shakes the world and rattles my bones as though an invisible herd of large animals are stampeding through the street.

A blast of scorching hot wind hits us. It burns my arms and throws us through the front door like dolls.

The monsters are loose, and they're eating us.

Our truck screeches to a stop, waking me with a startle. I remember putting my head down, but that's all.

Lou's hand reacts to my movement, holding my shoulder down and rubbing it the way Mum used to when I'm upset.

'We're here,' she says gently when I lift my head from her lap.

I thought it was just a nightmare, but upon waking, everything that had happened comes flooding back.

How am I still alive?

Lou checks my mask, and the soldier opens the back door to help us down. I don't know how long it's been, but after having slept, I feel a little better. At least my feet are on solid ground.

The grown-ups make their funny hand signals again, and the truck drives away, leaving the two of us alone on a dirt track in what seems like the middle of nowhere. The track leads through an eerie green forest. Eerie because, unlike everywhere else, it's not burned or destroyed. Instead, the lush forest surrounds us, covering the mountainside as far as I can see, making it seem like the last few cendecs *were* just a nightmare.

'Well, look at all that green. Isn't it beautiful?' Lou says, standing close beside me.

Coughing into the mask, I try to speak, but the pain stops the sound from coming out.

'Oh dear,' Lou says, 'let's get inside so we can remove these horrible masks and get you fixed up.'

Inside? Where is inside? It's just trees, track and mountain.

Lou clutches my hand, guiding me to a bare rock face, and pats the surface for something unseen. Her hand grasps what looks like rock, but moves like a curtain, and pushes it aside. Where there was solid rock now is the open mouth of a dimly lit cave. She tries to pull me towards it, but I'm mesmerised, unable to believe what I just saw. 'It's okay,' she says, waving her hand through the mountain-mimicking curtain. 'See, it's just camouflage. It mixes light to make it look like the surrounding environment. It's safe, I promise.'

The material ripples its surroundings, and when I touch it, it copies images of my hand across the surface.

After playing with the images for a moment, Lou leads me into the cave opening, and I hold my breath while entering the unknown.

Just inside the cave's entrance, the walls are all gouged and rough, like someone has chipped them away with a large fork. As we move deeper into the cave, my eyes adjust to the dim light coming from lamps hanging from big wooden beams holding up the ceiling. Soon, the passage opens up into a cavern with natural walls of uncarved stone, which bends off to the right just up ahead.

There, two people dressed head to toe in white baggy outfits and masks meet us. One of them carries a big black case.

They help my new friend shake out her dusty-brownish hair and assist her into a noisy white plastic garbage bag with arms and legs.

With plastic now covering her from head to toe, I can't help but point and give off a silent chuckle when Lou kneels before me, like a garbage bag monster. It's the first time I get to see her face without the mask. Bright emerald eyes shine like pretty jewels set against hard-worn, soot-covered skin. Even through all this, she's smiling at me. *Why?*

'Now it's your turn,' she says.

One of the white-clothed people dusts out my hair and removes my mask. 'Can you tell me your name, darling?' A woman's voice asks from behind a white mask that covers just her nose and mouth.

I try to tell her, but my voice only comes out as a painful whisper. 'Jayne, with a y,' I cough.

'Nice to meet you, Jayne, with a y,' the woman replies. She then looks up at her friend. 'Can you get out the Rad unit and check her out?'

'Yes, ma'am,' a male voice says.

The man opens the case and pulls out a black box that makes strange screeching and clicking noises when he waves it in front of me, but it squeals louder when he points it at Lou. 'The girl seems okay,' he says, 'but... I think you should see the doctor, Lou Tenant.'

'I'll be fine,' she says to him. 'Just make sure the girl's okay.' She then kneels in front of me again. 'So, Jayne, that's a lovely name. It suits you. Let's get you checked in and looked over by the doctor. You were out there for quite a long time.'

As the woman in white helps me into one of those enormous white garbage bag things, the man with the noisy box interrupts. 'Excuse me, Lou Tenant,' he says in a low voice. 'Can I speak to you for a moment?'

Lou replies, 'can it wait?'

'No, this is important...'

'Okay, then make it quick,' she says, standing and following the man in white, the plastic of her outfit rustling as she walks.

I shrug my shoulders and fake attempts to be helpful while trying to listen to the private conversation between Lou and the man.

'Hi Jayne, how you doing there?' the woman asks. 'You've been such a brave girl...'

Between the woman talking and the other noises of the cave, I get only bits and pieces of the conversation. '... high... fatal... doctor... treatment.'

'I will, in a moment,' Lou says, brushing him off. 'I'm fine for now. Are we done here?'

'Yes... but–' he insists.

'Good.'

'Well,' says the woman taping up my baggy plastic coveralls, 'you're good to go.'

'Follow me then,' the man says, leading us down the hallway.

Though they taped my coveralls to stop them from dragging on the ground, it still doesn't make it any easier to walk. We follow the white-clothed people along another rough-carved tunnel until we come to a section that widens out, where the stone turns into grey-painted concrete walls. Brighter lights up ahead reveal a small room where a large man wearing round glasses, a fishing hat and overalls sits behind a tiny table with thin metal legs. It seems he could use a larger chair as his bulk overhangs either side of it.

Three other people; two men and a woman, all holding guns, stand around him. They aren't wearing suits like the other two people, and they don't seem like soldiers either, just regular people in ordinary clothing, with guns. The only other notable things in the room are four large grey crates and a single metal door with a big wheel at its centre, which appears to be the only other way out.

The man at the table sits up when the two of us approach. His movement inadvertently knocks the table, spilling water from his mug, narrowly missing a book that lies open in front of him. He rests a scribe in its spine and glares at us over his glasses. 'Ahh, good to see you again, Lou Tenant Doe.'

So that's her last name? Doe?

'Remy, you're looking well. Have you lost weight?'

'Yer, a little,' he says without much emotion.

'How long's it been?'

'Must be five cycles now.'

'And Fayanna?'

The focus of his attention changes from Lou to the new puddle of water on the table. 'I was fishing with mates at Cloud lake not far from here when... well,' he recalls sadly.

'I'm sorry to hear that, Remy...' she says with a sad fondness, 'she was a good friend.'

Remy swallows with obvious discomfort, clears his throat and changes the subject. 'So, who is this darling you've brought with you?'

'Her name is Jayne. J-A-Y-N-E,' she says, glancing down at me.

He pushes his glasses in place with a finger, picks up his scribe, writes my name in his book, and then pulls his glasses down again to get a better look. 'Hello there, Jayne,' he says. 'Welcome to Gotthard.'

Lou questions, 'whatever happened to "The Sanctuary"?'

'Mapp changed it.'

'Of course she did. But Gotthard? Really?'

'That's the name of a Progenitor.'

'Thanks, Remy, I know that. I have read the *Book of the Progenitors*.'

He shrugs, 'she wanted something more *"spiritually significant."* Her words, not mine.'

'Ugh,' Lou huffs, 'and you all went along with it. I'm going to have to have a word to her.'

'Jayne... do you have a last name?' he asks, shifting his attention to me.

Embarrassed and scared, I hide behind Lou, gripping her hand.

'We have to leave Jayne's details off the records,' Lou says with a gentle tone, but also making it sound like an order.

Remy gives her a puzzled look. 'Why the secrecy?'

'People are looking for her.'

'And so is the case with all the children. Parents, guardians, extended family...'

'Please, Remy, I can't explain it now. Just use my last name, okay?'

Remy raises an eyebrow. 'Are you sure?'

'Just do it,' she replies flatly.

'Okay, *"Doe"* it is then.' He sighs and makes the addition to his book.

'Well,' he says, returning the scribe to its crease, 'it's lovely to meet you, Miss Jayne Doe. These nice people will take you to see the doctor now, get you checked out and settle you in. Hopefully, I'll see you again soon.'

At that moment, the man in the white suit steps forward and whispers in Lou's ear. 'We have to go.' I hear him say.

'Okay,' she replies, 'just give me a dec.'

He nods, then proceeds to the big metal door, turning the wheel at its centre to open it.

Lou steps back and crouches just out of arm's reach. 'Jayne,' she says, 'I have to leave you now, but you will be safe with Remy and the people here. They will take care of you.'

'No!' I squeal, attempting to throw myself in her arms, but one of the suited strangers holds me back.

Why can't I touch her now?

'I'm sorry, Jayne, but it has to be this way. You'll be safe here, I promise. You'll have an education and make new friends. Everything will be okay. Just wait and see.'

Only a whimper from my raw throat comes out, while a single tear rolls down my dry cheek. I silently plead in a desperate attempt to make my only friend; the person who cared enough to save my life, stay.

'It's okay,' Lou says, trying to comfort me.

When she stands, my knees wobble, and to stop her from leaving, I try to say, *I don't want strangers, I want to stay with you*, but the words come out as a rough crackle.

Lou turns and leaves through the metal door without looking back.

Fearful I'll never see her again, I run after her.

Remy calls out my name from the opening distance.

Beyond the door, Lou continues to stride down the hallway.

With every fibre of my being, I try to catch her.

Just as I run through the open door, a large woman appears in the tunnel, wraps a thick arm around my waist, and my feet leave the ground.

Wrenched backwards, I strain to reach for Lou, but sorrow replaces hope when she disappears around a corner.

'Ahh, Administrator Mapp,' Remy says, 'you caught her.'

'Remy. Who's this I'm holding?'

The woman sets me down, pudgy nose crinkling, giving me the impression she's looking at an insect, then her face cracks into a sickly smile. 'She's a dirty one, I'll give you that. Never mind, we'll have you cleaned up in no time.'

With a click of Administrator Mapp's fingers, the white-suited woman pushes me through the big metal door, hustling me down a corridor like I'm in a race.

The concrete tunnel beyond leads to a hallway painted in an ugly yellow-grey colour, lined with closed doors.

Further along the corridor, a single door is open, and I'm rushed through it into a plain room with Mapp trailing behind.

I'm led around an evil-looking metal table in the centre of the room to a shower where the woman turns on the tap. Without testing the temperature, she thrusts me under, clothing and all.

She tears away the plastic coveralls, and the freezing cold water soaks through to my skin, stealing precious air from my lungs. I squeal, but she holds me under, making sure all the dirt washes away.

While I wrestle against the hands that hold me, Mapp sits on a bed in the opposite corner, watching from a safe distance with that sickly sweet smile still on her face. 'Don't be such a baby,' she says above the sound of the rushing water and my gasps for air.

'I'm sorry,' the voice behind the mask says, 'the water has to be cold.'

It's cold, alright. If it were any colder, it'd come out as ice.

When things couldn't possibly get any worse, she pulls out a pair of scissors. 'Stay still,' she says. 'I don't want to snip off anything that's supposed to be attached.'

Shreds of my favourite overalls—the ones Dad bought me for my namedawn—and clumps of my long red hair fall to the floor as the woman cuts them away, forming a disgusting muddy heap at my feet. They may as well be washing me down the drain too, because that's where my life's going, not that anyone seems to care. With my clothes and hair gone, I have nothing left.

'Clean as she's gonna get,' the lady in the white suit says, turning the water off and scooping my life into a thick plastic garbage bag while I stand there, clutching my arms to my chest, dripping, naked and shivering.

Mapp dismisses the suited woman and throws a towel at me. 'Dry yourself off child, there are clothes here on the bed. The doctor will join you in five decs.'

A pink dress and pretty, strappy shoes. Two things I hate wearing the most. Give me pants and boots, and I'll keep up with the boys in the mud. The dress smells like the stuff Mum washed the floors with.

The door opens just as I finish dressing.

That wasn't five decs.

An overweight, balding man with a doctor's bag, a cane and sweat flowing down his face barges into the room, his white coat looking as grubby as him. When the door doesn't close, he kicks it with his heel, then pulls a cloth from his pocket to dab his forehead. Limping the short distance to the table, he grunts something about the heat and walking.

'Come child,' he says, in a gruff accent that's hard to understand. He pats the black surface of the table like he beckons a trained animal. 'Let me have a look at you.'

Unsure about him, I hold back.

'Quickly now, I haven't got all day.'

Reluctantly, I emerge from my safe distance to sit on the table beside him. This close, his foul smell makes me feel sick.

Maybe he's the one who needs a shower? He stinks like he hasn't bathed in a trey.

He drops his bag on the table beside me and rummages around inside, pulling out a stethoscope, which he puts around his neck, and a head mirror. Light reflected off the mirror blinds me while he fixes it in place on his glistening forehead, and I see dancing green fairies again.

'Now, let's look at you,' he says, reaching for me with both hands.

With the balled-up sweat-cloth still clutched in his grubby palm, I pull away in disgust.

'Hold still,' he snaps, forcefully grabbing my head.

The foul, damp rag touches my face. Its odour is worse than his, and retching, I struggle to get away.

'Stop squirming!' he demands, squeezing my head harder.

It sends me into a flurry of arms and legs.

A stray kick sends the doctor reeling backwards, releasing his grip to clutch at his crotch.

Face red with fury, he glares as though he'll rip my head right off. 'You worthless little brat!' he spits, striking me with the back of his hand hard across the face.

The pain in my jaw brings me to tears.

Unfazed, he grabs the straps of my dress, sits me up, and holds me firm.

'If you don't settle down...' he demands, 'I'll settle you down, you understand?'

All I can do is whimper while he shakes me to sit upright.

'Like it or not, you're getting this treatment. Now, be a good girl and stop struggling.'

Scared, tired and hopelessly sad, I relax, letting the examination begin.

'Good. Now that's not so hard, is it?' he says, releasing his grip.

The supposed doctor rummages around in his bag of torture equipment again and pulls out a nasty-looking metal needle and a tiny bottle of clear liquid.

That is the biggest needle I have ever seen.

He makes a show of filling the needle, holding it upright to flick it a few times, then, with what I can only describe as a sick satisfaction, stabs it deep into my arm. The liquid burns like fire as it floods into my shoulder, the pain spreading down my arm and to my chest.

The imaginary safety squashed under my bed in the dirt and dust at home now seems more appealing.

For what feels like ages, he forces me to endure his torture of poking and prodding, and then almost chokes me on a wide wooden stick.

When he's done, he reaches into his pocket and pulls out two enormous tablets covered in pocket fluff. 'Go on, take them,' he says, thrusting them at me with a cup of water.

Hands trembling, I take them and pick off the fluff. On their way down they choke me, scraping the insides of my raw throat and leaving me coughing and spluttering.

Now that's what swallowing rocks feels like.

'That's it,' he says, cheerily closing his bag when Mapp re-enters the room. 'She'll be fine.'

'And the radiation?' Mapp asks.

'I've given her iodine tablets. Like the others, she'll need to take them twice a day for the next few days, but other than that, the little monster will live.'

'Thank you, Doctor.'

'Oh, and you'd better watch that one,' he adds, glaring at me, 'she's trouble.'

I poke my tongue out at him in response.

'She's nothing I can't handle. Come on, Jayne,' the large woman says, 'time to meet your new family.'

Mapp pushes me out of the examination room and back into the boring yellow-grey coloured hallway. Voices echo louder along the hall the closer we get to a set of double doors, which open out to a large room filled with steel-framed beds. Spaced in even rows up to the back wall, many are filled with people of varying ages. They all stop and stare as we enter.

Mapp nudges me forward. 'Go pick a bed and stay put,' she says. 'Leave the others alone.'

Curious eyes follow us across the room while we plod past the rows of beds. All the other people have chosen beds near the front. I prefer a wall at my back, so I plonk myself down on a vacant bed at the far end. Once I've made my choice, Mapp stands at the foot of the bed with hands on hips. 'Settled then?'

I give an uncomfortable nod.

'Right, good. Now get some sleep,' she says, blunt as a brick, 'you're going to need it.'

With that, she stomps towards the door, stopping to bark at some children on her way.

Between the hard and lumpy mattress, the bright lights and a ticking clock echoing from its hiding place somewhere, I can't sleep.

I don't know why, but I envy that clock—going about its job without needing to know or care why. It certainly wouldn't care about the storm of fire outside.

Occasionally, a cry from one of the other children pierces the silence between ticks; tick, whimper, tick, cry, tick.

Nightmarish screams and pain drown me in a world of horrible memories, like seeing Amity's burnt face. I can't get her out of my mind.

Why wasn't she rescued too?

After tossing and turning for ages, I drape my blanket over the edge, grab my pillow, and climb underneath. It's cold and dusty on the concrete floor, but I don't care. To make myself more comfortable, I steal another blanket from an unoccupied neighbouring bed and curl up with it. The blanket curtain blocks out the alien complex, reducing my world to something more familiar.

Nothing will be as familiar again, like at home. But this is not home.

Why am I here? Under this bed?

I only want to see Mum and Dad and meet my new baby brother.

Why is that so hard?

A red–haired girl flicks up my curtain, disturbing my thoughts.

'Hey there,' she says.

Startled, I try to scuttle away, but the wall stops my retreat.

'What–cha doin'?' she asks with friendly curiosity.

I glance up at her smiling face. 'Umm... hiding?'

'Oh,' she replies, 'why?'

'I'm hiding from the monsters that burned the sky.'

'Monsters? What monsters?'

'You know, the monsters.'

She shakes her head. 'I'm not scared of monsters. Mum says I shouldn't be afraid of monsters. Let's go hunt your monsters, and then you won't be scared of them either.'

'Umm, you sure?'

'Umm, yer.'

'Okay.'

'My name's Ester. What's yours?'

'Jayne.'

02 – Watchtower

NC01

'Sir, an unusual, fast-moving weather front is coming from the south,' radar officer Junior Lieutenant Cristal Spriggs announced, turning from the radar console's monochromatic green screen to glance at her commanding officer seated behind her.

She couldn't tell if he'd heard from the breather mask and visor covering both their faces. After almost two cycles of wearing the thing, she was tired of it. With a gloved hand, she rubbed at where her mask strap held on to her balaclava and awaited her commander's response.

He rose from his oversized timber desk in the centre of the room, his head just falling short of the ceiling. Between him and that desk, they made the small octagonal room feel minuscule, and her along with it.

Spriggs continued, 'sir, it'll hit sometime around five eighty-three, half a cendec from now.'

He checked his pocket watch and spoke in a deep, resounding voice. 'Fifty decs before radar blackout, prepare for outage.'

'Aye, sir.' She watched him take the three short steps to the dead comms station, and the elongated window set into the wall behind it. As he often did, he gazed into the thick, sandblasted glass to observe the soulless reflection of the room. She only snapped her attention back to the radar screen when she spied him observing her.

After all this time working under you, we still address you only by rank, Spriggs thought. *But what's your actual name?*

For over two cycles, Commander and his motley crew of fourteen operated this intelligence and defence outpost; an inconspicuous cap of a concrete bunker high in the mountains called the Watchtower.

With its impenetrable position, dedicated power supply and state-of-the-art weaponry, it would have been a formidable military installation. However, the Watchtower had been scheduled for resupply three days before the war annihilated civilisation and blanketed the planet in nuclear winter, leaving its tired crew to survive on limited rations. And without a working comms station, they didn't know if they had a home or family to return to. With nowhere else to go, the Watchtower had become their prison.

Spriggs pulled her thick coat tighter to keep out the bitter cold and dust, and glanced over at the two hooded figures seated beside her. Illuminated only by dull incandescent desk lamps and the depressing green glow from the two remaining computerised consoles, they lazily monitored their stations, seeming oblivious to Commander, or her, watching them.

The scuffing of boots on concrete alerted her to someone else's presence just as Ensign Arendt Prow's moderate figure entered through the security door. He held a clipboard and wore a worn grey Cedreau Corporation Militia uniform, and obligatory breather, similar to Spriggs'.

'Sir, that report you wanted,' he said with apprehension, approaching the commander like the man was a vicious animal, quick to anger.

'Then report,' the commander boomed.

'Ahh,' Prow stammered, pushing back the hood of his thick jacket. 'Well, ahh, we have twenty-eight to twenty-nine days of rations.'

'Go on.'

'At our current rate of energy consumption, the atomic battery has 112 days of charge remain...' he trailed off when Commander straightened and slowly turned from his mirror reverie to face the ensign.

Prow continued, 'ahh... and there's approximately 120 decametas of fuel left per vehicle.'

At that, the commander slammed his fist down onto the comms station before him, making Prow jump.

'And the ventilation?'

'Sir?'

The commander grabbed the clipboard from Prow and scraped a pile of dust from the disused console onto the ensign's boots.

'Ah, that. Engineer Staff and me have done all we can. The filters clog up faster than we can clean them. They're pretty well fraxed, and there aren't no replacements.'

'Great,' Commander roared, 'you're telling me we have two to three tendaws of food remaining and just over a trey of power?'

'Yes, sir.'

'We'll be operational if you don't starve or suffocate us to death first!' The big man growled, throwing up his hand and making the ensign flinch. 'Send up the drone!'

'On it, sir.'

'This time, find more than just a small raiding party,' Commander said, taking the clipboard and returning to his desk.

'Yes, sir,' Prow said. He took a step back, preparing to leave.

'And Ensign,' Commander added. 'If you lose the drone again, I'll send *you* out next time. Dismissed.'

Visibly relieved, Prow struck his left pec with his right fist in salute, and without hesitating, marched out the door.

As the relief crew entered the command centre, Spriggs and the other outgoing shift stood and patted themselves down to dislodge the dust gathered in their clothing.

The replacement shift took their positions at the consoles. At the same time, Lieutenant Commander Lexi Colyar approached Commander, who remained standing at his desk, seemingly more interested in the provisions report than acknowledging her. 'Sir, I'm here to relieve you,' she said with assertion.

'You're dismissed, Colyar,' the commander replied, waving her away.

'Sir?'

'I said, you're dismissed, LC,' he repeated.

Colyar held her ground. 'Sir, you've been at your station for two shifts already.'

He turned from his desk to glare at her.

She stiffened her back and shoulders in defiance.

'I don't enjoy repeating myself, LC,' he growled. 'Are you challenging my authority?'

'No sir.'

He stepped closer, his solid, authoritative figure overshadowing hers. 'Then you're dismissed.'

'Sir, with respect, I will have to order you as the ranking medical officer—'

He spoke over her, 'because if you are, I would consider that an act of mutiny. Is this a mutiny, LC?'

'Sir, no sir.'

'Then get out of my Command Centre, Colyar!'

While the two commanding officers argued, Junior Lieutenant Spriggs drew her finger through the dust on the radar screen, summarising the latest activity to her replacement.

Long-Range Weapons officer Tillman wheeled his chair over to listen in on the conversation.

'Contact just appeared on screen. It moved from here to here,' Spriggs said.

'Radar?' Commander interjected.

Spriggs talked faster, trying to finish what she was saying. 'It then disappeared—'

The commander's time-worn desk lamp, mug and clipboard jumped as his fist landed like thunder on the desk.

All talking ceased.

Spriggs turned to face her superior. 'Sir, just about to hand over when an unidentified object entered atmo right into our blind spot. Don't think it was falling, changed direction and slowed before it disappeared.'

Commander straightened as though this was the most exciting thing that had occurred all day. 'Weapons, target it as soon as it returns to radar,' he ordered.

'We're going to—' Tillman began, but the commander cut him off.

'I didn't ask, Lieutenant.'

'Sir, yes sir,' Tillman replied, kicking the floor and scooting his chair back to his console. 'Contact is returning into view, it's moving slow,' Tillman said, watching the displays, his hands moving over the console to prepare the cannon. 'Sir, Peashooter is charged and target locked.'

Half a click away and buried in a bunker, the double-barrel rail cannon known as the Peashooter came to life. Its menacing metallic body, shrouded in the darkness, swivelled toward the object with controlled efficiency and tactical precision.

'Forward tracking of the target, sir,' Tillman called, 'ready to—'

'Fire!' the commander ordered without hesitation.

The weapons officer flipped a small grey cover on his console, exposing two red buttons. 'Fire in the hold!' He pressed the first button, then the second.

Dust rained on the crew as the bunker shook twice; metal mugs rattling off tables, spilling their precious water over the floor. The crew gathered around the radar and weapons stations, watching the blips on the screen and holding their collective breath.

Tillman broke the silence. 'Sir, projectiles no longer in flight. I think that's a hit.'

'Don't give me a think, Lieutenant. Give me a report,' Commander demanded.

'Yes, sir. I'll know more in a moment, sir.'

Engineer Lieutenant Quinn Staff sprinted through the door, pushed through the small crowd gathered around the radar console and darted straight to the Engineering station beside it.

He adjusted a dial to give a read-out of the power consumption, and when he saw it, his head dropped. 'Dust and debris!' he swore at the console. 'There's a reason we haven't fired that darned thing!'

He approached the commander. 'Sir,' he said, putting on his sternest voice, 'if we allow the Peashooter to recharge, it'll leave us with naff-all power and a functionally-frinx weapon. We won't be able to use it or anything else.'

Commander brushed off the engineer with disinterest.

'Sir, please, you can't ignore our situation,' Staff pleaded.

For an awkward moment, only the hum of the computerised consoles dared cut into the silence.

Staff moved around the desk, positioning himself between the commander and the radar console, boldly standing within arms' reach. 'Sir, we can't recharge the Peashooter.'

Commanders' large hand pushed the engineer's face out of the way, dislodging his mask. 'Radar, sitrep!' he shouted, brushing his hands while Staff retreated to fix his breather.

Spriggs replied, 'sir, the unidentified vessel has left radar and confirmed by seismograph. It crashed about one hundred clicks from here.'

Before saying a word, Commander retrieved his firearm from his desk drawer. 'All crew, shut down the equipment and pack your gear. We roll out at five-six-zero.'

Staff intervened once more. 'But, sir?' he exclaimed, and the commander glared down at him over the rim of his faceplate like a teacher scolding a nuisance child.

'Reverse the polarity... or whatever it is you do.'

'Sir, that's not the way...' Staff's voice trailed off as Commander leaned in closer.

'Enough. You have your orders, Lieutenant. Follow them!'

'Yes, sir,' he saluted, turning to power down the engineering console while muttering under his breath, 'anything to get out of this depressatorium.'

With the engineer out of his face, Commander turned his attention to the loitering Colyar. 'LC, make yourself useful.'

Colyar stood to attention.

'Send me a comms officer, then relay orders to the remaining crew. You and the other LC take a squad of six in the other vehicles. Dismissed.'

'Sir, yes, sir,' she said, saluting, then left.

'Ms Radar,' the commander said, addressing Spriggs, 'grab the portable, you're with me.'

'Yes, sir,' she replied, collecting her gear after being dismissed.

She reached under her console to grab the portable radar unit as Tillman, who had finished shutting down the weapons console, turned to the room, perplexed. 'Does anyone know what we shot down?'

Spriggs elbowed him in the ribs. 'Don't ask, just do.'

Three green and white camouflaged trucks bulldozed a track through the storm and toxic landscape, with Commander's vehicle leading the convoy.

Lieutenant Ezechiel Coxon, the cocky comms officer, sat by the door, holding a pencil torch up to a map, trying to navigate as the truck jostled its way over rough terrain to the crash site. Nestled between the two bulky men was the young, slender-framed Lieutenant Spriggs, with her boxy mobile radar on her lap, wired up to the battery under the bench seat.

For over a cendec, the crew endured a torturous ride. The combined cacophony of crunching permafrost under tyres, howling wind and the constant drone of the engine dulled their hearing. The engine radiated through the firewall underneath the bench, warming the cabin beyond a comfortable temperature.

Spriggs waved her hand, cutting the air horizontally, and Commander brought the vehicle to a stop, killing the headlights.

The engine idled while the wind outside continued to thrash up a whiteout of thick dust in the sub-zero temperatures.

Spriggs turned off the radar unit's display, allowing her eyes to adjust to what little light was out there, and examine something solid ahead, obscured by the storm gusts.

Commander let the vehicle roll forward a little.

'Sir, from the terrain on the map and radar triangulation,' Spriggs said, leaning forward to speculate at the solid form, 'it's a guess the crashed vessel is just over this hill.'

'Wait here,' Commander said, tightening the straps on his breather and pushed open the door with what seemed like ease. Numbing air robbed warmth from the cabin and froze perspiration in an instant, blasting them with grey, powdered charcoal.

Spriggs had been unprepared for the moment and shrunk into her coat, pulling its hood tighter.

Commander had been barely gone for a dec when Coxon broke the silence. 'Maybe we should leave him here, drive on.'

'And why would we do that?' Spriggs replied, unsure if he was serious.

'You heard how he treated Colyar. The guy's unhinged.'

'No, he's not,' she said in the commander's defence, 'besides, you don't know him.'

Coxon chuckled. 'And you do? We've worked with him for the last two-and-a-bit cycles, he's abusive and dangerous. You don't know him like you think you do.'

'Maybe not, but he's never properly hurt anyone.'

'You wanna bet? You see the stitches on Prow? The bruises on Montford?'

'Okay, so he has a strict temper. The way you lot carry on, why are you surprised?'

He chuckled again. 'Of course, you would say that, wouldn't you?'

'What's that supposed to mean?'

'Oh, come on, Cristal. We've all seen how you swoon over him. *"Yes, Commander, absolutely Commander, anything you say Commander"*. You're wet for him,' he said with an evocative retort.

'Am not! That's disgusting and completely inappropriate.'

'Come on, don't deny it. You are too.'

'What are you, five? You're just jealous that no self-respecting woman would go for a cocky, pimple-arsed, crud like you.'

'Ouch,' he replied, 'how would you know if I had a pimply arse, anyway? I could show it to you, and you can find out?'

'Shut up, Coxon,' Spriggs replied, turning her radar unit back on and ignoring him.

The comms gave a sudden click of static, and Coxon double-tapped the receiver, replying with a cryptic response, *"stopped for a bio, back soon."* In code, it meant, *"gone for a scout".*

More than ten decs passed. Bored, Coxon removed his gloves, unholstered the six-shooter pistol on his belt, and began fiddling with it, holding its balanced weight, fondling the cool metal and feeling the grain in its wooden grip between his fingers.

He began rotating the cylinder. *Click.*

Spriggs didn't take her eyes from the glowing radar screen. *Click.*

The engine coughed. *Click-click.*

She glared at him. 'Please don't.'

Click.

'Don't what?' *Click.*

Click. 'That.'

'Sorry.' He flicked the safety off. *Tick.*

'Put it away, you idiot, before you either shoot yourself or someone more important.'

The truck shook as though a large animal had rammed it, causing Coxon to drop the cylinder of his pistol in surprise. It hit the metal floor of the truck with a loud clang. A large bloodied glove slammed against the truck's windscreen. Then the driver's side door snatched open, and the commander clambered inside, seizing warmth from the internal cabin once again. As he closed the door, he noticed the cylinder of Coxon's pistol on the floor. 'Yours?'

Coxon dived for it, scrabbling over Spriggs' lap and head-butting Commander's tree trunk-sized thigh. His hand fumbled with the cylinder, dropping it again and causing the slugs to rattle free across the cabin floor. While Spriggs and Commander watched with dismay, Coxon grabbed the weapon part, dumped it in Spriggs' lap, then blundered for the slugs.

When he sat back up, she held the piece out to him. He took it, and with the clumsiness of a first-cycle cadet, pieced the weapon back together.

All the while, Commander didn't take his eyes from the foolery. 'Done?' he asked.

Coxon nodded, 'Yes, sir.'

'Nothing on radar, sir,' Spriggs said, breaking the awkwardness.

'Good,' the commander replied. 'Tell the others to follow at a distance and do what I do.'

'That your blood, sir?' Spriggs asked.

'Give the order.'

Coxon double-tapped the radio transmitter, then spoke into the mouthpiece, 'Bio over, could smell,' which in code meant, *'scout over, follow but keep your distance.'*

The commander flicked the headlights back on, straightened the truck, and climbed the short hill ahead, coming to a halt on the crest. The other two trucks stopped on either side.

From the hilltop overlooking the valley, the storm seemed more subdued. There, a shiny disc approximately one hundred metas in diameter lay at an angle, half-buried in a crumpled bedsheet of soil and dead, uprooted trees. Its massive size appeared to fill half the valley.

Beneath it, a campfire burned with its tendrils of flame blowing in all directions in the squalling winds. The disc's metallic surface reflected the dancing light, illuminating the surrounding area like it was magic.

'Now that's somethin' you don't see every day,' Coxon said.

Five figures busied themselves around the site.

'Seems we're not the only ones attracted to this thing,' Coxon added.

Without warning, the commander knocked the truck into gear and accelerated from the top of the hill at deadly speed toward the campsite. Silenced by the wind, not even the engine's roar could alert the camp's occupants in time as the truck barrelled into the camp. With a thud, two people in scrappy clothing disappeared beneath the truck's front wheels.

As the truck came to a jolting stop by the fire, Commander slipped out of the cabin and into the tempest. Coxon and Spriggs watched while Commander; a single menacing figure silhouetted by the fire, released his pistol free of its holster.

Flash, a person went down.

Flash, then another.

31

Flash, flash. Two more.

With the precision of an expert marksman, he discharged shots with deadly accuracy.

Before the crew had even left their trucks, the shooting was over. He re-holstered his weapon and surveyed his handiwork, while Coxon and Spriggs exited the cabin. Coxon bolted to the fire to keep warm, drawing his own pistol as though he were the one who cleaned up the camp. Cristal hung back, content to remain in the shelter of the truck. The others stopped not far away and were making their way towards them with weapons drawn. There was no telling what other surprises they may find out here.

A shadow stirred under the truck, and Spriggs jumped, startled to find an injured woman clawing herself away from the tyre tracks.

'Sir, this one's still alive,' she said, glancing beneath the truck.

Commander reached the vehicle in four long strides and dragged the maimed woman out by her jacket, pinning her against a massive front tyre. She screamed through her rough-built mask as her mangled leg flopped around.

He kneeled over her and ripped off her mask. In desperation, she tried to cover her face, but Commander slapped her hands away. 'How long have you been here?' he shouted over the wind.

She convulsed on a lungful of dust. Desperate for air, she gasped and violently coughed, choking the more she tried to breathe.

'Answer my question, and you'll get your mask back,' Commander yelled.

Through her barely comprehensible speech punctuated by coughs, she responded, 'just got here.'

He pressed his bloodied glove firmer into her chest, and seemingly satisfied by the woman's response, returned her mask.

She fumbled for it and placed it over her face, coughing before speaking again. 'Just got here, just lit the fire,' she said, glaring at the commander in terror. 'Please, I worked in tech-comms before the sky-fire. Hon'st, we lit the fire, started cookin'. Tracer, he went to check out the sky-disc. That's it. Hon'st. Please don't kill me.'

'Where's Tracer? Do I have to worry about him?' Commander growled, shaking her more violently.

'No,' she wailed, 'he's me mate. He went under your truck.'

'How low you fell,' Commander grumbled, shoving her into the tyre before letting go. As he stood, he picked her up by the front of her dirty jacket. She howled with pain as her hip seemed to separate from its joint. And like a piece of garbage, he tossed her away from the camp to be swallowed up by the darkness.

By this stage, the other Watchtower crew had gathered around.

'Get rid of the bodies,' Commander ordered.

Lieutenant Tillman yelled back, 'sir, what about the pris—'

Commander lifted his pistol at Tillman, whose eyes widened at the massive weapon directed at him.

'Sir, yes sir,' Tillman yelled back nervously, almost punching his shoulder in salute.

Without emotion, the big man fired. Tillman flinched as the round sailed past his head and hit a man hiding in the shadows behind a large tree root.

As though nothing had happened, Commander re-holstered the weapon, leaving Tillman visibly shaken. 'Set up while I crack this thing open,' he barked. Before leaving, he turned to Spriggs. 'Ms Radar, keep an eye out. I don't want any intrusions.'

She saluted, and Commander headed towards the unidentified crashed ship.

Spriggs returned to the comfort of the truck, setting the portable radar on her lap. Through the windows, she observed her commanding officer approach the half-buried ship, remove his glove and run his bare fingers along the hull. He took a moment to investigate the two massive gashes in its underside, remnants of the Peashooter's work. From where Spriggs sat, the openings appeared large enough for a person to crawl into, but he instead walked inward toward the disc's centre point, stooping as the space under the ship narrowed. When a panel of light opened above his head, he again removed his pistol and climbed inside.

Spriggs remained in the truck, splitting her attention between the radar and the crew gathered around the fire.

They all seemed more relaxed now Commander wasn't there.

Tillman and Colyar took their turn on patrol while the rest made themselves comfortable, stoking the fire with fresh wood and breaking open ration packs.

It reminded Spriggs she, too, was hungry. Breaking open a ration pack of her own, she couldn't recall the last time she ate.

While the crew sat quietly eating their rations and warming themselves by the fire, the icy wind gusted around them. After a while, it was Coxon who spoke first.

'Why are we still with Commander?' he asked no-one in particular. 'He's a murderous megalomaniac.'

Staff reset his breather and answered. 'Shh, you can't say that.'

'I'm only saying what we're all thinking,' Coxon said. 'He accused Colyar of mutiny. She's still shakking her...'

'So why do they say, "fire in the hold"?' Prow interrupted, diverting the conversation.

It was the more senior Lieutenant Commander Levvit who replied. 'Because about two-hundred cycles ago they used to mine a radioactive substance called megloinium. In those early days, they didn't know how volatile it was. You can dig it up fine, but over time, exposure to the environment would cause it to react. It was not uncommon for entire trains to evaporate from the explosions,' he chuckled. 'They quickly realised it needed to be transported in specially made, air-tight containers no bigger than the size of your head. Fires still happened, but not to the same reactive scale. So, whenever the rail engineers called out, "fire in the hold", you knew you had to get the flock out of there, fast.'

'How do you know that?' Prow asked.

'I was a mining engineer before the war. Megloinium isn't mined anymore; it's too difficult to stabilise on site. So that's where your word megalomaniac comes from, Coxon. It means large-lunatic.'

Coxon sneered, 'murderous large-lunatic.'

Staff threw a small rock at him, catching him in the back of the head. 'Better watch what you say. He wasn't like this half a trey ago. Now he has to put up with double-headed nimwits like you.'

Coxon laughed at Staff's insult. 'Double-headed nimwits? Seriously, Staff, is that the best you can come up with?'

Staff shrugged.

Levvit continued, holding his hand out in the thick air. 'It was only a matter of time before someone used it for this. Seems appropriate the thing that started the war should end it.'

'Megloinium didn't start the war,' Coxon interjected.

'Yeah, it did,' Levvit argued, 'we all know the story. Those Lib scrags stole a stockpile of the stuff from our research facility then blew it up, but not before poisoning the poor project director. Naturally, we retaliated.'

'We don't actually know she was poisoned, Levvit,' Coxon said. 'They said it was suicide. And besides, that wasn't the start of it. Megloinium wasn't the only thing they stole from us.'

'Oh, here we go,' Staff sighed. 'Man, you two gossip like a pair of teenage girls.'

'Piss off, Staff,' Coxon spat before continuing. 'You can't deny what they stole from us all those cycles ago didn't start this?'

'What are you blathering about?' Levvit chided.

'I think he's referring to the incident back in AP1925,' Quinn said.

Levvit scoffed, 'like he would remember that. Coxon, you would have been barely old enough to wipe your own arse.'

'Haha, Levvit,' Coxon said, 'I do read, and I know it was a crashed ship, kinda like this one. We found it and salvaged some stuff, but the Libs stole it. I may not know what it was, but it was definitely alien tech, and it *did* start the war.'

'Alien tech,' Levvit scoffed again.

'If you're so smart, Levvit, whaddya think that thing is?' Coxon asked, pointing at the half-buried disc.

'Now that, I haven't got a clue,' Levvit replied, 'that's not my area of expertise.'

'What about you, Staff?' Coxon probed. 'You're a proper engineer, yeh?'

Staff glanced at Coxon, then at the flickering surface of the crashed object and shrugged. 'I'm an electro-mechanical engineer, Coxon, not whatever engineer builds flying saucers. I haven't the foggiest.'

'But you do think it's alien?'

'Oh, for goodness' sake, Coxon,' Staff exasperated. 'You and your crazy conspiracy theories.'

'Come on,' Coxon exclaimed. 'You can't say you're not thinking it.'

'Yes, Coxon,' Staff grumbled, 'but I'm not stupid enough to say it at the top of my lungs. Whatever it is, it has Commander's attention.'

'Speaking of whom,' Levvit said, checking his wristwatch, 'it's been a while. I wonder what he's up to?'

Bassey echoes reverberated from the opening of the ship. 'Sounds like the commander's hand cannon is doin' its thing,' Coxon observed.

Levvit lifted his breather and took a few bites from his ration pack.

'Did you see what he did to that woman before?' Coxon said. 'I think he likes...' Jumping at the sound of crunching ground behind, he spun to face Commander's ominous figure and stammered. 'Sir, we were a little concerned for your safety in there,' he rattled off with unease.

'This picnic is over,' Commander growled. 'Get inside. We have work to do.'

As they entered the ship, somehow, something held the gritty air out, almost as if by magic. Beyond that, the mysterious disc's metallic grey interior walls curved around like the outside of the ship's design would suggest. The room didn't have any visible lighting, and it was as though the air itself glowed.

The ceilings were high, and all the doors had mounted plaques on them written in an unrecognisable language. Commander held his hand toward a panel and a towering door opened before them, revealing a room about double the size of the Watchtower's C&C, where five square, large metallic crates sat in a line along its centre.

Free from the consuming outside air, Commander removed his breather, and for the first time in a very long while, his crew got a good look at him. His was the face of a mountain; all sharp edges, square and cold hard.

His short-cropped hair was pitch-black and his eyes were almost as dark. He also bore a curiously tanned complexion for a man who had not seen sunlight in over two cycles.

The others followed his lead, removed their masks, and with hesitation, took their first breath of the alien air. It was the cleanest, purest air they had breathed in all their lives.

'Hey Montford,' Coxon remarked, taking a deep breath, then smoothing out his shaggy-blonde hair. 'I can't even smell your boots in here.'

Montford just shook his head as the others laughed.

'Stow your gear here,' Commander ordered. 'This is our staging area. Everything not attached to the ship comes here.' He then pointed to Coxon, Staff, Montford and Tillman. 'You four, bring your breathers and follow me. The rest spread out. Don't touch the displays or any of the bodies. Dismissed,' he barked and stormed off, with the four nominated officers running after him.

Commander and his contingent party of four passed through short hallways, reaching a circular room at the ship's centre. Various indiscernible coloured visualisations hung in the air, like high-tech dioramas, which appeared to be projected from an opaque black frieze-strip that ran along the room's walls.

But that wasn't the most interesting feature. Filling its centre and held erect by enormous clamps stood a massive, tubular-shaped object, which dwarfed everything else around it. Thick, vine-like cables flowed into its top, and an electrical hum emanating from within it brought the room to life. Commander reached out and touched the suspended object's smooth metallic surface, his face seeming to crack at the sight of it.

Nobody had ever seen this man smile.

He wasn't the only one. Staff and the others all gazed up at it in awe, wondering what it was and why it had elicited such a reaction from a man they thought was devoid of positive emotion.

Lieutenant Montford backed away for a better look, smoothing his mop of curly dark hair with intrigue. As he did, the door behind him, having sensed his approach, opened, emitting a hissing sound that immediately attracted *everyone's* attention. In an instant, Commander's head whipped up to glare at him, his angular face reset to its strict-as-usual expression. 'All of you, get over here,' he demanded.

Staff leapt to attention. 'Sir!'

'Gather up all spare cables, parts and equipment, and ready them for my truck. Touch nothing else.'

'Yes, sir,' the other three chorused.

The big man's gait put him out of the room and out of sight in just a few steps.

Montford had to jump to one side to let him pass.

As ordered, Staff started collecting equipment while the other three officers loitered about the room. 'Well, come on then, help,' he said in an annoyed tone.

Coxon and Tillman glanced at one another, then rushed over to help. Montford, with his mouth still agape in awe, instead inspected everything within the chamber. 'In all the twenty cycles I've served, I've never seen anything like this,' he said.

'You're old, Montford,' Coxon joked, reaching for a coil of cable on the floor. 'We get it.'

'And you're hilarious,' Montford said dryly. He was closely examining one of the strange projections depicting a wireframe diagram of the ship. 'I've never seen colour representations like these before. I wish we had this tech. You think we'd be able to take some back with us? How d'you s'pose we could get it off the wall?' he mused, reaching for a display.

'Don't!' Staff yelled, taking a step forward to stop him. But he was too late. Montford had touched it.

The ship rumbled and began vibrating.

A thudding echo grew louder.

The four men looked around with apprehension.

Then, like a wounded boart, Commander charged through the doorway, past Staff, spinning him into a wall and sending him collapsing to the deck.

By the time Staff's head had stopped spinning, Montford's face protruded through one of the projected displays with Commander's fist clutching at his coat. The big man stared into the lieutenant's panicked brown eyes with incensed rage.

'What did I say?' Commander boomed at Montford.

'Sorry sir,' Montford whimpered, immobilised against the ship's bulkhead by his superior's vice–like grip.

'WHAT. DID. I. SAY?'

From the wild look on Commander's face, Staff felt he was going to kill Montford. Without thinking, he picked himself up and rushed to his fellow officer's aid. 'Sir,' he pleaded, 'it wasn't Montford's fault. I was moving that reel of cable and accidentally pushed him.'

Commander turned to glare at him.

At that moment, Staff noticed faint metallic flecks moving about in the dark irises of his eyes. The engineer blinked to confirm what he was seeing.

With a grunt, Commander dropped Montford, and he collapsed in a heap, wincing as he touched a red sticky patch at the back of his head.

'GET UP!' the commander snarled. 'You have work to do.'

Montford wiped the blood on his pants and stood to attention, keeping his eyes level and doing everything he could to avoid further eye contact with Commander.

'Since you like touching things, get over here, touch ONLY what I tell you,' Commander said.

Montford hobbled over and stood at the projection next to his superior, flinching as the large man lifted his palm and placed it on the image.

He tilted it down to his officer's eye level, where Staff observed it was a schematic of the mysterious cylinder annotated with the same strange text he'd seen in the corridor.

'When I say so,' Commander continued, 'touch here and here. Then keep touching the red box until it disappears. Got it?'

'Sir, how do you know this?' Montford asked.

Commander just glared at him in response.

'Yes, sir,' Montford replied.

The large man stepped to the other side of the room, slid three of the displays together until they overlapped, and he began interacting with them, dragging information between the layers.

Staff followed Commander's hand movements with fixated curiosity as Coxon leaned in, asking, 'what's he doing?'

'I haven't the foggiest,' Staff replied.

'It looks like it could be a language from the North,' Montford said, keeping his eye on the display before him.

'But how did *they* get tech like this?' Coxon asked.

'The question you want to ask is, why don't we?' Staff said.

'No, the real question is, how does he—'

'Silence!' Commander snapped, cutting Montford off. 'Now!' he said, pointing at the lieutenant without moving his head.

Montford hesitated, then realising what Commander meant, did as instructed. Just as Commander had said, a red box displayed, and Montford stabbed his finger at the image.

Touch, touch, touch.

At certain angles, it gave Staff the impression his colleague was poking at thin air, but he saw the red box, and each time it appeared, Montford poked at the air again.

A loud bang came from high above the cylindrical object, startling the lieutenants and causing Montford to flinch.

'Don't stop, lieutenant,' Commander bellowed.

Montford continued his poking.

Every other touch of the display created another bang from the strange object. A mechanical whir released the cylinder of its clamps while the cables snaking from it ejected and fell away, all except the thickest cable that kept the thing suspended while it swung free.

As Commander's hands worked faster, manipulating objects within his projected displays, the floor below the massive swinging pendulum split open with a reverberating groan, revealing an invisible field separating the clean ship's air from the gusting turbid air outside.

'WOW,' Staff exclaimed, gazing into the shimmering hole in the floor. 'This technology is amazing. This would be great in the 'tower. After the last cycle and a half, I feel my mask has become a part of me.'

'You two,' Commander pointed to Tillman and Coxon, 'guide it through and lay it down.'

With their assistance, the strange cylindrical object entered the swirling vortex of dust and touched down onto the firm ground outside.

'Reset your breathers,' Commander said, fixing his own in place.

He waved a few more gestures at the displays, and with a muffled clunk, the support cable disconnected, releasing the device. The shimmering force field dissolved, and a cloud of foul wind blew into the room, covering Commander and his crew in dust.

Having completed his task, Commander stepped away from the display. 'Get out there,' he ordered his men. 'Take that to *my* truck, then come back. We're not done here.'

The large man strode from the room, leaving Staff and the others to wrestle with the object and his collection of items on their own.

Like a pack of predatory animals, the Watchtower crew methodically stripped the ship of all items of perceivable value and piled their findings up in the staging area. All the while Spriggs remained in the truck, eyes fixed on the display in her lap.

From out of the squalling dust, four figures emerged, struggling to carry some large object between them.

Spriggs swivelled in her seat to try to get a better view. With a thump, something heavy rocked the truck, followed moments later by the incessant whining of a winch reverberating through the cabin, and a blip.

A blip!

She almost missed it.

First time in a cycle and a half and I've had two contacts in one day.

Curbing her excitement, she suppressed the urge to investigate what was happening outside to observe the tiny green dot shuffling over her display.

Whatever it was, it was coming closer.

After watching the blip for a moment, she gathered her coat tighter and leapt into the fray, almost barrelling over Staff in the process.

'Are you almost finished?' Spriggs yelled over the howling wind.

Staff looked at her with surprise. 'Yer, we just have to strap it down and get the other stuff *he* wanted.'

'Hurry then,' she said, patting him on the shoulder before rushing off toward the downed ship.

When Spriggs arrived, she found Commander with LCs Colyar and Levvit in one large room. She marvelled at the fresh air, then set her attention on Commander, who was busy sifting through an eclectic collection of objects.

She waited in the doorway while Commander examined a pair of rimless glasses. The moment she set eyes on his unmasked face, she had to force herself to focus on the reason for which she was there. Though she could never recall him being so charismatic.

He put the peculiar glasses on and was looking at the auburn-haired Colyar, gesturing as though miming something in the air in front of him.

'Sir,' Spriggs interrupted, and he turned to face her. Tilting her head, she noticed the glasses had barely discernible lighting in the lenses.

'ARRGH!' he cursed, tearing the strange eyewear from his face and throwing them away. 'Ms Radar, what is it?'

She cleared her throat and continued. 'Sir, came to tell you, the seismograph has picked up ground movement. We've got company inbound. At speculation, we've about thirty decs before they get here.'

'Good...' he said, then something caught his attention.

He kicked aside some objects and bent down to pull out a small, hard-metal case. Embossed on its lid was a symbol depicting two serpents biting their tails intertwined like a double helix. With extreme care, he opened it, revealing foam-like padding with ten cylindrical slots. All except three of the slots were empty. He extracted an item from one of the occupied slots and held it up to the light. It was a small, glass vial containing a thick, black metallic substance that swirled as if it were alive.

Spriggs had never seen anything like it.

'Is this the only case like this?' Commander asked in a more subdued voice. 'Anything else from medical?'

Colyar, who was overseeing the collection, answered. 'Sir, we're not sure what medical looks like. This is all we found. I'm sorry, but there were no more cases like that. Just what you see here.'

He grunted and carefully returned the vial to its protective insert. Again, he reached into the pile of junk, this time pulling out a cylindrical object slightly larger than a pencil torch, but sizeable enough to fit a vial. After giving it a good inspection, he pushed it into a perfectly shaped slot in the lid's underside and closed the case.

Having delivered their package to the commander's truck and securing it, Staff and the others had dragged their aching muscles back to the ship and were ecstatic to have relieved themselves of their masks once again.

Montford felt at his head. 'See this dried blood, the commander did this. He's crazy.'

Staff retorted, 'Come on, Montford, he did tell you not to touch anything.'

'And I said I was sorry. Thank you for helping me, by the way. I really thought he was going to... you know,' Montford said, gesturing a cutting motion across his throat.

'Anytime, Montford,' Staff replied, 'But if it were Coxon...'

Coxon objected, just as the door to the staging area opened. 'Oh, go suck a bag of d–'

The commander was standing right there, examining a small pile of objects on the floor.

'A bag of what?' he asked, looking up, his voice mastering the acoustics of the room.

'Ahh,' Coxon stopped blank, 'a bag of datum, sir. Just playing with Staff, sir.'

He glared at them.

The moment he entered; Staff considered the collection of strange objects with the fascination of a child in a toy store. Much of it he'd never seen before, let alone perceive a use. Even the metal crates had their contents spilled out over the floor.

'You, engineer. Is the object secure?'

'Yes sir, it's snug,' Staff replied.

'Good. Get that stuff in my truck,' Commander ordered, pointing at a small pile by the door. 'Divide the rest between the other trucks. Engineer and Ms Radar, you're with me. We leave in fifteen.'

The Watchtower crew gathered their bounty from the downed ship and loaded it amongst the three trucks while Commander inspected his large trophy.

When everything had been packed, Commander turned the truck away and, without headlights, laboured up the long hill into the night.

In the large side mirror, Spriggs could see all was not well with the trucks behind them. One of them hadn't moved, its occupants buzzing around the engine, while the others were trying to assist.

'Sir? The others?' Spriggs queried, and Staff, who sat by the door, adjusted his posture to look as well.

'They'll catch up,' Commander replied.

'But sir,' Staff said, 'Aren't we going back to the 'tower?'

'No.'

The moment they reached the hill's crest, the valley lit up in a bright flash, followed by a shock wave that shook the truck.

'What was that?' Spriggs exclaimed.

Staff replied, 'a self-destruct? Maybe the others you saw on seismo?'

'Not possible. That contact is still ten decs out,' Spriggs said.

Commander simply turned on the headlights and continued driving.

'If we're not going back to the 'tower. Where are we going?'

'We are no longer pawns of a dead corporation,' Commander said, tearing the Cedreau Corporation patches from his uniform and tossing them out the window. 'We shall not be bound to them and their misguided vision. We forge our own road now, toward a more prosperous future. If this mission is realised, from ashes, a great empire will rise again.'

Spriggs loosened her collar to cool off a little. 'Never heard you talk like that before, sir,' she said with intrigue. 'If it's acceptable to ask, who are you anyway? We've worked under you for over two cycles, yet we don't even know your name.'

'I am who I am.'

'Yes, sir, but how may we address you?'

'I will accept sir or Commander.'

'But, sir, isn't that your title?' Spriggs asked.

'That is what I am.'

'As you wish, Commander. One other question. Do you really believe we can rebuild this world?'

Despite her question, Commander didn't answer. Instead, he continued driving on into the night, leaving Spriggs with more questions than she had answers.

Distorted sunlight broke through the horizon, revealing a gusty morning sky and burnt-orange haze. Spriggs awakened to the droning engine cutting to an idle and a blast of cold air entering the cabin. The morning light hit her face through her visor. She must have drifted off. Tightening the tie holding back her shoulder-length, light-brown hair, she adjusted her mask and leant forward to see out of the windscreen clearer. No one from the Watchtower had seen a sunrise in over two cycles.

As Spriggs moved, a momentary nausea overcame her. She waited for the feeling to pass before glancing around the cabin, noticing the embossed metal case Commander had collected now rested on the seat beside her. He was already gone.

'Where did Commander go?' Spriggs nudged Staff in disoriented confusion. Staff, groggy from having only just awoken, mumbled something inaudible, then opened the door and slipped out of the truck. Perplexed, Spriggs' gaze shifted between the case and the empty driver's seat, and touching a tender mark at her neck, she followed Staff out the door.

The two Watchtower crew stepped out to stand at the edge of the clifftop overlooking a barren valley of dead forest below. Despite the desolation, the lookout gave them a breathtaking view of the sunrise as fingers of golden morning sunlight reached out from the horizon, adding its warmth and light to the world and pacifying the icy dust fronts gusting around them.

'Wow!' Spriggs exclaimed, watching a stream of sunlight as it beamed down over the landscape, washing away her anxiety. 'It's beautiful.'

Her thoughts drifted to what Commander had said. Both she and Quinn glanced at each other, looking at the Cedreau Corporation patches adorning their chests and arms. Without needing to utter a word, they tore the patches from their uniforms and threw them to the wind.

No longer would we associate ourselves with a dead corporation, she thought as she watched the patches dance in the breeze. This was a new beginning.

Behind them, the rumbling of a second truck engine and tyres on frozen gravel came nearer. Spriggs and Staff turned to see a lone truck pulling up and stopping a short distance away. The six familiar occupants exited the vehicle and started walking towards them.

Colyar yelled through her mask. 'The other truck wouldn't start. We tried to help and raise you on comms... but... it looks like the ship self-destructed and destroyed the other truck when it blew. The others didn't make it...'

Commander stepped out from behind his parked vehicle and stood a few paces from the crew, Spriggs and Staff remaining where they were. They could only watch as Commander drew his pistol, and with lightning-fast reflexes, let the fury of its purpose smoke out six rounds, gunning down Colyar and the other unsuspecting crew where they stood. Muzzle smoking, he let the magazine drop to the crushed permafrost at his feet and reloaded. Spriggs and Staff froze in shock, neither able to consider the next option available to them for fear of what Commander may bring onto them. The wind buffeted against those who remained standing. The beauty of the sunrise forgotten by the bloody murder of the fellow crewmen before them.

'How's this going to play out?' Commander asked with nonchalant expectation.

Spriggs collapsed.

03 – Hard Times
NC01

'Found you!' I yell.

Ester complains from the depths of her hiding spot under a bed in a disused room. 'No fair! How d'you find me so quickly?'

'Not telling. Change of game, you're tagged.' Before she can crawl out, I slap her on the shoulder, turn, and run out of the room.

I make it out the door to the main corridor when Ester calls out, 'one to one hundred, I'm coming for ya Jayne.'

'That's not fair,' I shout over my shoulder. 'You didn't count a dec.'

'Goin' to catch ya.'

I dart around the next corner from the main hallway, pull tight to the wall and hide, waiting to spring my trap.

Ester sprints around the corner, but her long legs don't stop her in time. I shoot from my hiding spot, grab her by surprise and we scream, hug and bounce in an excited frenzy with each other's hair in our mouths.

'Can we be sisters, Ester?' I ask, admiring her fiery red hair like mine. 'I want you to be my sister, best friends always.'

'Yer, sisters, best friends forever, Jayne.'

'Yay, bestest sister-friends!'

My stomach gurgles, and we giggle. 'You hungry?' I ask, thinking of lunch.

'Yer, what time you think it is? The hall should be open now.'

'I dunno, but I'll race you.' Pushing Ester to the wall, I bolt for the dining hall.

'That's not fair,' she cries from behind, 'but I'll still beat ya!'

'You always do, you tree.'

Ester catches up in midecs, and giggling, slaps me on the shoulder. 'Tag you're it.' We take turns tagging each other, darting around corners and dodging people until we come to a section of the main tunnel where our laughter is drowned out by a strange knocking sound coming from above.

'You're it!' I tag her, but the strange noise steals my attention, and I gaze at the ceiling, curious as to the source. The sound seems to get louder, but all that's there is a dust-caked fan, some pipes and a hanging light globe.

'Got ya back,' Ester says, stopping to stare at the ceiling as well. 'Oh. I think we should be moving on.'

As I move out from under the section of pipe where the noise is loudest, a fine stream of water shoots out, hitting the light and causes its globe to explode in a shower of twinkling stars.

We double over in laughter as the crack in the pipe gets bigger, raining water down on us and the corridor. For a moment, I'm back in my yard again, where dad put on the sprinkler, and we dance, allowing the cool water to soak our hair and clothes.

'What in the Progenitors' names is going on here!' Mapp booms as she rounds the corner, and our excitement instantly dissolves. Ester and I freeze in her icy stare.

Standing behind Mapp, and filling the hallway, is an enormous man in cargo pants and big, black army boots. His short black hair, square jaw and huge muscly arms make me think he eats concrete for breakfast, bricks for lunch and cars for dinner. By comparison, Administrator Mapp, her short, pudgy shape in recycled Gotthard clothing, looks like a scruffy patchwork cushion. She glares at us with that fake smile, as though offering tei and cookies but forcing you to sit through a three-cendec lesson on how the water recycling system works.

'See, I told you I'd find her,' Mapp says to the enormous man, puffing herself up with self-importance. 'I can't help it she's sopping wet, though. These girls are always up to no good. That one, especially,' she says, pointing a sausage-thick finger at me. 'She's a destructive influence. I wouldn't be surprised if this is all her doing.'

Ester and I exchange worried looks.

'Ester,' Mapp calls, waving her hand at my sister-friend, 'come here, child.'

Ester shakes her head and tries to retreat, but something stops her. Mapp and the man-mountain seem to block the corridor.

'Come now, don't be silly. This nice man's going to take you to your new home.'

Ester doesn't move.

'I'm terribly sorry,' Mapp says with a croaky voice that's very unlike her. She rubs her palms together, clears her throat, and turns her attention back to Ester. 'Come on, child,' she says through clenched teeth, stiffening her back. 'Don't you dare embarrass me.'

'Let me handle this,' the man says, placing a knee on the floor and extending his hand to Ester. 'Ester?' he says, in a surprisingly gentle but strong voice, 'nice to meet you. Your mother sends her regards. She can't come but has asked me to collect you.'

Ester blinks, and her eyes dart between the grown-ups and me.

'Come now, child, you have to go with this nice man,' Mapp says more intently. 'We shan't be keeping your mother waiting. She's very busy and hasn't the time for your nonsense.'

'No!' I yell, grabbing Ester's hand, 'you can't take her!'

All my friends disappear when strangers turn up and leave through that door. I never see them again. I'm not losing Ester as well.

'Go away, Jayne!' Mapp yells with a scornful look, then turns to the man. 'I am terribly sorry, Commander? Is that what you said your name was? That's a very odd name,' she babbles. 'Anyway, that one's Jayne. Don't worry about her. I'll take care of her.'

The man, Commander, ignores her and continues trying to lure Ester over, reaching out as though trying to attract a stray animal with a piece of food.

With my heart racing, I hold Ester's hand tighter, afraid I'll lose her forever if I let her go. Her palms are sweaty like mine, and I tug at her arm, trying to get her to come back. 'Ester, Ester!' I cry, but she doesn't move. 'They'll take you like the others. Ester, come on!'

Goose-bumps run down her arm into mine, and her strength slips away as her shoulders slump into her chest.

'No, run Ester, we have to run away.'

'Oh, go bawl in a bucket,' Mapp huffs, slinking past the man called Commander to reach us. 'I said, go away, Jayne,' she growls, mocking my feeble attempts to pull Ester away. 'Go get some food. This doesn't concern you.'

Tears make everything go watery, and I clench my fists as Mapp picks up my only friend and carries her underarm towards the door, her legs dangling behind like overcooked vegetables.

'Ester!' I cry, charging Mapp, trying to tug at Ester's arm and almost causing Mapp to lose balance.

'Jayne, GO AWAY!' she growls at me one last time, her disgusting palm smothering my face as she pushes me to the floor.

'No! You can't. Don't take my sister away. She's my sister. Please don't take her away.'

'She's no more your sister than I'm your mother,' Mapp snaps. 'Now do as you're told and rack off, you filthy little wretch.'

She turns her back and steals Ester from my reach. The man-monster gives me a strange smirk, and they both leave me whimpering in a soggy heap on the floor.

From the cold concrete, the last glimpse I have of Ester is a mop of curly red hair and sad hazel eyes peeking from under Mapp's arm, disappearing through the dining hall and out of sight.

While I sit here to the sound of water gushing in the hallway, the hand in my lap reacts to a drip of water, and I lift it absently to wipe my face. The other hand helps, and they hug me, but without a voice, they can't help any more. With Ester gone, and no other family or friends, even in this tunnel prison of a thousand other people, I am alone.

The glowing red numbers of the bedside clock tick over to 1:81, and I toss again.

Unable to sleep, I sit up and rub my eyes. Hazy light streams through the vent in the bottom of the door, distorting the colours of the animals I'd hand-painted on the small circular mat at the end of the bed. This room is small, just barely big enough for a wireframe cot and wardrobe. A long, smeary mirror fixed to the wardrobe door helps make the room feel larger than it is. With the painted mat and a mobile of fairies I'd made from collected rubbish, I've tried to make it feel more like my room at home, but every morning I see those ugly yellowish-grey walls, hear the ticking fans and smell the horrible air, I'm reminded it's not.

Almost every night, the repetitive ticking of those fans pushing the funky air around awakens me.

I wish the fan would just stop, and I fixo in my sleep. That sounds better than living in this nasty place.

The fans may wake me, but it's the lights in the corridor outside that keep me awake.

Untangling myself from the knotted-up bedsheets, I reach over to the side table, open the drawer and, from its special hiding spot underneath, take out my secret weapon. It's a narrow tube with a self-made plunger, like a needle without the sharp bit. From the mug on the side table, I pull on the plunger to load it with water and pad over to crack open the door. The hinges creak, making me cringe. Holding my breath, I wait to see if anyone has heard. Then, taking aim at the light outside the room, I push in the rod.

A thin stream of water sprays out and hits its target dead-on.

The light explodes to the tinkling of paper-thin glass raining over concrete, plunging the hallway into darkness.

1:87; I retreat inside, climb back into bed, and return my weapon to its hiding place.

The door bursts open, and I'm awoken with a jolt.

Three silhouettes stand in the hall outside the door. One is obviously Mapp from her portly shape and high pitch shriek. Another is the maintenance guy with tools jingling and clanging from his belt, and the third sounds like Shibley, one of the wardens who looks after me—well, is supposed to.

'This'll be the third time this trey she's done that,' the maintenance guy shouts over Mapp, his silhouette waving its arms about wildly in the doorway. 'Last time, me and the others rewired this whole section, thinkin' it were a short. Dunno how she does it, but I know it was her.' He turns on my light, and I'm blinded by the sudden brightness.

'She's just a child,' Shibley argues in my defence.

Mapp yells at Shibley, flapping her arms. 'She's not a child. She's a destructive little—'

'She's a child,' Shibley cuts her off.

'Yes, well, if you kept her under control, we wouldn't be in this situation now, would we, Shibley?'

'And we don't have many globes left when she keeps destroyin' them like that,' the maintenance guy complains.

'Don't be so hard on her,' Shibley protests.

Mapp grumbles. 'You wardens are too soft. If I'd known you were going to treat these retched fiends like precious little gems, I would have hired someone with more mettle!' She yanks the cord on her dressing gown tighter. 'She needs discipline.'

Shibley glances at me, then pushes past Mapp and the maintenance guy, blocking their entrance into the room. 'Mapp, let me talk to her. I'll make sure she straightens out, okay?'

Mapp thinks about it for a moment, then glares at Shibley. 'I don't know where she gets it from, but this is her last chance. Got it, Shibley?' she stresses, poking him in the chest with one of her sausage fingers. 'Gotthard has limited resources, and we can't afford rebellious little creatures like her. She's your responsibility. If she acts up again, you're both out, got it?'

'If you insist.'

Mapp mutters something under her breath before sticking her nose high in the air and following it out the door, leading the maintenance guy away with her.

'Jayne, Jayne, Jayne,' Shibley says, turning to me and sitting himself down on the edge of the bed. He's a weedy man with thick glasses and fine brown hair that looks like there's not enough of it to cover his shiny round head. 'Jayne, you can't go about destroying things like that,' he says, avoiding eye contact by looking at the scrappy teddy on the side table. 'What's going on? You can tell me.'

'I can't sleep, not with that light on all the time.'

He sighs. 'Well, we can't help that. There are three times of the day; morn, noon and night, you know that. Some light must be always on. It's for safety, okay?'

'But how do I sleep?'

'You have to get used to it,' he says, reaching out a knobbly hand to touch my shoulder and then snaps it away just as quick to run it through his thinning hair. 'I don't know how you do that to the lights, but don't do it again, okay? I know you miss that other girl. What was her name? Ester? But you have to make new friends, okay?'

'What, out of cardboard tubes and glue?'

He gives me a blank stare. 'No, Jayne. The other children.'

'I don't like the others. I want Ester.'

'But Ester's not here anymore, okay?'

'I wish *I* wasn't here anymore,' I moan, tossing over to face the wall, away from Shibley.

'Okay,' he says, patting the bed, 'soon, the morn will turn on, and it'll be time to get up, anyway. Get dressed, and I'll see you in the dining hall. Today we're going to make some new friends, okay?'

'I don't want the morning to just "turn on". And I don't want to make new friends.'

'Don't talk like that, okay? Saying things like that will only make you sad, okay?'

'Do you say okay to everything? I said I don't want to make new friends. You can't make me, so go away, OKAY?'

'Oh... I can see you're tired and hungry. Come on, get up, get dressed. We'll go to the dining hall, o—'

'Arrgh...' I scream at the wall. 'You're not my mum, and you're not my dad. I don't want you to look after me. I don't need anyone. I hate Mapp, I hate this place, and I HATE YOU. OKAY?'

'Ahh. You're upset. That's o—fine. I'm trying to help you,' Shibley says with a quavering voice. 'But... Yes, um, dining hall. Okay?'

There's an awkward pat on my back, and the bed lifts as he stands and shuffles out the door. Leaving me alone in the room, I stare at the wall, imagining I could bore a hole in it just by focusing my anger. The adults don't get it. I doubt they ever will.

I wish I wish I wish I wasn't here anymore.

It's 3:55 in the morn, and I sprint to class.

From the direction of Mapp's office, the sound of raised voices echo around the corridor.

'You were gone for almost a trey...' Mapp—one of the voices, shouts in her high pitch shriek. 'Please...How was I to know you didn't send him?'

'Mapp,' another woman's voice roars with such fury, I almost feel sorry for her. 'You allowed a stranger to abduct my daughter...!'

A door slams, and the voices cut off.

I wonder what that was all about?

Miss Wolaver's glare follows me over the rim of her glasses as I enter the classroom. Nine other children of various ages sit with sad faces at rickety desks. There used to be fifty. All those empty desks serve as a depressing reminder of how much I miss Ester. That, and the gallery of student artworks stuck alongside the alphabet and maths posters lining the classroom's horrid grey walls. Among them is a picture of an outdoor scene Ester drew. It remains the only proof she even existed.

Where are you, what are you up to, and who are you friends with now? I bet it's better than here.

'Jaynnnne!' the short, stocky teacher barks from her desk at the head of the room. I scurry to a nearby vacant desk in the front row while the other students barely even give me a glance.

'Class b'gins at 3:50, or have you forgot'n that?' she slurs, pulling a large metal flask from her bag. She takes a swig and places it in her top drawer.

'Sorry, Miss,' I reply, slumping into the chair.

'Right,' she says, 'we were just going through your homework exercises. Because of your tardiness, you will tell me how many cendecs are in a day.'

Without thinking, I blurt, 'same as there was yesterday.'

Some other students stifle giggles, but Miss Wolaver frowns at me so hard, I think her face will crack. 'Think you're funny, do you, Jayne?' she scowls. 'Try again. This time, the correct answer please, or it's to Mapp's office for you.'

'Ten, Miss,' I huff. 'There are ten cendecs in a day.'

'Correct. But you've still earned yourself detention for being late.'

'Aw,' I complain, slouching over the desk. My wrist still hurts from last time.

Miss Wolaver pulls herself from her chair, wobbles to the chalkboard behind her and begins scribbling. 'In the decat time system, one hundred decs make up a cendec, and one hundred midecs make up a dec.'

'Jayne, I want you to stand and recite for me the decat date-time system.'

'Me again?'

'Yes, you. Maybe if you learn it well enough, you'll also remember to be on time.'

'Okay,' I reply, standing with the enthusiasm of a brick. 'A cycle is one revolution of our planet, Jorth, around the Aster sun.

There are 330 days in a cycle.

Three treys are in a cycle. Each is 110 days long.

Eleven tendaws to a trey.

Ten days in a tendawn.

One day is ten cendecs long.'

'Well done, Jayne. So, you've done your homework. Be on time in future. You may sit,' she says, contining to write unreadable scrawl on the board.

'One tendawn is made up of ten days. Who here can name the days of the tendawn?'

A girl with long blonde-haired two seats from me shoots up her hand.

'Yes, Kiya,' Miss Wolaver says, pointing to her, and in direct contrast to me, she almost tosses the chair back to stand.

'Lunaday, Annarrday, Triaday, Diosday, um,' she stops to think, then continues, 'Herlovday, Gottday, Freoday, Idunday, Drasilday and Asterday.'

'Excellent work, Kiya.'

'And who can name the three treys?'

Kiya blurts out the answer again. 'Reincarner, Centraal and Tenebrosity, Miss.'

'Smartass,' I mutter under my breath.

'What was that, Jayne?' Miss Wolaver snaps, and Kiya, glaring at me with a smug look on her round, pink face, pokes a tongue out.

'Nothing, just impressive, that's all,' I lie.

'Yes, it is. Thank you, Jayne, for that unnecessary commentary.' The teacher collects her flask from the drawer and takes another swig while Kiya flicks her hair with a snobby 'humph.'

'Right!' the teacher gurgles, 'grab your history textbooks and turn to page, umm...' Miss Wolaver goes over to 'little-miss-snooty,' picks up her open book and reads, 'page one-eight-two, Chapter eight: Anina Cleve's Journal. History says when this event came, bad things happened,' she says, holding up the book and pointing at the page.

Opening to the page as instructed, it describes a girl who hid out in an attic with her family for cycles. The teacher burbles in the background, but none of it makes any sense. With overwhelming disinterest, my gaze drifts to a picture of trees and mountains set into a fake window frame on the wall...

... escaping the confines of the tunnels.

Clear blue sky stretched overhead. The sun's long, slender fingers of golden light stroked my face while the fresh breeze, sweet after the rain, played with my hair and pushed leaves about on the grass. Aves sung songs about their day. Where am I? How did I get here?

A tree slurs my name...

'Jayne, Jayne! What on Jorth has gotten into you?'

The voice wrenches me from my enchanting daydream back to the old-scratched desk and that boring book. 'Jayne, have you turned to page one-eight-two like everyone else?'

'Yes, Miss Wolaver.'

'You have? Good. Then read the part I just asked you to read.'

'Sorry, Miss?'

The dumb classmates laugh, but I'm saved by a knock at the door that attracts Miss Wolaver's attention, and she shuffles to answer, speaking to someone just outside with voices too faint to overhear.

'Continue reading page eight-one-two,' she drones, closing the door on the way out.

While she's gone for a few decs, I wonder what this stuff is she drinks all the time.

The timber chair creaks as I stand and approach the teacher's desk. Listening for any noise on the other side of the door, I carefully slide open the top drawer. With curiosity, the other students watch on while I lift the metal flip top flask from its resting place. Its top makes a familiar rattling sound as I open it, exposing the liquid to the air under my nose.

'Ugh,' I cringe at the sharp toxic smell, like bad pickles in a jar. No wonder Miss Wolaver's breath smells so awful.

Taking a sip, I cough a spray of the foul-tasting liquid all over the chalkboard.

From the murmured laughter of the other students, at least they found it funny.

It tastes as bad as the smell of the stuff they pump into the trucks.

How can she drink this?

A loud thud reverberates through the wooden classroom door, and my heart skips a beat. Quickly, I set the flask back in its place in Miss Wolaver's top drawer and close it. But by the time she re-enters the room, rubbing her head, I'm left standing where I am, with the evidence of my activities in plain sight. The moment she sees me and the clean lines streaking down the chalkboard, she storms over and opens the drawer. As if knowing exactly what I'd been up to, she removes the flask, gives it a shake, and without looking up, roars, 'Jaynnnne! Get out of my class. Administrator Mapp is waiting for you in her office.'

'Yes, Miss,' I reply. Still bearing the welts on my hands from the last time I visited Mapp's office to taste her cane, I drag my heels over the concrete floor, toward the door and my fate.

I wonder what it's about this time. Maybe it's about last night or something else I did. Maybe she found my stash of knives I made from scrap materials?

Just outside the administration offices, Mapp finds me dawdling in the hall.

'Ah, good. There you are,' she grins, flashing her crooked, stained teeth and talking in a tone I don't think I've ever heard from her before.

'Come here, Jayne. You have a visitor, and we shan't keep them waiting.' She snatches my hand and drags me faster than I can keep up.

Her wrinkled skin feels rough on mine.

I want so much to be somewhere else. Maybe it's my turn to be taken. Maybe that monster man has come back for me? Or slave traders? I bet they have big warts on their noses and smell like they haven't washed in a cycle.

Walls with doors to places I'd never been in flash by. At the speed Mapp is dragging me, I struggle to keep up.

'Come on, stop being a lump and hurry,' Mapp protests, almost pulling my arm from its socket. 'Now, when you meet this nice lady, you must be on your best behaviour, alright? She came a long way to see you. So *don't* mess this up. Remember, best behaviour, right?'

I changed my mind—two cycles without a wash and three warts.

Mapp pushes me through a door into a room that could make a broom closet feel large. Three wooden folding chairs sit around a tiny cloth-covered table pushed against the wall, supporting a vase of dusty fake flowers. 'Sit there. Stay quiet,' she orders, pointing to one chair in the corner, and proceeds to sit on the chair by the door, her generous size leaving little space for anything else.

The constant ticking of the fans outside fills the silence. Mapp glares at me with that hideous smile, as though expecting me to do something upsetting. It almost feels as though she's trying to burrow into my mind to work out what I'm thinking.

A gentle knock at the door relieves the discomfort, and as it cracks open, a woman's soft voice flows into the room. It isn't a voice I expect to hear; it lacks the pain of time trapped in this place. Instead, it's calming and gentle and softens the feeling in the room like a light breeze on a muggy day. 'Wonderful, I have the right room,' the stranger says, the delightful smell of flowers flowing in along with her.

Her appearance is not like anything I'd seen at Gotthard. Long wavy brown hair pours down around her soft pale face and over narrow shoulders covered in a red coat made of an expensive-looking fabric. Under that, a delicate white flowery blouse tops a black layered ankle-length skirt, gathered to her left thigh by a black ribbon, so its length just brushes the tops of a pair of elegant, black, ankle-high, lace-up boots.

Even Mapp seems impressed, but she remains seated, filling the space by the door and pointing at the chair in the opposite corner. How she expects our guest to enter, I don't know.

'Excuse me, Administrator,' the stranger says.

'Sorry, limited space in this room,' Mapp replies.

The woman brings the two short handles of her hard-worn handbag to her chest, shrugs, and then attempts to squeeze into the narrow space behind Mapp. I can't help but giggle when she whacks the administrator in the back of the head several times. Eventually, Mapp gives in, stands and, with a loud huff, allows the visitor to pass, only then returning to her seat, holding her head, looking flustered and glaring at me, as though it were my fault. At least that stupid smile is gone.

The new woman doesn't react to Mapp as she inspects the spare chair, dusting it off with a brush of her hand before taking a seat.

'Hello, Jayne,' she says, sitting straight and tall, crossing her slender fingers with their bright, red-painted nails on the table in front. Her gentle brown eyes consider me with a sparkle lost from the residents of Gotthard. 'My name is Seraphin MonLantry. It is so nice to meet you.'

I don't care what her name is, pretty or not, she's not here for me, she can't be. No one cares about me. The man who took Ester didn't care about her, so why would this woman care about me? I bet she's just like all the other grown-ups.

With disinterest, I cross my arms. 'I'm not four anymore,' I huff, slumping in my chair. 'I'm not simple like the others.'

'Jayne,' Mapp growls.

Seraphin gives a soft laugh. 'My apologies, Jayne, I recognise that now,' she says, making a sidelong glance at Mapp. 'I shall correct that.'

'I'm sorry, Seraphin. I don't know where she gets it from,' Mapp says, attempting to regain her control.

'It is understandable. A mind without direction is a soul without purpose.'

'I don't know what you just said, but okay,' replies Mapp, 'the thing is, she's a troublemaker, a loose cannon, if you will. With strong discipline and hard work, I'm sure you'll be able to straighten her right out.'

Seraphin's expression changes as she turns to me. 'So, Jayne, is that what you want? Discipline and hard work?'

'Well... Miss, no. I just want my sister back.'

'Not this again,' Mapp huffs. 'She has no damn sister! Ever since that brat Ester was taken a trey ago, this one's been intolerable, moaning and groaning about losing her sister. She's got it in her twisted mind they were sisters. For Progenitor's sake, Jayne was brought here as an orphan! Had I known they'd cause so much trouble when they were together, I would have taken more care to keep them apart!'

'Administrator Mapp, she is a child.' Seraphin winks at me. 'A mature one at that who has had to grow up fast and adapt to many things no child her age ever should. Let her have her fun.'

'Why do people keep telling me that? She's just a child. Maybe, but I don't know how much child "fun" this facility can afford,' Mapp groans.

'Well, maybe that is where I can help?' Seraphin says with a smile of bright white teeth.

Mapp's eyes light up almost as bright.

'Let me have a chat with her. If she is what we are looking for, perhaps we can make you a deal?'

I don't like the sound of that. What kind of deal could she possibly be talking about?

Images of child slave camps come to mind where I'm taken away in shackles and chains to work in a mine.

'How does that sound, Jayne?' Seraphin asks, her voice echoing to me from the other side of my daydream.

'Huh? I don't want to be a slave,' I blurt.

Seraphin chuckles, 'Slave? No, nothing like that. Say, Administrator, would you mind please leaving us together for a moment? I would like to talk to Jayne alone.'

I can almost see the blood run from Mapp's chubby face.

'Um... That isn't advisable,' she protests.

'We will be fine, will we not, Jayne?'

It surprises me this woman, Seraphin, just asked me that. I shrug my agreement.

'Are... are you sure about that?' Mapp asks, again glaring at me.

What would have Mapp concerned like this? What could she possibly think I would do?

I attempt to copy Seraphin's posture, making myself look more confident and mature like her.

'Please, as I said, I would like to speak to Jayne alone.'

'Ahhh, I don't think that's... ahhh...' Mapp stutters.

'Administrator, we will be fine. Run along now. I will call you when we are done,' Seraphin insists, dismissing Mapp by calmly turning her hand over with a limp wrist and flicking her fingers towards the door.

Dismissed from her own meeting, Mapp's face flushes bright red. 'You have no idea...' she mumbles, standing and grimacing at Seraphin.

Seraphin smiles at Mapp in return, giving her a wave as she leaves.

The door slams closed.

Without Mapp, the room seems bigger, but the walls still feel like they're closing in. Only Gotthard's droning noises fill the space while this pretty stranger sizes me up, and I do the same with her.

I can tell Seraphin isn't as dumb as the other people here. There's definitely something different about her.

She inhales, her eyes catching and reflecting the soul-sapping green-tinged colour of the room. 'So, how did you destroy the lights?' she asks after a while.

I reply with as much child-like innocence as I can muster. 'What lights?'

'The ones outside your room, of course?' she smiles, flashing those perfect teeth.

'It's not my room,' I object, pouting and folding my arms again.

'Sorry? Whose room is it then?'

'It's not mine. I just sleep there. My room was in my parent's house, and that burned down. Besides, the lights were keeping me awake. How do I know you're not here to squeeze my secrets out of me, or take me off to work in a mine?'

She lets out another one of those quirky little laughs. 'Slave camps and mines? My, you have such a vivid imagination. No, nothing like that, and you do not have to answer my question.'

'What question?'

'About the lights.'

'Oh, I have a secret weapon, but I'm not telling.'

'Fair enough. Say, Jayne, do you have any friends here?'

'I did have friends, but Mapp fattened them up and ate them, one by one. Now, I'm left with the dumb and stupid ones.'

She leans forward and speaks in a quieter voice. 'Do you think she would eat you too? You do not look like they have fattened you up at all.'

'I'm resisting the terrible food they keep feeding me.'

'I see. Well, I can certainly understand that. As for your friends, surely you could make a friend out of the remaining children?'

'That's a good idea. Maybe I can borrow a saw from maintenance and stitches from medical to make one good friend.'

She gives another funny look. 'That is interesting thinking, Jayne, but not quite what I meant. Besides, you cannot do that. It would be unfair on the others you did not put back together.'

'Hmm, you're right,' I reply. 'But, I can't talk to the others. There's something not quite right about them. Something missing.'

'Something like...?'

'I don't know. They're boring.'

There's that laugh again. 'You have some fire there, Jayne, just the type of fire I am looking for.'

I fiddle with the tablecloth, and the dusty fake flowers become a distraction. Staring at them, I try to avoid looking at the stranger so she can't see me sad. 'An enormous man came and took my bestest sister-friend away,' I tell her. 'Mapp just thinks I'm being silly, but she doesn't understand. She doesn't care.'

'I understand,' she says with compassion. 'It is terrible when we lose those we care about. But sometimes, these things happen. All we can do is move forward. You see those flowers...'

Oh no, she's noticed me staring at them.

'They are beautiful yet neglected and completely unaware of their potential. They could have been part of a bride's bouquet at a wedding or adorning the table at a fancy restaurant, but here they are, covered in dust in this dank and musty room.'

Her comment makes me painfully aware of the dirty knees protruding from beneath my stained brown dress, and I try to cover them with my hands.

'There is no need to be embarrassed, Jayne. Had the flowers been living, they still would not have had the concept of anything greater than their own limited existence. They would only know what they are. You, on the other hand, are so much more.'

'What do you mean?'

'Well, I cannot say much about it here. Rest assured, I think you will fit right in.'

'And you're sure it's not a slave camp?'

'No, Jayne,' Seraphin laughs, 'it is *not* a slave camp, or a mine. I promise.'

'Then what is it?'

'How about I show you?'

'Nothing can be worse than here,' I mumble. 'And I'm pretty sure Mapp would be happy to get rid of me.'

'You have to look forward to the unknown. Excitement lives there. Besides, you will learn new skills and help make this a better world. What do you think?'

'Does a tomadai have long ears, fluffy tail and hop from place to place?' Not bothering to ask if she minds, I launch myself into her lap, and the two of us almost topple over.

'So that is a no then?' Seraphin chuckles as she embraces me with a firm squeeze.

I haven't felt this happy since my parents left.

'When do we go, Seraphin?'

Only this morning, I was being told off by just about every grown-up in this place. Now, I have the chance to leave, get out of Gotthard and see the outside world, I can barely contain my excitement.

The door bursts open, and I kick the small table in surprise, sending the sad arrangement of flowers crashing to the concrete floor. Its vase shatters into a million pieces, scattering shards in every direction.

'JAAAYYYNE!' Mapp howls through the doorway, her face burning red with fury like she would rip the door from its hinges. Her beady little eyes dart between me and the remains of the vase on the floor. I didn't think a person's face could get any redder. 'Get off her, you insolent little shak. I've had just enough of you and your intolerant, destructive behaviour.' She storms into the room with her hand extended.

Before Mapp can touch me, Seraphin, with super-fast reflexes, snatches the administrator's chubby wrist. 'That's enough,' she commands in a voice spoken as though to a domesticated animal.

Mapp clutches at her arm, struggling to pull her wrist free like a tomadai snared in a trap. Seraphin's grip holds tight. 'We do not attack children,' she says, not even flinching at Mapp's continued flailing. 'Jayne and I were having a lovely conversation. Now, if you settle yourself, we will tell you about it.'

Mapp growls, 'Let go of me!'

'Not until you calm down.'

'I'll calm you down, you crazy—'

'Calm, I said,' Seraphin insists, gripping tighter. From the look on Mapp's face, it's painful.

How is this woman so strong?

'Okay, okay,' Mapp says, unclenching her fist.

'Good,' Seraphin says, relaxing her grip so unexpectedly, it makes Mapp stagger backwards into the doorframe. 'Now we can have a conversation like civilised people.'

'Well, I never!' Mapp says, stunned, rubbing her wrist where a red mark has appeared.

'Anyway,' Seraphin continues in a matter-of-fact tone, 'it will please you to know that Jayne has decided to come with me. You will finally have her out of your hair.'

'She will do no such thing!' Mapp snaps. 'After this display, I've changed my mind. I'm rescinding the offer.'

'I have already accepted the offer. Besides, you were so insistent you wanted her gone in your response to my inquiry, I would think this should satisfy you. What was it you said? "This place cannot afford such a destructive little wretch"?'

'I know what I said,' Mapp says, nervously glancing at me. 'But now that I've seen how desperately she wants out, I've changed my mind.'

'I see,' Seraphin muses, 'let us ask Jayne what she thinks, then?'

'It doesn't get a say...'

'I want out of Gotthard, Seraphin,' I plead, happy at least one of them asked me what I wanted.

'It seems the vote is two against one.'

'I never...' Mapp protests with mouth agape. 'I'm the administrator of this facility. The decision IS mine, and I say Jayne stays!'

'That decision is no longer yours to make, Administrator. Jayne has already told me all I need to hear.'

'Has she now? And what lies has the little wretch told you?'

'Lies? The only lie here is yours. You give the impression young girls are well cared for when clearly they are not.'

'And you can do better? You don't know what goes on here. You've no idea—'

'Well, that is apparent,' Seraphin interrupts. 'Clearly, Jayne is wasting away here. That is all I need to see.'

'What you see is a little shak that needs discipline and control,' Mapp spits. 'I'm not convinced she will get that from you. So, she stays here, where I can watch her and make sure she gets what she needs.'

'Is that what you think this is, discipline and control? All you see is destructive misbehaviour and insolence. Do you know what I see? Ingenuity and innovation. Pure potential.'

'I don't care what you see. I've said I'm rescinding our arrangement, so she stays here, and that's final. Thank you, Miss MonLantry, but you may now leave.'

'Not without Jayne.'

'Or you'll do what?'

Seraphin's voice changes from sweet and kind to dark and severe. 'Are you certain you want to go down that road with me?'

'I... I have people I can call right now,' Mapp threatens, but her face says otherwise.

'Do you?' Seraphin replies calmly. 'That is lovely for you. Have you any idea of the organisation to which I belong? We *do not* take kindly to threats, Mapp. Do you want to cross me on something so trivial? Please, Administrator, this is the last time I will ask you politely. Release Jayne into my custody, *now*.'

Mapp stammers, but Seraphin doesn't wait for a response. 'Then,' she continues, 'you will assist Jayne with any of her belongings, and you will escort us both to the exit tunnel with no trouble. Do you understand?'

'I will do no such thing!' Mapp shouts, with sweat beading on her red brow. Next thing, she holds out her hand and a tiny pistol appears. Shaking, she points it at Seraphin. 'Now, I have asked you to leave. Jayne stays—'

Before Mapp can finish, Seraphin seizes her arm again and pulls it to the table, pinning it down. In one quick movement, she unbuckles a strap and removes the gun from around Mapp's wrist.

'Interesting,' Seraphin says, holding it up to the light while Mapp wails in protest. 'What are you doing with a weapon like this? Not to worry,' Seraphin continues, placing it in her handbag on the floor. 'I shall relieve you of it. Such a thing is not prudent in this place.'

'I will have your hide for that!' Mapp shrieks. 'How dare you!'

'That is what you get for threatening me,' Seraphin says in her calming voice, releasing Mapp and collecting her bag. In one motion, Seraphin stands, sliding me off her lap so I can stand, too. 'Come on, Jayne. Mapp was just about to show us to the exit.'

Mapp mumbles a few words under her breath.

'Do you want anything from your room?' Seraphin asks, reaching for my hand, but with her gaze still firmly fixed on Mapp.

'No,' I reply.

'Not even that teddy I heard about?'

I shake my head. 'Eww, not that horrible thing.'

'Are you sure? I heard a lovely lady made it for you.'

'That lovely lady got put in another part of Gotthard so she'd leave me alone.'

'Oh my, Jayne, that sounds awful.'

'Can we go now please, Seraphin?'

'I think so. Mapp has made it clear we are no longer welcome here,' she replies, raising her voice a little so Mapp can hear. '*Isn't* that right, Nanneral?'

'Nanneral?' I giggle. With a name like that, no wonder people always call her Administrator, Mapp or both.

Seraphin squeezes my fingers to stop me from laughing.

'See, Administrator,' Seraphin adds, 'I know more about you than you think. Should you try to cross either of us again, it would be wise for you to remember that.'

Mapp guides us through the dining hall to a green door. Excitement and fear bubble up into my belly. Seems that monster has returned, and it wants to eat me from the inside-out. Seraphin grips my hand a little firmer. She must've been watching me.

'Do not fear. I will keep you safe,' she says, her voice just loud enough to be heard over the hateful sounds of Gotthard.

I'm not going to miss that. I can't believe I'm finally leaving this hole.

It's been over a cycle since I've been in these parts. Vaguely, I recall the hallways all looking the same, missing light globes, putrid yellow-grey walls, dark windows and *that* doctor.

I wonder which room he saw me in?

Dirt trails piled up along the walls become thicker, and we come to a bend where a huge metal door with a large wheel in the middle blocks the way.

Mapp slides a bar across and turns the wheel. With a grunt, she pulls it open, then holds out her hand. 'After you.'

'You are the one showing the way,' Seraphin says.

Mapp huffs, and stepping over the metal threshold, waits in the dim light for us to follow. 'The front door is around that corner,' she says, pointing. 'Don't let it hit you on the way out. Now you have what you want, I have work to do. Goodbye.' With a creak of the door, Mapp is gone.

The darkened cave beyond the door looks familiar, like the one where I met Remy, and he signed my name into his record book. It's also the place I last saw Lou Doe, the woman who saved me and who gave me this name. The crates and Remy's table are all gone now. Only the rough-cut walls and floor remain. As the tunnel narrows, I think back to the day Lou brought me here.

'Is everything okay?' Seraphin asks.

'I'm not going to miss this place. I just want to remember the person who brought me here, that's all.'

'Oh?'

'Her name was Lou Tenant Doe.' As I say that, Seraphin missteps. 'I don't know where she is now, but I hope she's okay.'

'I'm sure she is,' Seraphin replies as she leads me to the door out.

Before she opens it, Seraphin goes over to a rucksack set aside in a corner, unzips it and pulls out two sets of protective overalls and gloves.

'Jayne,' Seraphin says, pulling a breather from the bag, carefully choosing her next words. 'Do you trust me?'

The question catches me by surprise. *How do I respond to that?* 'I don't understand?'

'Home differs greatly from Gotthard, and it will take time for you to adjust,' she says.

'What do you mean?'

'Best we leave that for another time. For now, before we go, you must know that it was not by chance I chose you. You are special. The lightbulbs and the syringe weapon you crafted to destroy them, the hidden stash of homemade weapons you kept concealed under your bed. You are not like the other children here, and that is what makes you special. You need to know that whatever happens, I will protect you. That is my job. Do you understand?'

How does she know all these things?

'Not really,' but I nod anyway. Something about her makes me feel safe, and I felt it the moment she stepped into that tiny room.

'Where I come from,' she says, kneeling to be the same height, 'I am called a Guardian. It is like a mother, but not. I know I am not your real mother, and I will never try to replace or spoil your memories of her. But I would like to think I can be as close to a mother as you deserve. For me to do that, I need you to trust me, and only me. Can you do that?'

The remaining light globe makes her brown eyes glisten, and I reply with a nod of confusion and excitement. I've chosen to be with her now, and there's no turning back. I have no idea where that'll take me, but I'm about to find out.

04 – New Beginnings

Gotthard's featureless metal plate door groans on its hinges as it pulls itself closed, pressing out one last breath of warm but stale air. With a sinister bang, it seals away that horrible place and pushes us out into the unforgiving cold.

Free at last, or am I?

Three hundred and fifty-four days I spent living in that wretched place. It lifts my spirits to finally break free, to see the sky and feel fresh air against my skin again. Although out here, it can hardly be called fresh.

A constant ash-filled gale blows into the short alcove, making the temperature out here much less comfortable than what I had just left behind. It strips away the warmth from my body, and I shiver.

Seraphin stands beside me, her white coveralls whipping about her in a frenzy. 'Ready?' she calls out over the noise.

'Seraphin, I'm cold,' I complain between chattering teeth.

I don't think she heard me because she grabs my hand and pulls me out into the nasty wind.

It cuts through my thin clothing, stinging like a thousand insects, and makes me second guess my decision to leave.

What am I doing? I don't even know this stranger, but she's dragging me through the cold to a place I don't know where.

Seraphin tows me along a road, through the forest of brown knobbly poles that used to be trees, now coated in grimy, grey ice.

Don't let go, or else she'll disappear. Then you'll be on your own.

The road meanders away to a stack of fallen trees, their twisted and knotted roots ripped out of the ground, blocking our path and sight of wherever it is we're going. My fingers and toes go numb, and without a cave or shelter anywhere in sight, the fear of freezing to death, never to be found again, brings back the monsters Ester and I chased away. Just like when I hid under my bed, they threaten to suffocate me and make my heart explode at the same time.

Clawing at the breather, I want to rip it off.

I need more air. I've got to breathe.

'You okay back there, Jayne?' Seraphin calls out, trying to keep the hood of her suit from whipping off her head.

Her voice snaps me back to reality, and I look around for my monster, but it seems Seraphin has scared him away. Well, at least for now. I know he's still lurking around out there, somewhere.

Seraphin's hand grips mine a little firmer. Her grip is warm and comforting. She pulls me in closer, then leans her shoulder into the wind and pushes on.

Beyond the fallen trees, a familiar rumbling sound grows louder, and we come across a patchy brown, grey and white truck hiding off the track amongst the surrounding landscape. The vehicle reminds me of the one Lou Tenent Doe had brought me in last cycle, only painted in different blotches of colour. Chains wrap around its massive tyres, and all I can think of is warmth.

The driver's door opens, and a man in a breathing mask, dressed in thick clothing coloured like the truck, drops to his feet. He wrestles the door closed as the wind attempts to rip it from him, and treading carefully, moves around to meet us.

'Welcome back, Ms MonLantry,' he yells over the gale. 'That was quick?'

'What did you expect?' Seraphin replies. 'The door please, Reg.'

'Hold on,' Reg says, opening the passenger side door for us. 'There's a bit of a breeze today. Oh, and who is this you've brought with you?' he asks.

'This is Jayne.'

For some reason, looking at Reg through his mask, with his fluffy grey eyebrows and soft wrinkles, he reminds me of Grandad. He politely extends his hand to shake mine. 'Hello, Jayne.'

'Pleasantries inside, please,' Seraphin says, pushing me toward the open door.

Reg's strong hands hold it back while I hoist myself into the cabin and slide across the springy bench seat. From here, I can see everything through the truck's windscreen, including trees bending this way and that as invisible giants only I can see, fight between them. Seraphin's gentle touch of my hand makes them disappear.

'You still with me, Jayne?' she says.

Reg scrambles back around the truck and clambers into the drivers' seat, not hesitating to close the cold out. 'Brr,' he says, furiously rubbing his gloved hands together while he adjusts the fan to make warm air blow harder through the vents.

'That's invigorating. How are you two doing? I know I have something around here somewhere...' he adds, leaning over and rummaging around in the void behind the seat. He pulls out a ragged but warm-looking blanket and wraps it over my shoulders. 'Would you like a block of koqua? Everybody likes koqua.'

The whole experience has me speechless, and I just nod.

Reg reaches into a dashboard compartment, pulls out a small foil-wrapped goodie and holds it out.

'How's that?' Seraphin asks, rubbing my arms vigorously.

While pulling the blanket tight, I reach for the koqua, and stammer, unable to keep my teeth from chattering. 'It's c... c... cold. But b... b... b... better.'

'The cold takes a little getting used to, I am afraid,' she says. 'An unfortunate side-effect of the bombs.'

'And the koqua?' Reg asks.

It's been a long time since I had koqua, and the sweetness sends tingles through my cheeks. 'It's not too bad,' I muffle through the dissolved creamy smoothness filling my mouth.

'You hear that?' Reg chuckles. 'She says it's only mediocre.'

A patch of blue pokes from between the clouds and the sparse leafless trees. 'It's the first time I've seen the sky in treys. After being cooped up in that place, I was beginning to forget what it looked like.'

'Ahh, looking on the bright side,' Seraphin smiles. 'I think you will do fine.'

'Will it always be like this, though?' I ask, hoping this winter won't last forever.

'I cannot say,' she replies thoughtfully. 'I have never lived through winter like this before. Nobody has. But over the last cycle, I can say the weather seems to have improved a little. So that is a promising sign.' With a quick flick of her wrist, she signals to Reg.

'Off we go!' Reg says, revving the truck, and rolls us out onto the track.

'I have been told we should be able to go outside without breathers in a cycle or two. Now that will be exciting,' Seraphin says with delight.

'That does sound exciting. Oh, to breathe fresh air again.' The shivers subside, and sensation returns to my fingers once again. 'Tell me about my new home?'

'Well,' Seraphin says, tugging on the blanket to make sure it fully covers my legs. 'Home is called Garret Gord. It once was a dry lake bed on a mountaintop called Garret Flats. Then a man named Elihus Kinton came and turned it into our home, taking in and educating stray girls just like you and me. Some call him a visionary. We call him the Patriarch.'

'The Patriarch?'

'There will be plenty of time to talk about that when we get home. Until then, just enjoy the ride.'

On the journey to Garret Gord, my new home, I gaze out the windscreen, watching with mixed wonder and disbelief as the changed world slides by. This used to be my world, but now with the barren landscape, charred remains of towns and grey snow covering everything, it's alien.

The narrow dirt road falls away into a steep descent through the dead, frozen forest.

Winding and rolling, we pass what used to be an old farmhouse, then a lake, with its surface frozen into thick white ice. This area should be lush and green, teeming with aves and animals, but now there's not a single living thing in sight.

'Jayne,' Mum calls out from the other room, 'your brother is crying again. Can you please go find out if he needs changing?'

'In a moment.'

'Now please, Jayne!'

'Okay.' Leaving my toys where my story had been interrupted, I rush out of my room. There, lying in the hallway, is a broom and a brick. Why is there a brick there?

The door to my brother's room is closed, and the handle is warm. When I push open the door, the walls are missing, and the sky swirls a deathly red cloud above my baby brother, who lies screaming in his cot.

I turn away to get mum. Then everything is gone except a burning pile of rubble and an arm reaching out for me...

The truck drops into a pot-hole, awakening me with a jolt. When I open my eyes, the road has become a windy track, and it climbs ever higher up the side of a mountain.

Seraphin is resting her head against the door with her eyes closed. It seems she's fallen asleep to the motion of the truck as well.

'Oh, you're awake,' Reg says, looking over at me. 'Just in time, too. Check this out. You better hold on.'

The truck turns a bend, and stretching out in front, the track disappears, leaving only cloudy sky.

Seraphin stirs, opening her eyes. 'Ohh, I love this bit.'

We tip over the hill, and my stomach leaps into my throat as Reg lets the truck go. With nothing but sky in the windscreen and angled trees whipping by, it feels like we're flying.

'Wheee!' I giggle with excitement.

Reg has done this before.

Like a diving ave, we continue our descent towards what looks like thick, grey cloud clinging to the mountain. It appears to cut off the road ahead, and I can almost feel the air get colder as we plunge beneath it. There, at the bottom, the track flattens out into a low, narrow ridge, just wide enough for the one truck. On the left, the forest gives way to a flat area, stretching as far as the eye can see, and on the right is burnt woodlands made up of more leafless poles.

Just when I thought I'd seen the end of the ride, the road ahead shoots straight up a hill so steep it disappears through the cloud again and into the sky.

The moment we push above the cloud, I can't help but marvel at the view. For here, there are no trees, only a mountain carved into gigantic curved steps, and at the very top, an island made of solid rock.

'Wow!' I say, leaning forward to get a better look.

'Impressive, hey?' Seraphin smiles, seemingly not at all surprised by my reaction.

From all the things I have seen today, this is the most amazing, and I can't take my eyes off it.

The truck slows on the slope, crawling up the skyward facing road for what seems like ages. At the top, we pull to a stop at a pair of enormous steel gates set into a sprawling fence made of solid tree trunks rammed into the ground.

Reg lets the window down, flushing the warm air from the cabin, and speaks to a guard wearing a uniform like his.

They wave us through, and as we pass the armed guards at the massive gate, past two more parked trucks painted like this one, and I imagine this place is a fort.

I'm going to be living in a fort?

Seraphin nudges me. 'We are home.'

'This is home?'

There's not much here, just a big flat patch of bare dirt with eight small concrete shed-like boxes not large enough to live in, dotted nearby. Beyond that, there's more fence running off into the haze. All this bare open ground gives me a sick feeling I'll be living outdoors in this terrible weather.

Seraphin places a hand on my shoulder and says, 'you will spend plenty of time outside soon enough, but for the moment, we better get inside before you catch a cold.'

Inside? How could there be? There's nothing here?

We cross the compound and enter the second shed to the right, going down three flights of stairs to a landing, stopping to remove our masks and protective coveralls. It feels good to be out of that ridiculous outfit again. Not only was it uncomfortable, but the mask also kept fogging up, and the coveralls made swooshing noises as I walked; it felt like I was wearing a garbage bag.

Seraphin drops the dirty suits into a large basket.

The lighting here is less annoying than at Gotthard, but the walls are still painted in that same unimaginative creamy-grey colour.

It seems I can't get away from that repulsive colour scheme.

Seraphin lets her hair out and whispers, 'when you are in this hallway, keep your voice down. Other families live here. And another thing, never go into another apartment, even if invited. This is important, do you understand?'

'I don't want to live in another Gotthard, Seraphin.'

'Do not worry, I will explain. For the moment, just do as I ask of you, okay?'

I can't keep my eyes off Seraphin's silky, brown hair, admiring it as my short red hair bounces in front of my vision.

I want hair like Seraphin's. I don't like my red hair anymore. I miss Dad.

At the end of the long hallway, Seraphin unlocks a wide door, pushes it all the way open and strides inside, holding it open for me to enter.

Inside the spacious apartment, plants and flowers mesmerise me with their vibrant greens and reds and colours I don't even have names for.

'Well, come on in then, this is *our* place,' Seraphin calls, rousing me from my trance, and I wander in as though entering a fantasy world.

This is unlike any place I have ever been before. The enormous circular room doesn't have a straight wall. Big green leafy plants and beautiful flowers in hanging baskets and pots as tall as me make the apartment feel like a natural wonderland. And at the back of the room is a dining table near a large kitchen where there's a big blue table off to one side, with edges restraining multicoloured balls strewn around its top.

Compared to Gotthard, this place is a mystical palace filled with light that streams down from square windows in the ceiling, giving life to vibrant paintings of shapes and patterns hanging on the white walls. It even smells beautiful, like Seraphin.

'Wowskis!'

She smiles, 'You like it? I was hoping you would.'

Taking in the wonder, there's even a visiontube.

'You have a visiontube!' I shout with delight. 'But nobody has those anymore. They all broke with the bombs, like everything else.'

Seraphin gives a soft laugh. 'Not here. There are many pre-recorded shows playing at certain times on the VT. We also have many educational, leisure shows and features. Everything needed to expand growing young minds. The Patriarch has thought of everything.'

'The Patriarch?'

'Yes, as I said before, he founded this place.'

'That's a funny name. Why do you call him that?'

'The Patriarch is our father, our saviour. He has a dream for the future, provides for us and protects us.'

'Oh. Okay then. Will I get to meet him?'

'He will meet you when the time is right.'

My excitement fades, noticing the green couch facing the VT, and I take a seat, wiping my hand over the texture, trying to remember how my parents' couch felt.

'Oh, is there something wrong?' Seraphin asks.

'I had a green couch, as well. I mean, mum and dad had a green couch. I remember sitting on it while they cooked and listened to my wild stories.'

'I am so sorry, darling, I did not know,' she says, sitting next to me, gently stroking my shoulder. 'I shall have it replaced on the morrow.'

'No, please don't,' I sniff, gazing up at her. 'I love it.'

'Are you sure?' she asks, looking puzzled.

'Please keep it. I want you to keep it.'

For a moment, she sits with me in silence. 'Okay, we will keep it.'

'Sera...' Her name sticks in my throat, and I look away with embarrassment. 'I'm sorry.'

'It is fine. It has been a bit of an emotional ride for you, I understand. You know what? you can call me Sera if you like. I like the name.'

'Okay, Sera,' I sniff, wiping away a tear.

It feels strange, crying in front of her, but I also feel better. But I still have a lot of questions.

'Sera, what are people like here? Will there be others like me?'

'You will meet them soon enough.'

At that, I grin with excitement.

'Jayne,' she continues, her voice turning serious. 'I am not going to lie to you. It will be hard work for the next few cycles. But I think you may find it gets easier. You see, we live by a strict but necessary set of rules. In time you will come to learn them all. For now, we must start with the most important one; respect your Guardian, trust none other. Do you understand?'

'That's an odd thing to say.'

'This is serious. Even here, people are wicked and are not to be trusted. They will try to take advantage of you.'

'Does that include you, Sera?'

'Here at Garret Gord, I am your Guardian, and that title carries a certain amount of authority. Like you, I do not always stick to the rules. I do not expect your trust or respect straight away. I want to earn it, and I hope someday I can. But know this, Jayne. Trust is not the same thing as respect. Respect may be demanded, but trust cannot be forced. That is yours, and yours alone. It is safest not to trust at all.'

'What about other people, though? When will I meet them?'

'Eventually. For the moment, I am your family.'

What sort of place have I gone to where I can't trust anyone?

'That reminds me, I have some clothes for you to wear. I had them made especially for you. They are in your room.'

'I have a room?'

'Yes. Behind the kitchen, it is the door to the left.'

Excited, I bound across the room in search. More doors hide behind the wall of plants, and I burst through the door described.

Unlike all the walls at Gotthard, this room is painted in a calming and airy, pale blue. Bright sunlight streaming through one of those rectangular windows in the ceiling makes the room feel light and comfortable. And in its centre, strung with fairy lights, is a large, aged, white four-poster bed, with a storage chest at its foot, side tables, dresser and wardrobe in the far corner, all matching the style of the bed. This room is easily three times bigger than that miserable cupboard at Gotthard. There's even a bookcase, desk and chair along one wall—plenty of space to put my things, if only I had any.

'Do you like it?' Sera asks, standing in the doorway as I run laps around the room with newfound energy.

'I love it!'

'You can decorate it however you like, and if you do not like the furniture, I can see if we can trade it for something else. And we can repaint the walls if you do not like the colour.'

'Sera, it's wonderful. It's not cream, white or grey,' I cry, throwing my arms around her waist. 'I really do love it. I'm going to keep it just the way it is.'

'I am glad you like it. Now, go shower. You are a little on the nose.'

'Sera...?'

'Next door,' she adds, pointing to the left. 'You will find a towel and some soap already in there. Now go, you smell like a garbage chute.' She smiles, mouthing the words, 'hurry up.'

It's the longest shower I've had in treys. In Gotthard, we were limited to only two decs each, using only boring soap, which smelled like drain cleaner and old itchy towels.

Here, I emerge from the bathroom dressed in a fluffy white robe smelling of rainflower and elderwood, scents similar to the perfumes mum used to wear.

The aroma of something cooking draws me to the kitchen, and I find Sera stirring a pot and flipping something in a pan.

She glances up. 'There you are,' she says. 'I was beginning to wonder if you had dissolved and washed away down the drain. This is almost done, so you might want to get dressed.'

I scurry to my room, put on some of my brand-new clothes, and take a moment to admire them in the full-length mirror on my wardrobe door. For the first time in a very long while, I'm wearing clean, comfortable clothes. I twirl on the spot to watch the folds of my dark blue slacks and loose white top flow like ripples across water in the mirror.

By the time I step out into the kitchen, Sera's busy serving up something yummy on a pair of plates.

'Whaddya think?' I ask, spinning to show off my new outfit.

'Looking good. What do *you* think?'

'They're beautiful, thank you!'

'I am glad you like them. I was unsure about your taste in fashion, but if you are happy, I am happy. Come on, dinner is ready.'

Laid out on the large wooden dining table is a pair of dark purple placemats and the shiniest knife and fork I have ever seen.

'What's this?' I ask, looking at the neatly arranged food on the plate, taking my time to breathe in the aroma.

'It is just simple pot beans and eggs on toast.'

'This isn't like any beans and eggs on toast I've ever had before.'

'Probably not. I am not surprised seeing what gruel they fed you in that place, but I think you will find things are very different here. For a start, at Garret Gord, we are self-sufficient. Everything you see here, we either grow, catch, or make ourselves. The pot beans are my own special recipe.'

My mouth waters and I realise I hadn't eaten since the koqua earlier. Steam rises from the plate as I shovel some beans into my mouth. 'Ah, hot, hot, hot!' I yelp when they scold my tongue on their way down.

'Careful, they have just come off the stove.'

'I don't care. They're yummy!' I say, in between piping hot mouthfuls.

'I am glad you like them. Just the thing for a growing... say Jayne, how old are you? Sixteen, seventeen?'

'No silly, I just turned eight,' I reply, looking up from the full fork.

'Eight! Wow, really? Did they do anything special for you?'

'No, not really. Besides, without mum and dad, namedawns just aren't the same anymore. Administrator Mapp—Nanneral came to see me, gave me a hug and some small tasteless cake, two colouring pencils, and then she left. That's about it.'

'How beastly,' Sera replies with aghast, 'that simply will not do. We must make up for your misspent namedawn then. An eight-cycle-old deserves a decent namedawn, do you not agree?'

A smile virtually cracks my face in two.

At that, Sera stands and walks over to the kitchen to retrieve a small rectangular parcel, neatly wrapped in brightly coloured decorative paper and a red ribbon tied off in a bow. She places it on the table in front of me.

Curious, I glance at her for approval.

'You do not have to ask. I gave it to you. Open it.'

A worn black box rolls out into my hands as I discard the wrapping. Lifting the lid, nestled within, is a set of three slender, oddly-shaped metal knives with holes in their handles, and three old coins.

I look up at Sera in confusion.

Nobody has ever given me a box of knives before.

'They are practice throwing knives. They used to be mine. Now they are yours.'

'Throwing knives?' I grin, wondering if she's serious. 'And the coins?'

'Where I come from, gifting a knife is considered bad luck, as it can cut friendships. The coins are to buy away the bad luck.'

'Oh, Sera, this is the best namedawn present ever!'

'Not so fast. You will have to learn how to use them first.'

'I will learn how to use throwing knives?'

'Yes, among other things. Until then,' she says, replacing the lid, 'they will remain in their box.'

'Aw, but...'

'Consider this your first lesson. Every weapon must be respected. All things, including that fork, have the potential to kill when used with malicious intent or disrespect. Therefore, only use weapons when we must, and with trained hands and mind. For now, we will put the box here,' she says, placing it on a shelf just out of the kitchen. 'When you are ready, their care and potential will be yours. Anyway, happy belated namedawn, Jayne.'

Correction, best day ever!

05 – A Little Hope

Excerpt from Book of the Progenitors:

It is said, the leader of the Dragons, Xisnys Kacir, steals the souls of the vanquished in combat and recruits them to her own destructive purpose. She stands on her feet and fights with hands, like a person, yet her breath is pure fire. Her ferocity is something to behold. If only the armies of Gaia could tame her.

NC02

The weak sun was setting over the refugee camp Hope, as Sage Solon hurried flat-footed over the slippery ground, braving the blistering cold to deliver his urgent message.

With heart pounding in his ears and puffing heavily into his breather, he hastened along the main street through the centre of the camp, his icy path lit by twilight and dim blue bio-luminescent liquid lamps strung up on wooden posts. On either side, he passed huts made of salvaged scrap material; homes for the displaced and destitute, each one as depressing as the last.

People who recognised Sage's prominent, red, ankle-length coat either waved in passing or tried to engage him in conversation. This night, the message he carried was far more critical than to be hijacked into a discussion about toilet paper rations. So, he changed his route to avoid them, choosing a slightly more perilous path, plunging into the shadows between the shacks, to traverse an obstacle course of rubbish, angled building supports, and ropes pegged into the frozen ground. His destination was a shack toward the western end of camp. It wasn't larger or fancier than any of the other refugee huts, but it was humble for the camp administrator.

Taking shelter in the alcove by the door, he paused briefly to gather his breath, glance around the street to ensure he wasn't followed, then knock his identifiable pattern.

A moment passed, then the door cracked open, and a familiar, middle-aged man with a caramel complexion and a warm, comforting smile greeted him, widening the gap to allow him to slide through. 'Grace even,' Gaius Sempro stuttered.

Once inside the warm, dimly lit living room of Gaius's home, Sage removed his mask, revealing the rugged face of a man who had seen more grief in the last few cycles than he had in the entire thirty-four cycles of his life. 'Grace even,' he replied, placing his fleece-lined cap and heavy loaghtan wool coat on a peg by the door.

The unique, red-dyed coat had been gifted to him from a loaghtan herder after he saved one of the hooved animals from a ravine a trey ago. It quickly became one of his most treasured possessions and now served as his hallmark; a symbol of his respected position as vice-administrator of their small but growing community.

Gaius had seen many more cycles than Sage, and it showed in the creases around his brown eyes and grey-flecked, dark brown hair. He ambled across the quaint living room to a small table supporting a bio-luminescent lamp and turned the dial on the wooden base. A bladed fan in the liquid began stirring, generating more light the faster it turned. He adjusted it until it illuminated the single room, revealing a worn-out bed in the back corner where a couple in their forties and a boy aged about eight huddled under the blankets. Sage nodded to them in acknowledgement, and they responded in kind.

Opposite the bed by the door was a single-seat wingback chair with its footrest and a few crates forming a makeshift bed where Gaius slept. The rest of the hut comprised a simple kitchen, with a plain, round wooden table and an oil heater with a warming plate that was keeping a jug of water from freezing. Gaius picked up the jug, splashed some water into two ceramic mugs, and handed one to Sage.

'What can I help you with this even?' Gaius stuttered, taking a sip of the water.

'Sir, a comms report from the Watch. Five trucks are cutting their way through our barriers on the other side of the river. They're progressing faster than we would expect. Watch suggests we have about half a cendec before they arrive.'

'Hmm,' Gaius mused, 'do we know who or why?'

'No, sir. But Watch thinks they might be military. We have to assume they're hostile.'

Gaius's nickname of the "*smiling administrator*" held true. It never ceased to amaze Sage how, no matter the news, the man calmly accepted it.

The older man finished his drink and set down his cup. 'Get everyone to the cave. Then, go do your thing.'

'Do you want a silent alarm?'

'We're too big now for door knocking. Use emergency protocols.'

'Understood. What about the Topes?' Sage replied, glancing over at the family in the bed, where three sets of eyes reflected at him in the low light.

Gaius glanced at them too and bowed his head. 'Garan is unable to walk...'

'Don't worry. I'll send over two strong people to help.'

'Good man. Oh, and if you see the council, send them to the overlook.'

Sage nodded. 'I'll make sure everyone gets to safety, then I'll find you at the overlook.' He turned to leave, but hesitated. 'Sir, when this is over, I need your permission to train more people.'

Gaius patted Sage on the shoulder. 'Yes, of course, we'll talk about it.'

'Thank you, and for the water,' Sage said, draining the cup. As he nodded to the Topes and prepared to leave, Gaius added, 'be careful. We need you.'

Sage rushed towards the centre of camp, his destination standing out like a windowless castle in the middle of a village of shacks.

'Whoa,' he muttered to himself, slipping on the ice. He waved his arms to steady himself, and regaining his balance, came to a stop in the dip leading up to the community hall.

The refugee camp was founded upon the ruins of this old stone building. Erected before the war, it once was a circedoma; a place of worship to the Progenitors, a powerful race thought to have once inhabited Jorth but left for the stars eons ago.

The humble circedoma had been part of a small, remote mining town, abandoned for so long, the name had since been forgotten. Only the circedoma, with its solid hardwood timber frame supporting rough-cut stone walls, remained. Dilapidated, burned and decaying, it too would have been forgotten in time if it weren't for Gaius and his late wife, Rika, stumbling across it one freezing night. The two rebuilt it, reinforced it with timber and metal sheeting found from other destroyed buildings, and converted it into their home.

As more refugees discovered the camp, it became a shared home. When the sizable two-room building became inadequate to house everyone, the pacifist war veteran, with the aid of his wife and others, expanded the camp. Gaius and Rika moved out so the building could become an in-between house for newcomers and finally converted it into a community and council hall to support a refugee camp. Little did they know that it would eventually accommodate over five hundred people. Most of the refugees brought nothing, clinging onto the only thing they treasured most and what brought them here in the first place.

For this reason, they called their new home Hope.

Sage made his way up the gentle slope and pushed through its rough timber doors.

Only a handful of chairs and a podium of simple construction occupied the room, leaving most of the timber floor vacant. With his feet on firmer ground, Sage jogged to the storeroom behind the podium. At the rear of the storeroom, filled with boxes, chairs and folded tables, he lifted a loose plank in the floor and pushed a concealed button.

Outside, horn-shaped loudspeakers mounted on light poles wailed their warning, alerting the camp's residents of impending danger until Sage released his finger and waited for the twelve area wardens to stomp through the door.

'Thank you all for coming so quickly,' Sage said, greeting the twelve people wearing light coloured bands on their arms. 'We've done this before, and sad to say, this is not a drill. Hostile trucks are inbound, and we must assume they're armed. Righto, make sure every house is empty. Don't forget your training. Remember, watch for strays and backtrackers. Get everyone out. Pipkins, that also means your ex-wife. Eastman, you're with me. Dismissed.'

The wardens all voiced their compliance and filed out the door. Sage followed to greet the twenty-two assembled target shooters, standing in an arc, carrying rifles slung over their shoulders. The long, slender barrels of their weapons towered over their heads, and the stocks disappeared into their shaggy grey and white fur coats. It made them look like formidable ursus, the beastly mammals from which their coats were made.

'This is not a drill,' Sage ordered. 'Take your kill box positions and hold your fire until I give the call.'

Another armed man pushed through the dissipating group of beast people towards Sage. Despite his tall, athletic physique, he seemed small compared to the bulk of the target-shooters. 'Reporting for duty,' he said, his thick, knee-length brown coat whipping in the wind behind him.

'Jaxson, thank the Progenitors you're here. How goes the evacuation?' Sage asked.

'So far, so good. Looks like those drills really paid off. People are already leaving their homes and heading for the caves,' Jaxson said.

'Good,' Sage nodded. 'I'll head there once all the wardens report back. I won't be happy until everyone is safely back in their beds after this is over. Take Eastman and report to Gaius. He needs help with Garan.'

'No problem. You'll be right by yourself?'

'Yes, I don't expect too much trouble. And I won't be alone. I'll have the wardens with me, but keep your watch. We can't be too careful. When you're done helping Gaius, find me at the shelter.'

'Right you are,' Jaxson replied and left Sage watching the tired, single-file march of refugees snake their way towards the evacuation assembly area.

Headlights glinted over the camp from the mountain road on the opposite side of the frozen river. The trucks drew nearer, labouring through their roadblocks of fallen trees and boulders. Sage monitored the last of the stragglers, herded by the wardens and those beams of light, pressing urgency.

Sage did his best to keep up morale, dropping into the moving procession and chatting to the stragglers.

There was old Edsel with her bad back, hobbling beside her grouchy husband Bronal, the nurse Marra carrying her adopted son, Tobias, whose parents perished in the bombings just after he was born, and Aubine, the middle-aged history teacher with her ancient, stubborn ways.

Despite Sage's best efforts, many still voiced their complaints about the weather and their wishes to return to their heated shacks as they passed.

'Come on, folks, not much further to go,' Sage called, clapping his gloved hands a few times, more for keeping warm than for an audible hurry-up. 'Soon, this will be all over, and you'll be able to return to your homes. I just need you to get a hurry on, quickly now.'

The headlights reached the opposite bank of the river. Soon they would be upon the camp.

Sage approached just as Jaxson was exiting the cave, the custom-made metal spikes on his shoes gripping the icy ground with ease.

'Gaius and the Tope family have been looked after.'

'Good, thanks,' Sage said, his relief concealed by his mask. 'Is this everyone?'

'I think so.'

'Better be. That's the last of the wardens—time to move. Gaius needs us at the overlook. The target-shooters will look after the camp now.'

As they walked away, Sage admired Jaxson's footwear. 'I think I need a pair of those.'

'After all this, I'll make you a pair.'

From the sheltered, rocky cliff called the overlook, Sage and the other councillors watched with apprehension as the convoy of vehicles rounded the last corner before the camp. Their headlights glistened off the frozen road, stopping to investigate a roadblock before resuming their slow crawl along the main street.

When the convoy stopped outside the community hall, a lone person, clad all in black, climbed down from the second vehicle, glanced in all directions as though waiting for a greeting party, then moved towards the hall.

The moment Sage lost sight of them, the small tabletop comms unit beside him crackled to life. The voice on the other end whispered, 'Shooter four. The person has entered the hall. Out.'

'How are the Tope's going? How's Garan?' Sage asked Gaius while waiting for another report to come over the comms.

Gaius spoke slowly, trying not to stutter. 'Not well. The boy needs food. Not good during a growth spurt. Garan's getting worse. Lexi's doing the best she can, but he needs better treatment, or his leg will rot off.'

'Shooter four. They came back out. They're not moving, maybe waiting. Out.'

Sage sighed. 'So Ferne's salve didn't work? That's disappointing.'

'We'll make do. Just grateful you and Lexi found us. Don't know where we'd be without you.'

'Us? Are you kidding?' He touched Gaius's shoulder to deflect the attention away from himself. 'Anyway, how are you holding up?'

'Can't wait for winter to finish. Everything hurts.'

'Shooter fifteen. He's calling for the person in charge. Out.'

'I'm two-thirds your age, and I know what you mean,' Sage said.

Gaius chuckled into a cough. 'Rub it in.'

'Shooter fifteen. He's calling for the administrator again, says he has a proposal. Out.'

'Sir, I can go talk with him,' Sage said.

'You're too valuable. I can't risk losing you,' Gaius stuttered. 'I'll go.'

'And you're not? No, I should go. You're more important than me.'

'Shooter fifteen. He says he's asking one last time. Out.'

Gaius stumbled over his words. 'What do you think?' he asked, turning around to seek advice from his colleagues. They all murmured with worry.

'Gaius,' Sage insisted, 'that guy doesn't look all that dangerous, and maybe all he wants to do is chat. Either way, with your limp and stutter, no offence, you should stay here where it's safe. Let me handle this.'

'I can't have you risking your life,' Gaius said, but he didn't get much more of a chance to object, as Sage had already disappeared down the slope.

Sage reached the first target-shooter. The camouflaged figure rolled over, aiming a pistol toward the sound of footsteps, nodded at Sage, and resumed his sentry posture.

The man in black stood in the bio-luminescent lit street, peering into the darkness. As he drew nearer, Sage noticed the man was wearing tailored clothing; his long, expensive-looking coat and stylish pointed boots gave him the air of a man who didn't know struggle. He didn't appear to be armed.

Sage pulled out his pistol anyway and took cover in the shadows.

The stranger removed his breather momentarily. 'If the administrator isn't willing to talk, I guess you don't want all this food and equipment,' he yelled out, pointing at the trucks behind him and replaced his breather.

'What do you want?' Sage yelled his reply.

The man in black turned to face the direction from where Sage's voice had come. 'I want to talk to the administrator.'

'You can talk to me,' Sage replied.

'I don't want to talk to someone in the shadows, or the administrator's errand boy.'

'How do we know you're not here to kill us?'

'If I wanted to kill you, I wouldn't have come in five noisy trucks, would I? Now, errand boy, go get your administrator.'

'Who says I'm not?'

'The administrator? Nope, you're not. You already told me you weren't. I'm not talking to you anymore. Go get your boss and let the adults talk,' the man in black chided.

Sage burned up a little at that remark, then turned to leave to find Gaius and Jaxson standing beside a tree in the dark.

Gaius limped closer. 'You knew I had to come after you,' he whispered.

'Sir, he says he has food in those trucks.'

'I heard. What does he want? Nobody makes that kind of offer without wanting something in return.'

'Hmm, you're right. I'll find out what he wants.'

Gaius tipped his head.

Sage tightened his grip on his pistol, stepped through the rough ground, away from Gaius and the headlights. He knew the layout of the kill box; he'd designed it, and entered the area so as not to block a shooter. 'There needs to be some trust here,' he yelled out.

'Not you again. I thought I told you—'

'Yes, you did,' Sage interrupted, stepping out into the light.

'You want to talk about trust? What about that toy you're holding?' the man in black said, poking his mask at Sage's pistol.

'Self-defence. You think I'm going to come out here, unarmed?'

The man in black held his hands far from his body. 'I did. Have it your way. Let's do this pre-talk thing. But make it snappy. I haven't got all night.'

Sage took his time covering the distance, and without diverting his eyes from the stranger, stopped a truck's length away. 'Open the trucks,' he demanded.

'You open them.'

Sage held two fingers high, then pointed to the ground in front of the strange man. The ground ice chipped away in two directions. 'As you can see, I have target-shooters everywhere. They're well trained.'

The outsider chuckled. 'Then, the question remains. Why do you need that toy?' He approached the rear door of the closest truck and opened it. A few cloth bags fell to the ground. The stranger picked one up, looked inside, resealed it and threw it to Sage. 'See, it's just food. That truck has a deconstructed greenhouse. The others have water filtration and more food for your, whatever this is. You can keep that bag as a gesture of good faith, even if you choose not to accept my generous offer.'

'Who are you, and what do you want?' Sage demanded again, holding the bag.

Movement in the dark behind the man in black caught Sage's attention.

'Now that look is either your armed cronies coming in to take my offering by force, or, Gaius Sempro and stooge. Knowing how soft Gaius has become, I would say it's the latter.'

Unable to handle the tension any longer, Gaius limped out into the light toward the stranger. 'Do I know you?' he asked as he closed the gap.

'Aaand, there he is,' the man mocked. 'Yes, Gaius. I know who you are. Your reputation precedes you.'

'And you are?' Gaius asked, raising a concealed eyebrow.

'Voltaire Catlow, at your service,' the man in black said, giving a flamboyant bow.

'Now that the formalities are out of the way, the adults want to talk,' he said, directing the remark at Sage.

Sage grimaced. 'This way.' And he gestured toward the hall.

Gaius, Voltaire, and Sage entered the community hall one after the other, with Jaxson and Voltaire's burly bodyguard jostling to enter last, neither wanting to turn their back on the other. Voltaire, noticing the silent comical display, turned to his bodyguard. 'Will you stop dancing and just get in here!' he said, pointing to the vast space inside the hall. His man, like a trained pet, complied, much to Jaxson's apparent satisfaction.

As the doors closed, Voltaire's bodyguard and Jaxson took their positions on either side of the room, considering one another with professional interest, while Sage turned up the four bio-luminescent lamps.

The dust in the air fell to the floor, and everyone removed their breathers, revealing their faces and allowing Sage to finally see who they were dealing with.

Without his mask, the short little man in black had a well-shaven face, chubby cheeks and a mole under his left eye. His slicked-back black hair gave him the air of a snooty, well-to-do businessman. He lifted his head to glare down his nose at Gaius with repulsion, a look that made the hair on the back of Sage's neck raise on end.

Sage carried two chairs from the row against the wall into the centre of the room; one for Gaius, the other for himself.

'You didn't get one for me?' Voltaire remarked.

Sage pointed to the row of chairs. 'You're capable.'

Voltaire smirked. 'Okay then,' he said, motioning to his bodyguard with a click of his fingers to fetch him a chair.

The brutish grunt retrieved one and set it down in front of Voltaire. He looked at the seat with disdain, brushed it off with his gloved hand, and then wiped his hand down the brute's chest before sitting. Voltaire inspected the room from his rigid posture, gave a slight nod, and reached inside his large coat.

Jaxson jumped to attention, covering his pistol, while the brute drew his own pistol halfway from his holster in reaction.

The little man saw the tension between the two. 'Relax,' he said dismissively, continuing to pull out a small insulated flask. 'This is just to drink.'

Jaxson eased when Voltaire unscrewed the cap, inverted it as a cup, and poured out a steaming dark brown liquid. 'See, it's just kahwah,' he said, blowing over the steaming cup toward Gaius and Sage. 'You know, kahwah?'

The aroma wafted across the short distance. Its familiar fruity, nutty fragrance brought back memories for the both of them, from a time before the war when the coveted dark beverage was plentiful. Neither had had so much as a sip in over two cycles.

'Ah, kahwah,' Voltaire swooned. 'Elixir of the Progenitors. I'd offer you some, but it seems my flask holds only enough for one.' He reclined in his chair and took a slow sip. 'Those were the days,' Voltaire continued, completely ignorant of Gaius and Sage's unimpressed expressions. 'Where I grew up,' he trailed off, amusing himself, 'we had kahwah trees. Every day I picked berries, dried them out and roasted the beans until—' he cut himself off. 'From the pathetic looks on your faces... you can have some, too. Out there, in one of those trucks, I have brought you some, if you should be so inclined.'

Sage interrupted. 'Mister—'

'Catlow, Voltaire Catlow,' Voltaire interjected.

'Whatever, get to the point.'

'Please, Mister Catlow,' Gaius stuttered, trying to maintain his calm. 'You didn't come here to drink kahwah in front of us. What do you want?'

'W..w..w..w... w... what?' Voltaire mocked.

'Hey,' Sage objected.

'It's okay, Sage,' Gaius said.

'Say, why are a stuttering cripple and a misguided boy-ranger running this place?'

'I said HEY!' Sage yelled out again, this time rising from his seat. Gaius put his hand out, motioning Sage to calm himself.

Sage sat back down, but glared daggers at the weedy little man.

'You better put a leash on him,' Voltaire chided.

Sage scowled.

'I didn't invite you in here to insult us,' Gaius said, his voice flat and unwavering, being careful not to stutter.

'Yes, you didn't invite me. Yet here I am,' Voltaire said condescendingly.

Gaius continued, 'you said you had an offer for us. Make it.'

Voltaire sighed. 'Look at what I have been reduced to. And to think I was once the great Voltaire Catlow. Before the war, I spearheaded a very successful company, selling goods across the world.' He sniggered. 'I made an insane amount of credits, at least until everything burned, then credits became both priceless and worthless. I still have a few stashed away until they get used again. But war is unkind, so here I am, cavorting with peasants.'

'Is that it, Voltaire?' Sage growled. 'You came here to do what exactly, insult a few refugees? That's very big of you. What do you want?'

Voltaire sighed again, set his cup on the floor beside him, and leaned forward. 'I wouldn't have dealt with scrap before the war, but it seems there's not much business taking place at the moment. So, you want to get down to business, as you wish,' he began. 'My *employer* has commissioned me to make you a deal. You see, they see something in this little shak-hole of yours. And it is a shak-hole,' he said, taking another look about the hall with disgust.

Sage's blood began to boil. It would seem Gaius had noticed the tension and rested a hand on his knee to steady him.

Voltaire looked from one to the other and continued. 'But you have something they want, and they have offered to compensate you handsomely for it. If it were up to me, I would burn this retched place to the ground.' He smiled and gave Sage a sidelong glance. 'But fortunately for you, it isn't up to me.'

'Then why are you here?' Sage demanded one last time through clenched teeth.

'I'm so glad you asked,' Voltaire smiled again, taking satisfaction in watching Sage fume. 'My employer wants access to the caves in those mountains.' He pointed in a random direction.

Gaius blinked. 'The caves?'

'Yes, the caves. And by that, they mean *exclusive* access to *everything*, including the old mining tunnels and catacombs.'

'Exclusive?' Gaius repeated.

'Yes, Gaius, exclusive. That means restricted. To you.'

'Why the caves?' Gaius asked.

'That's privileged information, for us to know and you to none of your business.'

'But...'

Voltaire raised a finger. 'There's more. They also wish to use your town as a central point, where the workers can come and relax, eat, drink and have their choice of gendered flesh.'

'Gendered flesh?' Sage retorted.

'Yes, you know,' Voltaire gestured something provocative in the air that made Sage's face go crimson with anger.

'No!' Sage shouted, 'Certainly not.'

Gaius continued, clearly hiding his disgust. 'And what do we get from this "deal"?' he cut in, diverting the conversation.

'You've already seen the trucks out there,' Voltaire said, pointing at the door. 'As I said to boy-ranger here, they're loaded with enough food and supplies to feed a town. One of those trucks has a greenhouse and seeds, enabling you to grow your own food. This is to get you started, and we can expand it more later. My employer seeks to establish themselves as patron of Hope. Consider it an investment in your future.'

'Why us?' Gaius asked.

'Because you, my ignorant friend, are sitting on a rather nice reserve of goethite. You have no use for it, and my employer wants it. This is what they are offering for it.'

Gaius stuttered, 'G... goe—'

'Yes, Gaius, goethite,' Voltaire interrupted, 'to make metals. Did you not know what the mine was there for? Or did you just think it was useful for stuffing people into whenever you have uninvited guests?'

Gaius let that pass. 'I know what it is used for. Why here? Why now?'

'As I said, that is none of your business. All you need to know is the mines will be used again, and you stand to benefit. If you accept the offer.'

'But that will make us dependent on you,' Sage said. 'As we stand, we're independent.'

'Yes, but my employer has a vested interest in your welfare. This would be a symbiotic relationship. You provide the grunt and the resources; we keep you fed and help you grow. It's that simple.'

'And the gendered flesh?' Sage interrupted.

Voltaire shrugged. 'What can I say, we must cater to all appetites? From where I'm sitting, Gaius, even a decrepit old fool like you and your whiny pet boy-ranger should see this is a reasonable deal.'

With that, Sage couldn't take it any longer and leapt from his chair, ready to grab Catlow by the front of his expensive-looking coat. He wanted to wring the little man's indignant neck, but Gaius just raised a hand.

'I've heard enough!' Sage roared. 'Who do you think we are? Inane minnows so desperate we would allow you to just come in here, take what you want and do whatever you please with us? Your deal is rubbish, and you are insane.'

'Hey,' Voltaire said, recoiling back into his chair, arms out wide in feigned innocence. 'I'm just the messenger. These are my employer's orders, not mine, remember? Back in the day, I wouldn't have even bothered coming here to ask, and I certainly would not be this generous.'

'Generous my backside. How do you do it? Go from one insult to another without taking a breath?' Sage demanded, turning to Gaius, who was doing much better at maintaining his composure than Sage. 'Gaius, you can't possibly be seriously considering this? This guy is an idiot,' Sage yelled, waving a hand at Voltaire, who remained seated with an amused expression on his face. 'Gendered flesh! What sort of place do you think this is?'

'You didn't even notice I used the word "town" for this dump,' Voltaire added, smiling.

Sage raged. 'You have—'

Gaius grabbed his arm, cutting him off. 'Mister Catlow,' Gaius said calmly, with carefully considered words. 'I might stutter and walk with a limp, but that does not make me simple. I can see when I'm being had, and we don't need someone like you coming here, throwing around his riches and insults, trying to do us out of what little we have. This is not a town. It's a refugee camp, we're doing it tough, but we're managing just fine without your help. Thank you very much, your offer is g... generous, but we don't need it.'

'Tell that to the guy whose leg is about to fall off,' Voltaire retorted, 'or his poor, hungry son, curling up in your rotten share-shack every night. Come on, Gaius. You're either deluded or lying. We both know you need our help.'

Gaius opened his mouth to speak, but Sage cut him off. 'If you think you know us so well, what makes you think your offer is worth what you ask?'

Voltaire stood, took his time to straighten his coat, and made a slow but calculated step toward Sage. 'Because we also have medicine, my dear hot-headed friend,' he said with a smug grin. He pulled out a green pharmaceutical bottle labelled *Deplacillin* and handed it to Sage, while at the same time placing a sly arm around the shoulder of the fuming younger man. 'Painkillers, anti-virals, antibiotics, whatever you need, we have lots of it. Right now.'

Sage pushed Voltaire away in disgust, the small man taking a few steps back to stay on his feet.

'Now I know you're lying. Nobody's seen any *Deplacillin* since the war finished. How do I know this is real?' Sage asked, waving around the bottle.

'There's a lot more where that came from.'

Sage turned to Gaius and could tell his attention peaked when medicine had been introduced to the conversation.

Voltaire's voice changed, becoming serious, as though insulted. 'I have been called many names, some I can't even pronounce, but never have I been called a liar.'

Gaius rose from his seat, placed a hand on Sage's shoulder and said with a mild stutter, 'I think what my apprentice is saying is, we need some time to consider the offer. Would you excuse us?' he said as he directed Sage to the storeroom at the rear of the hall. Jaxson followed close behind.

The two men stood in the tiny storeroom with Jaxson posted at the open door, cramped in amongst a city of stored items. Gaius turned to Sage, 'I know you are angry, but keep it under control.'

'Forgive me, Gaius,' Sage replied, 'but to be perfectly honest, the guy is a self-absorbed ass. I think he'd sell his mother if he could mass-produce at a profit. The deal sounds enticing, given our current situation, but it stinks, and I don't trust him.'

'What choice do we have?'

'How do we even know he's telling the truth? I mean, look at this,' Sage said, handing Gaius the bottle of antibiotics. 'Where did he even get this from?'

At that, Jaxson stepped forward, a little apprehensive. 'Sirs, if I may?'

'What is it?' Gaius asked, motioning to him to join them.

'I hate to admit it, but I used to work for Voltaire,' he said, his admission not unexpected. 'I never worked with him directly, but I heard he had a reputation as a notorious businessman. At first, I didn't recognise him, but the moment he started talking, it was unmistakable. Rest assured, he is the Voltaire Catlow I know from afar. Anyway, if he says he has *Deplacillin*, trust me, he's got it.'

'What company was it?' Sage asked.

'You really want to know?'

Sage nodded.

'Asunder.'

Both Sage and Gaius gasped.

'The weapons company?' Sage exclaimed.

'I know what you're thinking,' Jaxson said. 'But it wasn't like that. I worked as a bodyguard for one of the Asunder board members who also happened to be a close friend of Voltaire's. I had nothing to do with the weapons. It was a job, and it allowed me access to privileged business information. Since the war ended, I figured, so had my contract.'

'We all had jobs before the war,' Sage said. 'Is there anything we can use against him?'

'Aside from cavorting with my client's wife and general business activities? Not really. It seems as though he's back to his old deeds again.'

'What sort of deeds?' Gaius asked.

'He enjoyed getting into bed with big "global domination" types— the class of people who start wars and drop nuclear bombs on innocent cities. My bet is, he found himself on the wrong side of this war and is trying to crawl his way back. If that's the case, he won't hesitate to step over you to do it. He wants Hope. I don't know why, but I'd be careful with him.'

Sage scratched his head. 'Well, that just confirms it then, doesn't it?'

'Confirms what?' Gaius asked.

'That we can't go ahead with this,' Sage said. 'It would be nice to have food, medicine and maybe even some brick buildings and civility for raising children, but at what cost?'

'We cannot go on like this, Sage,' Gaius sighed. 'Where else will we get this chance? Look at Garan. He needs this,' he said, looking down despondently at the bottle of antibiotics in his hand.

'If we take this, we are effectively selling our souls to Xisnys. There's no knowing the true price we'll pay. I say no.'

Gaius hung his head, conflicted by the need to provide for his people and the need to protect them. 'Jaxson,' he said, turning to his security officer. 'As a citizen of Hope, what say you?'

'Sir, I can't ask you to trust Voltaire. He's a cunning, self-righteous despot. But you do what you need to do. I'll accept and support your decision, whatever it is.'

Gaius and Sage exchanged pensive looks, then the three men exited the storeroom to find Voltaire standing, waiting impatiently outside the door.

'So!' he exclaimed. 'What will it be? Will you accept my generous offer?'

Gaius stood his ground, straight-faced, took a deep breath and spoke as calmly as he could. 'Hope is not for sale,' he declared. 'We will not accept your offer, however generous it may seem. It isn't worth the price you're asking.'

'Hmmm,' Voltaire mused. 'That is disappointing. Are you sure?' He turned his back, ambling towards the centre of the room, with the three men following at a distance.

'Yes,' Gaius asserted, and Sage felt they had made the right decision.

'Then you misunderstand,' Voltaire said mid-stride, turned, adjusted his coat and brushed a few flecks of dust from his lapel. His voice deepened to a more threatening tone. 'This is not a negotiation,' he said, curtly, 'it's a peace offering. Take it or leave it. But if I leave here tonight with these supplies, I will only return tomorrow with a new set of trucks, and I will take this place by force. Either way, my employer *will* get what they want.'

The three Hope residents glared at Voltaire dumbfounded as though he had dropped a house on them.

Voltaire continued, 'they didn't have to send me here to this stinking, Progenitor-forsaken place to make this offer to you. They just wanted to try it the nice way first. But if you choose not to cooperate, I cannot be held responsible for what happens next. The lives and the welfare of your people are in your hands. So, I ask again, will you accept my generous offer?'

'So,' Gaius said, considering the weedy man with incredulity. 'You are holding us to ransom?'

'Yes, I guess I am,' Voltaire grinned. 'But put it this way, if you decide to take our generous, one-night-only offer, you not only get to keep your position and this stinking place, you get food, medicine and all the resources you need to build a town, and you can do that all however you choose. All you have to do is supply us with what we need, do as we say when we ask and keep out of our way. It isn't that bad when you come to think about it. Refuse, and you lose everything.'

Gaius blinked at Sage. He, too, had a look of absolute shock on his face, combined with rage and barely contained desire to tear Voltaire's head from his shoulders. Sage had never seen that look on his face before. Gaius may have been a pacifist, but Sage could tell he was doing everything he could to refrain from ripping the man apart himself.

'This is the face of business I miss. Exciting, isn't it?' Voltaire gloated, grinning a maniacal grin and rubbing his hands together with obvious pleasure.

A moment passed, and Gaius spoke, his stutter returning. 'All right,' he said, conceding defeat, 'we accept your terms, Mister Catlow. But on one condition. You leave my people alone. If you want this "town", you protect it too.'

Sage added, 'I swear, if you do anything to harm this community, you'll find yourself face down in a—'

'I'm not in the position to make any promises, Mister Sempro,' Voltaire interrupted, turning to face Gaius, 'but I'm fairly certain you will have everything you need to do that yourself.'

With that, Voltaire took Gaius's hand and shook it vigorously. Then he motioned to his bodyguard, who slipped outside, returning moments later with a person holding a yellow envelope under their arm. The brute closed the door as the newcomer patted themselves down and removed their mask to reveal the soft face of a woman in her late twenties, with layered jaw-length brown hair and aquamarine eyes.

'Excellent,' Voltaire announced. 'Gentlemen, I would like you to meet Ms Cristal Spriggs, attaché to LunaTec Enterprises, my, and soon to be your, employer.'

Cristal set down her mask on a chair and approached Gaius and Sage with an outstretched hand.

Still dumbfounded, they politely introduced themselves.

Voltaire continued, 'Cristal has your paperwork. Once signed, she will be your contact and representative with us. You need anything, she'll sort it out.'

He added, speaking behind a cupped hand. 'She's both brains and body of this outfit, if you know what I mean?'

Sage and Gaius both cringed.

'Hi,' Cristal said in a polite and friendly manner, her presence immediately setting Sage and Gaius at ease. 'Don't mind him. We all think he's an ass,' she said with a pleasant smile. 'Do you have a table? We can get this sorted.'

06 – Beyond Innocence
NC03

The wind snapped the sails open, accelerating the Fenix beyond the cannon-shot splashing in the water to the aft. Ajee Yond stood beside Captain Nash on the aft deck, target-rifle slung over her shoulder for the next close pass to the defended shipyard.

Branton, the ever bold and fearless captain, stood at the helm, defiant against the solid shot whistling past him and their splashes showering the ship. He adjusted the front of his double-breasted red leather coat, its knee-length tails flapping in the wind.

High on a defensive stone wall, adorned with enemy flags flicking in the breeze, a soldier ran to a swivel-mounted cannon.

Ajee stepped to the railing. 'Keep it steady, Captain,' she yelled as she aimed the loaded long-barrel rifle at the soldier ramming the cannon with powder. She pulled the hammer back and adjusted the slider on its sights. Ajee aimed, took a slow breath, and braced for the recoil. The custom-made long-barrel kicked hard into her shoulder, smoke billowing from its end, and the man dropped from sight. 'Ready, Captain,' she yelled out, reloading the rifle.

Captain Nash ran his hands down the wheel like he was climbing a ladder, swinging the ship starboard hard into the changing winds, the sails catching the full power of the breeze. The ship jolted as the broadside cannons came in line with the gates. They barked in unison, and the timber gates exploded inward, shrapnel...

'Jaaayne,' Sera calls from another room, interrupting the fantasy world in which I had been immersed.

She drifts into my bedroom, wearing a huge smile.

'But I was just about at the good bit,' I complain, dropping the book in my lap.

'You have read *"Be Yond the Horizon"* so many times, I would think you could narrate it to me by now. From the looks of it, I would guess you are at the shipyard where they find that message.'

'The Dragon is awake, the Fenix has risen, don't burn the Ashes,' we recite together.

'Yep, that's where I'm up to. Shame the first and last chapters are missing, though. Is this the only copy we've got?'

'Afraid so. Look at it this way, it forces you to make up your own exciting ending, does it not?'

'Do you know who wrote it? Did they write a sequel? Do we have a copy?' I ask expectantly, the questions tumbling out almost all at once.

'Whoa, Jayne!' she says, startled by my enthusiasm. 'I do not know. There is no library here, just a small collection of books we share around. Without knowing who the author is, I cannot ask.'

'Oh. Okay,' I sigh and wonder if I'll ever learn what happens to Ajee Yond.

'Cheer up,' she says. 'It is not that bad. There are plenty of books around that have endings. Hey,' she adds, her face lighting up with that smile again. 'Guess what?'

'What?'

'I have a surprise for you,' she says, sitting on the edge of the bed beside me and pulling a little wrapped parcel from behind her back.

'Happy namedawn, Jayne!' She hands me the parcel, her voice beaming with pride.

With everything that's happened in the last cycle, I'm both stunned and delighted she remembered. Tears well as I stare down at the beautifully wrapped present. Sera loves her little details, hand decorating the paper with my favourite colours of green and blue and tying it off with a gold bow. She's even curled the ribbon for effect.

Sera leans in, wrapping her arms around my shoulders in a firm hug, squeezing until I hug her back. For that moment, I'm the happiest person in the world.

I try to slip the ribbon off without damaging the bow, but the anticipation causes me to shred the paper away, burying the coverless book in my lap. After all the wrapping, only a small brown cardboard box remains.

As I lift the lid, resting amongst a nest of shredded paper is a charcoal grey woven bracelet.

'Jewellery? Nobody's ever given me jewellery before. But is it meant to be that colour?'

'It is a fire bracelet,' she says, removing it from the box to fasten it around my wrist. 'These two clasps contain flint. Strike them together, and you can make fire wherever you go.'

'Wow! That's cool. Thanks, Sera. I thought you'd just got me a boring bracelet.'

She giggles. 'There is more. How would you like to get out of here and I show you how to use it?'

'Go out?' I ask, grinning from ear to ear with excitement. 'Where?'

'I thought we would go camping. There is a lake near here I have not been to before and thought it would be a nice place to go visit for a few days. Want to go check it out with me?'

'Um, yeah! I'd do anything to get out of here.'

'Wonderful, we have permission to leave the Gord for up to six days, starting from ten decs ago.'

And just like that, I'm throwing things into a backpack and getting changed into my outdoor clothes. Within thirty decs, the two of us are taking our first steps outside the gates of Garret Gord in over a cycle.

Relishing in my bottled freedom, I take in the environment like a newborn entering the world for the first time. It's amazing how much can change in a cycle. For one, there is not as much dust in the air, although it's still not clear enough to take off our breathers. There's less ice, the horrible icy wind is gone, and at my feet, sparse patches of greenery peek through the permafrost to greet the sun's brighter light. Life, it seems, is getting back to normal, even if that grimy grey sludge still covers almost everything in sight.

I zip my coat tighter and adjust my scarf. These clothes may seem light and camouflaged in the same bleak grey-brown colours as the landscape, but I'm grateful they're comfortable and warm.

'Sera?'

'Yes?'

'This is the best day ever! I was going crazy cooped up in the apartment.'

'Even with your studies?'

'Yeah, about that. Haven't we run out of books yet?'

She chuckles. 'There are a lot more where those came from. Are you bored?'

'There's only so many times you can do the same thing before it becomes a chore. I've watched about everything on the VT, and I've even played *"Weighted Affect"* on the games console so many times I'm beginning to feel like the game is playing me.'

'I see. What about the knife-throwing and shitak'na lessons?'

'I reckon I could hit the centre target blindfolded now, and as for shitak'na, I know all your tells.'

'You do, do you?'

'Yeah. Like you take a quick breath through your nose before you do a leg sweep, and you crinkle your nose before you throw a left hook.'

'Oh, right,' she says, a little bemused. 'Just as well we got you out here then, hey?'

'Yeah. So, what's a lake like? I mean, before the winter? I've never been to one.'

'Never?' she replies, taken aback by my admission.

'Well, no. My parents never had the time. They always took me to cities when we went on holiday.'

'That is a shame,' she says. 'They are one of the most beautiful things in nature. In some places, trees grow right up to the water's edge, and the sun would ripple off the surface like a melted mirror. It was common to see animals come out to drink, and on a long hot day, you could strip down and cool off in the water serenaded by aves singing songs to one other, catching insects or...'

'That sounds amazing. I hope I get to try that one day.'

'I hope you do as well.'

All this talk of lakes gets me thinking. 'Why doesn't Jorth have oceans like in *"Be Yond the Horizon"*?'

'It is just a fantasy book. Someone's imagination.'

'I know, but do you think there's a planet somewhere that's got oceans?'

'Certainly. That is how we know about them. The closest planet the Aster system has to oceans is the water planet, Vositer. It is one big ocean. Vositer may even have had land, like Jorth. We have just never been there to find out.'

Sera catches her breath. 'We will talk later. There is a long way to go before nightfall, and we still have to find something for dinner.' She unfolds the map, checks the compass and returns them to her jacket pocket.

By the time the sun goes down, we had gathered a small collection of root vegetables, and I watch on with eager curiosity as Sera investigates the spaces between rocks and fallen logs.

'Found some,' she whisper-shouts, waving me over and pulling back a thin branch in a pile of debris.

'Found some what?' I ask, bouncing forward to look over her shoulder.

'Tracks and droppings,' she says, pointing at some scuff marks and a small collection of brown pellets on the snow. She picks up a pellet and shows it to me. 'See this? This is a tomadai scat. It looks like it might use this area as a run. If I set a trap here without disturbing the area, we might be fortunate to have some meat on the morrow.'

Sera reaches into her backpack and pulls out a length of thin wire. Together, we set up the trap beneath the branches and leave it for the unfortunate animal to return.

Once the trap's set, Sera points up at one of the surrounding trees. 'See how the branches run perpendicular to the ground? That is where we sleep tonight.'

'A tree? Why not a nice tent or hammock?'

'All in good time.' She marks the tree on the grey, frozen ground and dusts her hands off on her pants. 'Right. Let's go make a fire.'

Out here, she seems to be a different person, methodical and skilled, like she has done this many times before.

We reach a low spot in the landscape, hidden by fallen trees and boulders.

It's hard finding anything dry in this place, but the two of us gather up enough small branches and bark to build a small fire. Sera demonstrates how to build it, then, setting the last log, steps back. 'Okay, now is the time for your bracelet.'

I remove it from my wrist and, under Sera's guidance, strike the two end clasps together. Sparks shoot forth, catching in the tinder, igniting it and licking to life as fire. Within moments, we are warming our hands by the low flames.

As we sit, enjoying the heat, I reach for another stick to feed the flames, but Sera stops me. 'Not just yet. This is one important lesson you need to learn and that is, big fires attract unwanted attention. We just want to cook, then go. Never cook near your bed.'

'Okay.' I nod, not quite sure what she means.

'If you want to do something, sweep the dirt off there.' Sera points with her knife at a low point running along the ground. 'Use this to chip away the ice and collect it in your tin mug.'

'From where?'

'That creek.'

'There's a creek there? How'd you know that?'

'Experience. Now hurry before we run out of timber.'

Sera reverses her knife and presents it to me. I grab the milky-white and green flecked handle and withdraw the massive weapon from its soft leather sheath. With a blade as long as my thigh, it's much bigger and heavier than I expect, and Sera lets off her little giggle of amusement as I almost drop it on the ground.

It's stunning.

The light from the fire doesn't do it justice, but I'd seen nothing like it before. With intricate feathers engraved on its opaline handle, its blade with majestic images of predatory aves etched into the surface, and reverse barbs lining its spine; it's both menacing and beautiful at the same time.

'And Jayne, be careful with that. I don't want you to lose a finger,' she says, her eyes glistening. 'Then you can cut the vegetables.'

It's hard work chipping ice, but I get almost enough to fill the cup. Once I'm done, I hand the knife back to Sera, and without hesitation, she re-sheaths it, shoving it carelessly back into her bag.

As dinner cooks, Sera gives me a lesson on survival. 'The fire should not be visible in a crevice or trough. Even if people smell it, it is still hard to find,' she says, but while she speaks, my attention drifts to the knife handle protruding out of her bag.

After a while, I gather the courage to ask, inadvertently cutting her off mid-sentence. 'Sera. Where'd that small sword come from?'

That playful giggle of hers slips out. 'Oh, my knife, you like that, do you?'

She slides it out of its sheath and rotates the handle between her thumb and forefinger in quiet introspection. 'I did some work a while back. This is what they gave me when I completed my assignment.'

'What was your assignment?'

'Ahh, I am not going to talk about that.'

'Well, it must have been important, whatever it was, especially if they gave you something like that?'

'Yeah, a real honour,' she says with obvious sarcasm.

'What's wrong?'

'Nothing, you would not understand.'

'I want to understand. How could you not be impressed by something like that?'

'Jayne,' she says sombrely, re-sheathing it once more and shoving it deep into her bag, out of sight. 'I do not wish to talk about this.'

Before I can question her further, the pot on the fire boils over onto the coals, shooting red sparks into the air. 'I think the food is cooked,' she says, leaping to retrieve the vegetables, and I get the sense the conversation has been buried. Without saying anything more, she drains the water into our cups for drinking and wraps two parcels of food, passing one to me, then quietly extinguishes the fire.

Relative darkness engulfs us with the fire's fading embers, and the envelope of cold returns. Only patchy moonlight provides us with visibility now.

It doesn't take long to retrace our steps, footprint for footprint, back to the marked tree.

'When was the last time you climbed a tree?' she asks, looking up at it, then at me.

I shrug.

'Because this is your next lesson.'

'I honestly can't remember the last time I climbed a tree, but I do know I've never done it in the dark, in a forest filled with all sorts of nasty, bitey things.'

'Watch carefully and learn,' Sera says, scaling the trunk like a siamang. After a few unsuccessful attempts, she hoists me up beside her. She then pulls a rope from her pack and uses it to secure us both to the branch.

'Why are we sleeping on a hard branch?' I can't help but ask.

'Have you seen a soft branch?' From the way she just said that I'm sure she just gave me a sly grin. 'There are wild animals and other unpleasant things out here, and they will not think twice about taking you or me as a midnight snack.'

'Oh, okay, but why must you tie this so tight?'

'Eat your dinner, Jayne,' she says.

'Alright.'

While I graze on the little bundle of veggies, the temperature plummets, and it's a good thing I packed my skin-lined thermal blanket. It may be the only comfort I get lying here.

'And try to get some sleep,' she adds, 'we have got a big day ahead of us on the morrow.'

A gregarious, black and white feathered ave perches on a limb beside my head and lets out a loud screech. If it hadn't been for the rope tethering me in place, I might have ended up face down on the cold ground.

To say it's strange sleeping tied to a tree is an understatement, but if it means not being eaten during the night, I suppose I can get used to it.

As the sun rises on a new day, we climb down and go check the trap. To our delight, we've caught something; a small brown and grey furry creature with long ears, large hind legs and a fluffy tail. Sera was right; it's a tomadai, the first one I'd ever seen in, well, real life. We restart last night's fire, and Sera shows me how to prepare and preserve the meat for later.

The wind changes direction about a cendec after we finish cooking, and a grey snowfall consumes the valley, reducing visibility by the midec. The steady slope down becomes harder to hike. With our steps floundering over branches and rocks hidden beneath the thickening snow, we seek shelter.

Sera touches my arm and points toward a darkened upside-down V shape in the near grey-out. To our relief, it turns out to be a hollowed-out tree bole with just enough room for the two of us to sit cross-legged with our backpacks on our laps.

Snow gathers around the small opening, collapsing into the confined space.

'I hope this old trunk has wood rot,' Sera says, looking around in the limited light, 'or we will fixo if the snow covers our exit.'

That's a word I haven't worried about since leaving Gotthard.

We lose track of time sitting there in the dark. The air becomes stale but remains breathable.

When the howling wind dies down, Sera uses her hand trowel to dig us out of the deep, newly packed snow, and we push our way to the surface.

A fluffy grey carpet covers everything in sight, proving impossible for my little legs to traverse. With each step, I drop thigh-deep into the snow.

Sera giggles. 'I have an idea,' she says, lifting me onto the top of our tree stump and trudges off through the knee-deep snow. After watching her scurry around, breaking branches off trees and stripping them of bark, she returns with an arm full of wood. Then, removing a coil of rope from her pack, she begins separating the strands and weaving things together.

'What is it?' I ask, watching with amazement.

'It is a snowshoe,' she says, holding out what looks like a flat basket-weave club. I help her make three more, and when we're done, she uses the last of the rope strands to tie them to our feet. 'Okay. Try them out.'

Cautiously, I lower myself onto the snow, and to my surprise, I don't sink, the shoes nicely spreading my weight over the consuming ground, and we continue to make our way up the mountainside.

An eerie stillness falls upon the frozen forest of decomposing trees, the fresh snowfall muting all sound, making it feel like we're the only living organisms on the planet.

Further up the mountainside, the snow cover subsides, and with our snowshoes falling apart, we remove them. They've served their purpose anyway, and we leave them behind for our journey onward.

By the day's end, I'm tired and looking forward to a good night's sleep.

The sunlight fades, and we talk very little, performing the same tasks we did the previous night, finally retreating to our chosen high perch to sleep.

The cold, salted meat is tough and chewy but satisfying. Much tastier than the vegetables, which I insist could use some flavouring.

'You have learned well,' Sera compliments. 'A few more trips like this, and I'll make a decent ranger out of you yet.'

Even through my gloves, I can feel blisters forming.

'We should reach the lake on the morrow. It is just over that ridge,' she says, pointing south.

'Is it far?'

'No, I think between two and three cendecs, then we can spend two nights exploring the lake before going home. What do you think?'

'I think—'

'Rusty, you stupid...' a voice yells, carried by the wind.

Sera puts a hand on my arm and holds a finger up to her mask for quiet.

'I smelled the fire coming from this way. Must be a camp,' a different voice yells, this one sounding gruff.

Ice crunches and twigs snap under our tree, and I hold my breath, daring to look over the side of the branch for the source of the sound.

A man in rough clothing stands at the base of our tree, fumbling for something in front of him. 'Ahhh,' he sighs, glancing up to the sound of liquid splashing against the trunk.

To avoid being seen, I quickly pull back out of sight.

A crunchy splat interrupts the man from his business. 'Tur'coo, you's dumb boart,' the man yells. 'You's could've earned a slug in the chest for that.'

He stomps away, and from the darkness, calls out again. 'Got you's now, I'm gunna make you's eat that snow.'

Sounds of a scuffle break out from that direction, and another man's voice joins the altercation. 'Jarrek, you punch like a child.'

A different, but more commanding voice cuts through the scuffle. 'Get up, you stupid tomadai's...' The changing wind muting the rest.

When I think the noisy party are leaving, six dark figures lumber under our tree. 'We're eating meat tonight. I hope you grags like little girl,' a woman's voice says in a distinctive accent.

They all laugh and grunt like animals, carrying on at the thought.

Another woman snickers over the others. 'We's gunna miss the bes' bit. The screams make it taste all th' much sweeter. So hurry up, you's lazy rumps. I'm hungry.'

Howling with delight, the party stomps like a herd of eudur toward where our cooking fire had been.

Once they're out of earshot, I turn to Sera, utterly disgusted. 'Who were those horrible people?'

'Raiders,' she says. From the way she says it, I can tell the disgust is mutual. 'They are savages that live in these parts. Unlike you and I, they did not find peace after the war, instead turned to scavenging and cannibalism to survive. They are one reason we do not sleep on the ground.'

'They really eat people?'

'Yes, they do.'

'So, what they said back there was—'

'Just eat,' Sera cuts me off. 'Do not worry about them. If we keep out of their way, they will hopefully stay out of ours.'

Not surprising, Sera's words offer little comfort, and I find I've lost my appetite, deciding to put my food parcel back in my pack for later. At least the rope makes sense now, and as though it's my only lifeline, I cling to it and try to get some sleep. My mind swirls with images of raiders hunting us, laughing and carousing around a campfire, and in its centre, tied to a spit, is me.

'I hope you grags like little girl.'

111

The early dawn light creeps over the horizon, and I awaken to find Sera already untying herself.

'Beautiful dawn,' she says. 'Did you sleep well?'

'Not really. After last night and sleeping on this branch, I couldn't rest. My mind kept racing.'

'That is not good. Do you think you will be alright to move on?'

'Yeah, should be good.'

'If you are okay with continuing, I would like to get going in ten.'

'Where are we going?'

'I think we would go see where our friends from last night went.'

'But I thought we were going to avoid the raiders?'

'Avoid, yes, but we can still look. We have to be silent, though.'

After eating, we collect the empty traps, take care to check each other over for loose or rattling items, and erase all traces of our camp.

It's still early in the morning when we find the trail leading toward the raider camp, stopping on the crest of a hill and hiding behind the remains of a stone wall to survey the area. Through the atmospheric haze, a dirty but beautiful expanse of ice extends to a shadowy grey area just visible in the distance.

The raiders' camp is a dump of crates and garbage which sits on a slope leading down to the ice. There's a makeshift lean-to made from stacked crates and a large canvas sheet, and a rusted old truck with some form of crude construction on the back, but there's no other shelter in sight. It stands to reason the occupants are passed out in rough, animal skin bedrolls, scattered around a dying fire in the centre of camp.

'I count about seven,' I whisper to Sera, eyeing the camp for signs of other raiders.

'Eight,' she corrects me. 'There will be at least eight. One thing you have to remember about raiders is they travel in couples. If you see an odd number, find the missing one, they could be standing right behind you.'

'Ah,' I reply, snapping my head around to check.

'See that lean-to,' she continues, pointing to the canvas sheet. 'I bet that is where the leader and his mate will be sleeping. So, my guess is, there are ten.'

Just beyond the lean-to and closer to the lake's edge is a detached trailer with a rusted cage on the back. It contains a few blankets on the floor, and a pile of fresh bones lay scattered outside the enclosure as though someone had carelessly tossed them.

Inside the cage, the blankets shift.

'Look,' I say, pointing at the cage, 'there's something in there. Sera, they could be people. We have to go help them.'

I start to shuffle around the wall and towards the camp, but Sera puts a firm hand on my shoulder, sitting me back down.

'Jayne,' she says in a calm, low voice, 'I am sorry, but we can't.'

'Why?' I protest.

'Because we are just here to observe, we cannot interfere.'

'But they're going to die!'

'I know. But it is impossible. We do not want to end up in there with them. Besides, we do not have any backup or weapons.'

'They're asleep, and they've got weapons.' Before Sera can grab me again, I shuffle over a rock ledge and out of reach.

'Jayne, no!' Sera exclaims from behind, but I lose her voice as I descend towards the camp.

I reach the first sleeping raider. His homemade mask is dislodged, and the drool track down his cheek is caked with dust.

Careful not to disturb him, I pick up a short rifle and a crude knife lying next to him on the icy ground, then make for the cage.

As I approach, the acrid smell of rotting flesh, blood and unwashed bodies is overwhelming, and it makes me dry retch.

With the point of the knife, I lift the edge of a disgusting blanket to find five people wearing limited clothing and no breathers. Their blue faces turn to glare at me, blinking with confused eyes.

'Where are your clothes and breathers?' I ask.

They don't respond.

Something moves in the corner of my vision, my heart skips a beat, and I lift the rifle.

Then Sera sticks her head around the corner of the trailer. She peers through the bars at the cold mass of bodies under the blanket and shakes her head, whispering, 'they are dead already. Their bodies do not know it yet, but you can see it in their eyes. Come on, nothing can save these poor people now.'

A gruff voice yells from the other side of the trailer, 'where's me rifle?'

'The raiders!' Sera exclaims.

Beyond the cage, the raider from whom I had taken the rifle points and runs straight towards us.

'Oi, you's, wot you doin' there then?'

'Quick, run!' Sera yells, grabbing my jacket, and we both bolt towards the shadowy area over the ice.

The instant I take my first step out onto the lake's frozen surface, my foot slips and slides like oil on glass, and I drop to my backside. With the raiders now lumbering around on the bank, it's only a matter of time before they shake off their grogginess and come after us. I frantically struggle to get up, but my feet keep slipping. From out of nowhere, Sera's hand grabs my forearm and yanks me up. 'Come on,' she says, and together we run, trying to get as much distance between them and us.

'They've got me rifle,' the man yells.

Glancing over my shoulder, he's followed us out onto the ice and is rapidly closing the gap.

'Jayne, stop,' Sera shouts. 'Take the shot!'

I look over at her in confusion. 'What?'

'Take the shot. Call it practice,' she yells, bringing us to a halt.

A crowd of raiders now gather by the lake's edge and take unaimed shots with their odd collection of firearms.

'Kneel here,' Sera yells, with slugs whistling past. 'Quickly, aim, then take the shot.'

Hesitantly, I follow Sera's instructions, kneel on the ice, and tuck the unsophisticated rifle into my shoulder.

'Remember,' Sera coaches, 'tuck the elbow under, take a few breaths, then squeeze the trigger.'

I'm Ajee Yond, brave on the deck of the Fenix, feeling the weapon, the stock buried in my shoulder, the forestock nestled gently in my left hand. I gaze down the sights of the barrel at the enemy on the wall, aim, take a deep breath and...

The rifle kicks hard, and the short barrel peels in three.

'Ah frak! That hurt,' I curse, throwing the now useless weapon aside, sending it skittering across the ice.

The shot catches the raider off guard. He loses his footing and goes crashing to the frozen surface. Our momentary advantage is fleeting, though, as some other raiders rush out after us.

Sera helps me up, and we run as fast as our feet will take us.

Out here, it's other-worldly; if only I had the time to stop and enjoy it. But with the ruckus coming from behind, it doesn't leave us much choice, and we race across the ice with the band of mad raiders in frantic pursuit. At first, our footfalls make a crunching sound, as though walking on solid frozen ground, but then the sound changes, like aves chirping in a cave.

'You destroyed me rifle,' the man howls after us. 'You'll pay for that.'

Sera's long legs steadily put her in front, but mine just don't seem to want to keep up. 'Keep running, I'll catch up,' she yells, veering off, and I slide past, turning back to see why.

A short distance behind, the raider and Sera collide, and the two spill onto the ice.

They're not the only ones. The sudden movement causes me to slip over too, and I hit the ice hard.

Brushing off the pain, I climb to my knees and look towards Sera. She's on her back with the sizable raider climbing his way up her body.

They wrestle for dominance. Sera throws jabs into muscles and tendons like she'd taught me to do. He tries to grab her arms, but with all that thick padding, her attacks only make him laugh.

'Ya got some fight in ya, haven't ya,' he mocks Sera, pressing her body firmly against the ice. 'Gonna enjoy chewin' on ya bones tonight. But first, I'm gonna have me some fun.' And then he looks over at me. 'With both of ya.'

To most, it would seem like an unfair fight, but I know Sera; she's waiting for the right time.

Or is she?

'Fight back, Sera,' I yell in desperation. 'Fight!'

'You just wait right there, little girl,' the horrid man growls.

Again, she pushes him away. This time he whips off his mask and rips away hers, too. In an abhorrent show, he palms her jaw to one side, leans in, and licks her from neck to forehead. 'Mmmm, fresh meat,' he laughs, flashing grotesque yellow teeth and groping at Sera's chest while the other hand moves towards the front of his pants.

With only the knife I stole from him, all I can do is watch and hope.

But Sera continues punching her palm against his dirty breastplate. It does nothing, and he laughs his callous laugh again. 'You're mine now.'

In frustration, Sera hits the breastplate once more, and then there's that subtle look I know; the tell she knows something he doesn't. She lifts her hand to the man's throat. And Pop!

A cloud of red sprays from his neck, and the raider stops fighting. He clutches at his throat with a startled look where deep red blood is seeping between his fingers. He falls sideways off Sera and, for a moment, struggles, holding the wound and smearing his blood all over the ice.

As Sera reaches for her mask, he makes one last feeble grab at her wrist but lets that go in favour of the gushing wound. Clambering to her feet, she puts her breather back on and gives the man a firm kick to the head on her way over.

'He won't be a problem for us anymore,' she says, a little short of breath.

'What happened?'

'The pistol wouldn't eject.' She lifts back her sleeve to reveal the tiny pistol Nanneral had previously owned.

'Well, that came in handy,' I chuckle as Sera reaches down to help me up.

'I thought I told you to run.'

'But... Sera, the truck!' I yell, noticing we have another problem. 'It's on the ice!'

Ice screams under tyres as the rusty truck from the camp races past the raiders on foot and barrels towards us.

We're running again.

The ice echo continues now, intermixed with the rumbling sound of the truck gaining from behind. What was once choral singing becomes a reverberating groan. In the distance, the tree line makes our destination seem that much further away.

There's no way we can make it in time.

With the truck bearing down, we run as hard as we can. My lungs burn, and struggling to breathe through the restriction of the mask, my pace slows. Sera, holding my hand, encourages me to push on, but all I want to do is take off this restraint and breathe freely.

The truck slides sideways past us, spinning multiple times and lurching to a violent halt about a hundred metas away.

Four raiders leap from the vehicle, landing on the ice, two from the rear, and two from the front cabin, cutting off our escape.

Sliding to a stop, we face off with them, our dilemma punctuated by the ice complaining underfoot that gives off a long, jarring groan.

All four raiders hold rifles at their hip, pointing them at us and advancing, yelling indiscernible taunts whipped away by the wind.

The ice groans once more, its sound resonating like a quake underfoot. All of a sudden, there's an almighty crack, and the truck's right front wheel drops through the ice, throwing the unsuspecting occupants inside against the windscreen.

The four, armed raiders standing before us cease their taunts and turn to watch as their truck, leaning at a precarious angle, continues to tip onto its side. Powerless to assist, all they can do is stand by while the widening hole consumes their truck. The cabin enters the freezing water, and it rushes up to engulf half of the compartment. Trapped inside, the two raiders claw at the upper window trying to escape, but their vehicle drops further into the icy abyss.

Cracks continue to radiate on either side of the hole, breaking off and parting away, flooding the truck with water.

Within midecs, it and its occupants disappear beneath the surface, unleashing a bevy of frothing ice water.

From out of the four raiders left standing, one of them loses his footing and slides into the freezing water.

In a disastrously comical display, the remaining three take tentative steps toward the hole. They peer over the edge to see where their friend had gone but get too close, and the ice breaks away beneath their feet, plunging two more in after.

Dropping his rifle, the last lonely raider snatches for the hand of the person beside him, catching only air.

His companions flail and splutter, fighting to remain above water while he desperately reaches out to save one of them. In their mad panic, they yank him in as well.

With the raiders splashing in their pathetic attempts to clamber out of the hole, we run. Only the Progenitors can save them now.

The shadowy area we'd spotted from the camp turns out to be the edge of a forest on a small island, its foliage long dead like everything else. While we allow time to catch our breath, three hazy figures advance toward us, followed by a massive, fast-moving wall of swirling grey.

From all the commotion, we hadn't noticed the storm, and it now looms upon us like a ferocious beast with a mighty vengeance. The wind whips up debris and sends it flying towards that roiling dark grey front.

The three raiders seem to have lost interest in their pursuit and are rushing to reach the island. But with all the dust being kicked up by the swirling wind, they vanish from sight.

'We have to find shelter, now!' Sera shouts above the cacophony.

'But where?' I ask as we run along the shore, searching among the dead trees for any sign of shelter.

'A cave, a hollowed-out tree, anything,' Sera yells.

In no time, we make it to the island's lee side, which offers a little more protection from the weather.

There, a rock formation juts out from the shore, its shape looking like the bow of the Fenix in Ajee's story. We run for it, finding a crevice near the frozen water line, and dive inside. Within, it opens up into a cave large enough for two.

Outside, the wind, sleet and thunder rages on while we make ourselves comfortable in our cosy little shelter. With a continuous light breeze blowing through, it offers little warmth, but we are dry and safe from the storm, and man, am I happy about that.

'Sera,' I complain, my teeth chattering uncontrollably. 'If I don't get warm soon, I'm going to freeze like those...' I can't bring myself to finish the sentence, shivering more thinking about the poor people in the cage.

Sera gives me a hug, rubbing my arms to generate warmth. 'I think it is safe to light a small fire,' she says, looking around for anything to burn. She gathers up all the dry material in the cave, but there isn't much. 'Stay here and stay warm the best you can,' she says, collecting rope from her pack, tying one end around her waist and the other around a rock at the cave's entrance. 'Tug this three times if you need me. I will be back soon.' And like that, she ducks out of the cave and into the storm.

I awaken, wrapped in a blanket, and find Sera sitting by a small fire burning in a nook. 'Hey, sleepyhead,' she says. 'Are you warm?'

Nodding, I move closer. Sera has a small pot of vegetables bubbling over the fire, and the smell of it makes my stomach rumble, reminding me of how little I've eaten. As I nibble on my last piece of cured tomadai meat, I'm glad I left it for later.

Sera sits by the fire, unstrapping the little pistol from around her wrist. 'Useless piece of rubbish,' she curses, tossing it across the cave floor.

'What'd you do that for?'

'It is all bent. I cannot use that now.'

'I might be able to fix it,' I say, collecting it up. 'At least we know the thing works.'

She shrugs. 'Take it then. It is useless. If you can fix it, it is yours. But Jayne,' she says as I shove it into my pack. 'Remember what I said about weapons. Be careful with that. Do not tell anyone I let you have it. They would have my head if they found out I let you have a firearm so young.'

For two days, the ferocious storm rages on. We shelter in place in the cave, taking turns to watch the fire while the other rests, leaving only to gather more wood. On the second morning, I awaken to a dim stream of light shining through the cave's entrance and Sera's muffled voice calling my name.

'Jayne, get out here! Hurry, hurry!'

Terrified the raiders have found us, I jump to attention, grab a knife and dash for the cave opening.

'What's going on?' I yell in panic.

Sera doesn't reply.

No! The raiders have found us. They've detected the smoke.

Gripping the knife handle tight, I crawl toward the exit.

'There you are,' Sera says, making me jump in fright when her head appears in the entranceway.

'Sheesh, you startled me.' I clutch my chest in relief.

Sera grabs my free hand and pulls me outside. 'You have got to see this.'

The moment I step out into the light, it's blinding, but as my eyes adjust, the storm has eased, and the snow is no longer falling in heavy sheets. Sera points at a shimmering ray of sunlight beaming through a gap in the clouds, making the slow-moving dust in the air below glow like gold. It's like something out of the *Book of the Progenitors*; as if Aster, the sun mistress herself, reached out and opened the clouds, impressing upon the world the time has come for rebirth.

We stand in silence, enjoying the tranquillity, watching as the finger of light dissipates over the frozen surface of the lake.

'So,' Sera asks, as the last stream of light is consumed by cloud. 'What do you think of the lake?'

'Um,' I shrug, relishing in my first and only real opportunity to look at it since coming here. 'It's nice, I guess.'

She wraps an arm around me and pulls me closer.

'This is not what I had in mind when I thought about bringing you here. But all things considered...' she trails off.

'Sera, it's nice. Thank you.'

'Well, we better be heading back. We are already late, and those clouds still look menacing.'

We grab our belongings from the cave and head back out onto the ice towards the raider camp.

Half-buried in the fresh snow, a female raider lies face up, about one hundred metas from shore. Her frostbitten face stares at the sky, and we give her a wide berth.

'Seems an appropriate end for someone who commits another to die the way their captives did,' Sera spits.

'Probably the one who bragged about eating girls, too. Good riddance.'

'Come on,' Sera says, 'we need to keep moving, else we will end up like her.'

A dark smear across the horizon in the distance promises solid ground, but without having had much food for the last two days, it may as well be twice the distance.

We navigate around snowdrifts and the refrozen churned ice from the truck and eventually step off the ice into the raider camp.

The heap of frozen blankets lies still in the cage, and littered about the camp are smashed crates of useless pre-war paraphernalia. Even their bedrolls are still where the raiders up and left them. Only junk and rotting food is all that remains, so we head for the lean-to toward the back of camp.

Inside, there are some wood crates, a mouldy two-person mattress, a pair of bedrolls, blankets, an assortment of other rubbish and, to our surprise, covered by a tarpaulin, a car. It's painted green and has four doors, two bench seats and wheels much smaller than a truck's. Besides the colour, it looks a bit like the one my parents had.

Sera dances on the spot with joy, then rushes to open the driver's door, ushering me inside. The car is freezing, but I'm fortunate to find a few musty blankets on the back seat. Grabbing two, I wrap one around myself and hand another to Sera as she closes the door.

The engine splutters when Sera attempts to start it. 'I think it is out of fuel,' she says, pointing to the fuel gauge on the dash. 'Wait here. I thought I saw fuel cans outside.'

I wait for what feels like ages, and when Sera doesn't return, I leave the relative comfort of the vehicle and go looking for her.

As I leave the tent, Sera is struggling with a male raider. They fight over a pistol the raider holds aloft above their heads, and she's pummelling him with short, sharp shitak'na jabs to the armpit.

Then they notice my presence.

The raider fumbles, and Sera uses the distraction to shoulder-barge him away, delivering a knee to the groin. He drops the pistol and stumbles backwards. Without thinking, I reach for the crude knife at my belt, and in a single fluid motion, release the unbalanced weapon from my hand. Unlike my throwing knives, it clumsily tumbles through the air, but it does the job, striking my target in the throat.

He grasps at the blade sticking out of his neck and keels over backward, gurgling on his blood.

'Good shot, Jayne!' Sera compliments. 'For a handle-heavy knife, you got the throw right.'

'Thanks, but I was aiming for the chest.'

Without warning, Sera drops to the ground, grabs the raider's pistol, and fires a single slug in my direction. The shot whistles through the air, dropping something like a dead weight behind me. When I turn around, a female raider lies crumpled with a slug hole in her forehead.

'Gord damn!' I exclaim, kicking her to make sure she's dead.

'Remember what I said about raiders?' Sera says, tossing the weapon away. 'That's why we should always be prepared. That should hopefully be the last of them.'

We make our way back to the car with the cans of fuel, and that's when I notice it.

'Just a moment,' I say. 'There's something I have to do.'

I break off and hurry toward the rusty old cage holding the poor, freezing captives. As I approach, none of the occupants are moving. Instead, there is an inert mass beneath the rotting blankets. Sera was right. It looks like, in their last moments, the prisoners were trying to huddle together to share their limited body warmth, but the elements won out in the end. Seeing them like that makes my eyes involuntarily well up. I remove my mask to wipe away a tear as Sera's gentle footsteps come up from behind. She places a comforting arm around me, and I can't hold it back any longer.

'I'm crying, and I have no idea why,' I babble.

'It is okay,' she says.

'But I don't even know these people.'

'It is natural to feel remorse for the loss of your own kind, especially for those who in your eyes did nothing to deserve it.'

'It isn't fair!'

'No, it is not.'

For some reason, her voice remains steady and flat, and to a degree, it annoys me how calm she is being.

'Don't you feel it too?'

Sera drops her hand and looks at me so I can see the sincerity on her face. Even behind the visor, I can tell her eyes are heavy.

'Yes, I do. But I have experienced much more of this than you can ever know. It does not get easier, but you learn to handle your emotions in time. This is not a lesson I can teach you. It is one you must learn on your own.'

Sera's words leave me speechless. Instead, I put on my mask and look forlornly at the poor captives in the cage; victims of their own innocence.

'We can't leave them like this,' I say. 'We just can't. We have to set them free.'

'But Jayne...'

I don't wait for her permission or help. Instead, I run around picking up everything I can find; crates, logs, the raiders' belongings, everything, and pile it in and around the cage. Sera picks up on what I'm doing and decides to help. In no time, we amass quite a sizeable mound.

'I want this to be seen from the Gord,' I declare.

Sera pauses, deep in thought, then presents a can of fuel. 'We do not need this much,' she says, handing me the half-empty can. 'This should do.'

I douse the pile.

'Okay,' she says, holding out a stick, its end wrapped in a fuel-soaked cloth. 'Light it up. Set them free!'

One spark from my fire bracelet and Sera's stick becomes a torch. With a sense of satisfaction, I take the stick and throw it onto the pile. The mound ignites in a whoosh, and the whole heap goes up in flames so intense I back away from the heat.

'Nobody is going to harm them anymore,' she says, watching the bonfire burn. 'If you have finished here, let us get out of this place, shall we? I think we have had just about enough fun for a few days. It is time we head home.'

And with that, we drive off toward Garret Gord, a plume of black smoke billowing behind us from what used to be the raiders' camp; a beacon to any who shall pass.

Justice was done here.

07 – Acquaintances

Two khaki green ex-military trucks ploughed through the freezing early morning.

The leading vehicle breached the last steep section of the mountain crest, its engine coughing on the last fumes of fuel from the climb.

Orian brought the vehicle to a stop and tapped the fuel gauge with a finger. 'Have to refuel again,' she said, looking at Anaska sitting in the passenger seat.

Orian checked her breather and braced for the influx of freezing air.

For the fourth time since their departure, she left the engine running and climbed out into the cold to check the fuel tank while the other truck pulled up alongside. She removed the cap and knocked it against the tank. The echo sounded deep.

With all the spare fuel canisters empty, she had hoped there would be more. As she trudged around to the reserve tank, the other truck's driver side window opened. 'What's the fuel situation?' the driver asked.

'We're running on fumes,' Orian replied. 'I've just flicked over to the reserve. That'll give us about a cendec. After that, we're walking.'

'I wish I could help, but we switched over a little while back.'

'Thanks anyway,' Orian said, climbing back behind the wheel.

'I take it we've seen better days?' Anaska asked.

'We just better hope we find this place soon.'

The limited convoy resumed their descent down the steep and windy mountain track.

'What's the possibility we're looking for a ghost town in all this?' Anaska asked, motioning at the depressing landscape.

'I'm not sure, but that is the third destroyed roadblock we've driven through now,' Orian replied.

'Should we have remained at Gotthard?'

Orian sighed. 'We had to leave. The ventilation system was failing, and when Mapp refuted there was a problem, I had to act.'

'How do you know this place is even out here?'

'I don't. Normally, I don't hold stock in rumour, but when I heard about this refugee camp, I saw it as our only remaining option.'

'And Mapp, what did she have to say about this?'

'You know Mapp. Buried her head like she always does.'

'I'm surprised she gave us the trucks then,' Anaska said.

'She didn't.'

Lazy sunlight broke over the horizon, filling the valley and plains with a glowing haze. Anaska leaned forward to stare out the windscreen. 'I think I saw something down there,' she said, trying to rub the sleep out of her eyes.

'I think that must be lack of sleep. I didn't see anything.'

'Perhaps you're right. I'll let you focus on driving. I don't want to take the fast way down.'

It's gotta be around here somewhere, Orian thought, as they rounded a bend where a meandering, flat path cut its way through the low sections of the landscape.

As they drew nearer, Anaska pointed towards a clearing by the edge of the path and pylons that looked like the remains of an old bridge. 'Pull up over here,' she said. 'I think that's a river.'

Orian nodded and brought the vehicle to a stop. The two women fixed their breathers on tighter and climbed out.

Even in her rough, plain, handmade Gotthard garments, Orian had an air of style about her. Wrapping her knee-length patchwork blanket coat around her tighter, it helped keep out the wind. At the edge of the river, she bent down to inspect the ice. White and glassy, it looked solid enough.

'Do you think it will hold our vehicles?' she asked.

Anaska joined her at the river's edge, the ex-engineer inspecting the ice more meticulously before stepping out onto it. 'It's hard to tell the depth of the ice, but it appears solid enough. I think it'll be fine to drive on. I can see tyre tracks where other vehicles have driven on it before. They look fresh, and they're headed that way.' She pointed to a gap in the dead trees on the opposite riverbank.

'This might be it then,' Orian rejoiced.

'Don't get too excited. We're not there yet.'

As the truck duo drove slow and steady over the frozen river, a shiver ran up Orian's spine. 'Do you feel that?' she asked.

'What, the pairs of beady eyes staring at us from the bank?' Anaska said. 'Yes, I caught someone watching us a little way back. They're not too discreet about it either.'

'Keep your wits about you. We don't want a repeat of yesterday.'

On the other side of the river, fallen logs forming triangular-shaped barricades lined the narrow track. Corralled between boulders and standing trees, their vehicles were forced forward along the winding roadway.

'I'd say we're getting close,' Anaska said as they drove around another boulder set on the inside of a bend.

The dirt road soon widened, and several shacks constructed from an assortment of materials came into view.

Orian's heart fluttered.

Maybe they'd finally found it.

Anaska reached back to bang on the wall dividing the cabin from the trailer where their precious cargo of passengers rode. 'We're here!' she yelled. 'We made it.'

Orian marvelled at the hundred or so shacks nestled along the rough, impacted gravel main street lined with light poles—it was much more advanced than she had expected. People emerged to catch a glimpse as the convoy drove past, some wary, others curious.

The Gotthard trucks pulled up outside the largest building on the main street, where two people obstructed the roadway. One was a man wearing a red ankle-length coat and nursing a rifle, while his dark and brawny companion rested his left hand on a holstered pistol at his hip.

'Stay here,' Orian said. 'I think it best only one of us says hello.'

Anaska nodded, 'no arguments here.'

Orian climbed out, trudged towards the two men, and stopped at a comfortable distance. 'Good morn, my name is Orian Gracyn. Myself and twenty-nine other refugees are looking for Hope.' As she made her introduction, she gestured at herself and then at the trucks.

'Then you have found it. I'm Vice-Administrator Solon, and this is my Head of Security, Jaxson Yanez,' the man in the red coat said. To Orian, they looked stern but not threatening. 'Ms Gracyn,' he said in a level tone, 'I don't suppose you mind showing me the contents of those trucks?'

This wasn't the warm welcome she was expecting. Then again, she wasn't sure what kind of reception she was expecting.

'My people need urgent medical attention, but if you must...'

'If you don't mind, please, Ms Gracyn,' he insisted.

Orian turned and led the men to the rear of the truck, keeping a close eye on them with every step. As they passed the passenger's side, Anaska watched with both hands in plain sight on the dash.

Rounding the rear doors, the vice-administrator raised his rifle. Careful not to cause alarm, Orian lifted her hands and slowly unlatched the catch, swinging the doors open to reveal thirteen sets of depressed and weary eyes peering back at them through the dappled light.

'Good dawn, folks. If you don't mind staying where you are,' the man said, then turning to Orian, 'we'd like to check out the other truck now.'

'Haven't you seen enough?' Orian pleaded.

'Not until I've seen the other truck,' he insisted, escorting her around to the rear of the other vehicle.

He readied himself again, this time with the barrel of his rifle not held as high. Orian released the back door. Forlorn faces looked up at them from a person lying on the floor.

'What happened?' Orian asked with shock.

A voice in the dim light replied, 'Ma'am, it's Vic. He didn't make it.'

Orian's heart sank. 'Put that murder stick down,' she snapped between gritted teeth at the man in red. 'Now, do you believe me, or do you want to autopsy Vic for weapons?'

The vice-administrator lowered his rifle and handed it to his companion. 'Go get Doctor Colyar and Ferne.'

'Yes, sir,' Jaxson replied, slinging the rifle strap over his shoulder and taking off between the shacks.

After watching his man disappear, the vice-administrator lifted his breather and shouted, 'I need some help out here!'

A small crowd filtered out onto the main street and assisted Orian's people down from the trucks, starting with the wounded.

'I'm sorry about that,' he said, turning to Orian. 'It's a bit of a necessary formality.'

'Understandable, Vice-Administrator,' Orian replied, concealing her frustration at the delay.

'The name's Sage, by the way,' he said, raising his hand to shake Orian's. 'Welcome to Hope.'

Sage escorted Orian through the large doors of the moderately lit community hall, past neatly set up tables and chairs to one at the far end.

Orian removed her breather and massaged her face, relieved to breathe without the aid of a mask.

'So, you were expecting us?' Orian asked, commenting on the setup and the local people buzzing around.

'Our scouts alerted us to your arrival as soon as you crossed the Codan ranges,' he replied. 'We're used to people appearing out of the ether. Just they're not always the friendly type.'

She observed the curious mix of people streaming into the hall, including the two who slipped in with Jaxson. As they set to work attending to the wounded, Orian assumed they were the doctor and Ferne.

The others carried canvas cots, bedding and an assortment of supplies. It surprised Orian to see so many people braving the cold. 'Is it customary to be so welcoming like this?' she asked.

'We were all in your shoes at some point,' Sage replied. 'Well, most of us. The administrator and his wife had the hardest job building this place from rubble. They had to do it on their own. When I arrived, there were already about fifty people in the camp.'

Orian was captivated by his charming, youthful appearance and thought it rather strange a person like him could be vice-administrator.

'So, you're the vice-administrator? Will the administrator be joining us?'

'He will be with us shortly,' Sage replied. 'In the meantime, my people will help you out with whatever you need. So, where are you from?'

'Gotthard,' she said in a flat tone.

'Hmm, a few of us have come from there.'

'There may be a few more coming,' Orian said. 'As we were leaving, the place was falling apart, but now that we've found this place, I can send word back. If there's room, of course.'

'Friendly faces are always welcome, and we do what we can to help. So, are there just the two trucks or are there more on the way now?'

'There were originally three,' she said in a sombre voice. 'But a group of thugs dressed in shabby clothing and brandishing weapons ambushed our convoy. We never saw them coming. We lost many good people that night.'

'Raiders,' Sage said with disgust, 'they infest these parts.'

'Raiders?'

'Bands of savages who attack people like you and me for food, among other things. We've had run-ins with them from time to time. I'm sorry, Orian,' Sage said with a sympathetic tone, 'I'm sure Gaius will—'

'Who?' she asked, jerking her head back in surprise at the name.

Just then, a grizzled, silver and brown-haired man limped through the doors to the hall, removed his breather and the instant Orian saw his face, her eyes widened.

He froze.

She stared at him in disbelief.

Gaius's face flooded with conflict as he looked at the door, then to Orian, then back to the door, before taking his time to meander through the exhausted crowd.

'Gaius? Is that you?' Orian said before Sage could introduce her.

'Orian?' Gaius said, his words escaping him. 'But I thought...?' The incredulity in his voice, coupled with the expression of disbelief, mirrored hers. He stood on the other side of the table like an eudur caught in a truck's headlights.

Sage's face reflected his confusion.

Gaius's smile wavered. 'I am sorry, but if you excuse me...' he stuttered, then turned and ambled away.

'I'm sorry, Orian, but I have no idea what just happened,' Sage said, reaching for his mask. 'That wasn't like Gaius. Let me go—'

'It's okay,' she said, catching his arm. 'Leave him be. I imagine my presence here would upset him.'

Sage's eyes darted between Gaius leaving and Orian, her comparatively calm demeanour masking her own internal conflict.

'Do you know him?' Sage asked after a moment.

'Knew him, yes,' she said, not diverting her attention from the closing door at the opposite end of the hall. 'It's a long story. Perhaps I'll tell it to you some time.'

The little community hall became a buzzing hive of activity with several of Hope's residents, dressed in neat, comfortable-looking garments milling among the new arrivals. They offered warm welcomes, food, bedding and clothing. Orian marvelled at the practised efficiency and care with which they went about their duties.

Sage was about to leave to attend to other matters when a sweet-faced woman in her mid-thirties came over carrying a covered tray. A delectable aroma wafted from its contents. Trailing behind her was a boy, aged about ten, bearing a neatly folded stack of blankets and a towel.

'Welcome to Hope,' the woman said to Orian with a gentle smile. 'I'm Abril Tope, and this is my son, Rodi. You must be Orian?'

Rodi gave a cute grin, handing Orian the pile before bounding off toward a young girl with frizzy, dark brown hair.

'That's right,' she replied.

Abril uncovered the tray, revealing mugs of steaming hot liquid and an assortment of baked goods. 'You must be hungry. Can I offer you something to eat or drink? I have kahwah and hot tei.'

'Did you say kahwah?'

Abril nodded with pride.

Orian smiled. It surprised her how such a simple gesture could lift her spirits. She selected a cup and a small, warm, soft bun that smelled divine. 'Thank you,' she said graciously, 'we really do appreciate it.'

At that point, Sage spoke up. 'I apologise, ladies, but there's something I need to attend to. I'll leave you with Abril, Orian. It was a pleasure meeting you.' He took a bun, then strode away.

'He seems like a good fellow?' Orian said, watching Sage with his long coat flapping behind him.

'Who? You mean Sage?' Abril replied, glancing in his direction. 'Yes, this is all his work. Of course, these days, we don't get many newcomers, but over the treys, with him and Gaius, we've honed this down to a fine art. I think people miss it.'

Gaius, Orian pondered. Now she'd seen him, she couldn't shake him from her thoughts. 'Do you mind if I ask you a question? How long has Gaius been running this place?'

Abril set down the tray and replied. 'He founded Hope. Why do you ask?'

Orian raised an eyebrow. 'No reason,' she lied. 'I just knew him in a former life and wondered what had become of him.'

'I see,' Abril said. 'If it weren't for him, many of us wouldn't be here, myself included. It's been a long few cycles.'

'You're telling me. That reminds me, Sage told me about raiders. How often do you get them around here?'

Abril thought about that. 'We get the occasional attacks, I think, but Sage would be able to answer that. He looks after our defences. I heard you encountered a mob of them on your journey here. Can I ask what happened?'

'It's still a bit of a tender subject, but if it helps in any way, I don't mind telling it.'

Abril nodded with a sympathetic expression, and Orian began.

'It was our fourth night,' she recounted, trying to keep herself calm, 'and we were looking for a safe place to stop and rest. The sun had set when we suddenly heard a loud noise, like a pack of ferocious wild animals, but they were carrying torches and weapons. I still can't believe how heavily armed they were. They had rifles and artillery like you would expect of an army. Before we could react, they were on us, attacking the rear truck in our convoy.' Orian swallowed her grief. 'They hit us so fast, and so violently, the truck was on fire before any of us could even let off a single round. We tried to fight them off, but there were so many of them we didn't stand a chance. The only way we could survive was to run.'

'Progenitors save us, are you okay?'

'A little rattled, but I'm sure I'll be fine. I'm more concerned about the others.' Orian scanned the room, observing her companions. They all bore more than physical injuries. Despite getting help from the Hope locals, their faces still wore their grief. Those were the faces of people who had seen death coming and somehow survived. Orian sensed a part of them remained behind with the friends and family they lost that night.

'You're in good company,' Abril said, placing a gentle hand on Orian's arm. 'Here in Hope, we all help one another. It's what we do. We've all been through it.'

'Thank you.'

'You're most welcome. It does give us cause for concern, though. I'm really glad you told me.'

'Oh?'

'That doesn't sound like a typical raider attack. They sound too organised,' Abril mused. 'If I showed you a map, could you point to where they attacked you?'

'Sure.'

Abril led Orian over to a pre-war map stuck to the wall. It showed Hope marked as a hand-drawn red cross and the local surrounds. Orian considered it, then pointed to a winding black line depicting the road between Gotthard and Hope.

'There,' she said.

'That's a little close for comfort. Wait here,' Abril said, and hurried off to Sage, who was deep in conversation on the other side of the hall. Shortly after, she returned with the vice-administrator in tow.

'This is where she said her convoy was ambushed,' Abril said, pointing to the place on the map.

'How many did you say there were?' he asked.

'We didn't get a good look at them,' Orian replied, 'but I'd say about thirty or more.'

Sage pursed his lips in contemplation. 'That *is* unusual, but nothing we can't handle.'

Abril gave him a doubtful look. 'Are you sure?'

'Our target-shooters are well trained. They can deal with a few raiders. I don't think it's anything to worry about.'

'I'm not so sure,' Abril objected.

'Abril, they're my people. I think I know what they can handle.'

'But these aren't just raiders. From Orian's description, they sound like a small army.'

Sage was getting annoyed, his previously calm voice becoming short and stern. 'I said we can take care of it,' he insisted, trying to end any further argument on the matter.

'At least raise it with the council,' Abril said. 'Let them decide. They should at least be made aware.'

'Alright,' he conceded with a sour expression, 'not that it will do anything, but I'll call a meeting.' He then promptly turned and stormed away.

'Thank you,' Abril called after him, 'and make it today. This can't wait.'

He waved in acknowledgement and kept on walking.

'I'm sorry about that,' Abril said, turning to Orian. 'He can be a bit stubborn at times.'

'It's okay. I've dealt with my fair share of stubborn ones in my day,' Orian said. 'True stubbornness is a bunch of knuckle-headed politicians bickering over a bill. By comparison, I'd bet your council would be civilised.'

Abril laughed at that. 'Say, would you mind addressing the council? Maybe you can tell them what happened. They might listen to you.'

'I don't know...' Orian objected, thinking about encountering Gaius more than anything.

'Please, Orian. If you can just tell them what you told me, you might be able to convince them to take this seriously. I've been trying to tell them for ages to get their heads out of the dirt and do something about the raiders, but they won't listen to me. You heard Sage, sometimes he can be a bit...' she trailed off.

Orian considered the idea some more. If this was going to be her home, she was as much responsible for its safety as they were. Abril had a point. Perhaps telling her story may sway minds in Abril's favour. 'Well, if you insist,' she agreed, 'I can only try.'

'That's all I ask.'

Seeing that the hall was now filled with noisy refugees adjusting to their new surroundings, the council, with Orian, decided to hold their impromptu meeting in Gaius's hut.

Four well-dressed, official-looking Hope residents filed into the tiny hut and took a seat around the small circular dining table. Orian stood in the dim light behind Gaius and Sage by the heater.

Gaius placed out cups of water and set a lamp in the centre of the table, turning it up to illuminate the faces of Sage, Abril and another man Orian had not yet met, taking their seats.

'Why is Niklas Martell always late?' Abril grumbled.

'Is he that important?' Sage asked in a snide tone.

At that moment, a draft of cold air had everyone grab their coat collars as the door opened, and a younger man with tufts of brownish hair poking out below a grey, loaghtan-fleece hat strutted in with his cane. He removed his breather, and adjusting his coat, took the last chair. 'What's the big deal?' he said arrogantly. 'I'd just started eating my breakfast. Why aren't we using the hall?'

Orian adjusted her footing in the darkness.

'And who is she?' The young man questioned, pointing at Orian.

'Don't be rude to our guest, Niklas,' Abril scolded him. 'This is Orian. I invited her.'

Gaius cleared his throat, then took his seat, shrugging off the rude comments. 'Thank you, everyone, for coming on such short notice. Abril has raised a rather concerning matter she wants us to discuss. Abril if you please.'

'Thank you, Gaius,' Abril announced, sitting forward in her chair so her soft, round face was clearly visible in the light. 'As you know, thirty new refugees arrived this morn from Gotthard. We have received some disturbing information from them about a potential threat to Hope. I want to make sure we're prepared—'

'Which we are,' Sage interrupted, crossing his arms.

'Be that as it may, Sage.' She shot a sidelong glance at him, but his steely expression didn't seem to faze her.

Abril continued. 'I've invited the source of that information to the meeting today so she can tell us herself what happened. Then, we can decide if we should act. Everyone, this is Orian Gracyn.'

Five sets of eyes shifted to Orian. To be the centre of attention in a political meeting wasn't uncommon for her, but with Gaius in the room, she had shivers like someone dropped ice down her back.

To Orian's astute observation, it looked from Gaius's nervous disposition, he desperately wanted to run, but no one else seemed to notice or care. *Maybe that was normal for him now?* she thought sadly. 'Thank you for the gracious invitation, Abril,' Orian said, pushing aside the thought. She stepped into the circle of light and began recounting the events leading up to and including the vicious raider attack on her convoy, describing how the assailants seemed prepared and emphasising the terrible loss of those sixteen lives along with the third truck.

'You need to be aware; they were on the road heading this way,' she concluded.

'How do we know you didn't lead them this way?' Niklas accused.

'Niklas, watch your tone,' Gaius snapped.

'I think we need to hear what she has to say, Niklas,' added the other, as yet unnamed man.

'Thank you, Garan,' Gaius agreed, addressing the weathered, sandy-blonde haired gentleman seated beside Abril. 'Please continue, Orian.'

'How many of you have been along that track on the other side of the mountains?' Orian asked. 'Have you noticed how little room there is for turning around? I just finished explaining to you, we had stopped for the night when they attacked us from behind. It was an ambush. They found us, not the other way around. If you don't believe me,' she waved an arm toward the mountains, 'go see for yourself.'

'But you said there were thirty or more of them?' Niklas asked.

'They had military-grade weapons,' Orian said, 'and they used them like someone had trained them. They knew exactly when to hit us. We didn't stand a chance.'

'Yet here you are,' Niklas retorted.

'Thank you for your information, Orian,' Sage cut in. 'Don't get me wrong, we're grateful and very sorry this happened to you, but respectfully, you were a caravan of sitting water-aves. That attack sounds opportunistic to me, and it's regrettable you were the ones to face it. But the fact of the matter is, we're simply a village of refugees. There's nothing of interest here. And even if there were, we have a very well-trained team of target-shooters and scouts. I personally assure you we have nothing to worry about.'

Orian brushed a hand through her thick mane of greying-brown hair and rolled her eyes, stepping back into the shadows, removing herself from the discussion.

'And we also have LunaTec,' Niklas added, stifling a snicker. 'They're supposed to protect us, aren't they?'

Abril scoffed, 'LunaTec, pfft. What have they done? They haven't so much as offered a single pistol to help. And, where are they? They're not even here!'

'Did anyone even bother to invite Cristal?' Sage asked, looking at Abril.

She shrugged. 'I sent a message to Ms Spriggs, but it's not up to me to babysit her, Sage. If LunaTec had an interest in this place, they'd be here.'

'And what do you suppose they'd do?' Sage rebuffed.

'Help defend us, that's a start,' Abril replied. 'Since they came here and made their demands, they've barely said boo to us.'

Sage was incredulous. 'I don't like LunaTec nosing in on us any more than you do, but at least I can see the benefits. You've got food, haven't you?' he argued, 'And new clothes and Garan's still alive.'

'Hey! Hey!' Abril objected. 'That's not fair.'

'No, it isn't,' Sage interjected. 'But we're alive.'

'How long for?' Abril spoke over Sage's last word.

Sage blurted, '*And* they built that bunker for us. My people—'

'Say what you will about LunaTec,' Garan raised his voice, joining the argument. 'They came through for us. I, for one, am grateful.'

'No thanks to Gaius and Sage selling us out, though,' Niklas piped up, sitting back in his chair with his arms crossed. 'Nobody consulted me about that decision.'

Sage knocked back his chair as he stood, fury written all over his face. 'You weren't there, Martell,' he accused, 'because if you were, you would have made the same decision we did. We didn't have a choice!'

Niklas scowled, 'I still think we got cranked, and that would not have happened if you consulted with me.'

'Whatever, it was the right decision!' Sage yelled, slamming his hand on the table.

'Can we get back on topic?' Abril shouted; her voice drowned out as the Council erupted into a raucous shouting match.

Abril's voice paled against the argument as she tried, and failed, to redirect the conversation.

Niklas shot to his feet, his chair striking the wall in a counter show of bravado. 'How do you know if it was the right decision?' he yelled.

Garan slammed the table to make his point just as valid, pointing a finger at Sage and then Niklas. 'You don't know what you're sayin', both of you—'

Orian watched with disbelief as volleys of heated words fired across the table, and the meeting descended into chaos. It was plain to her Gaius, despite his position, was powerless to stop it. Like a fish, his mouth opened and closed, trying in vain to get a word in, but the barrage of insults continued. Orian thought she'd seen worse. Maybe she was wrong?

Niklas pointed his finger back at Garan and shouted over him. 'You take that finger away before I break it off and shove it—'

'ORDER, ORDER!' Orian bellowed, stepping forward and slapping her hand hard on the wooden table.

All argument ceased, and five pairs of eyes stared at her in shock.

'Are you children or councillors?' she demanded, rubbing her stinging palm.

Their expressions remained icy, but the question gave them pause.

'You are the leaders of Hope, are you not? Is Hope not a place where the desperate and vulnerable come in search of peace and refuge? Yet here you are fighting like spoilt children over the last biscuit. You have assembled here to discuss a credible and imminent threat to your lives. At the very least, you must take that threat seriously and consider the consequences if you fail. Please, tell me I'm wrong!'

The startled council members glanced at each other and back at Orian, their confusion replaced by embarrassment. She had called them out, and they knew it.

Gaius spoke up. 'Orian is right,' he said, doing his best not to stutter, but overwhelmed by emotion, he couldn't help it. 'We must consider the safety and welfare of our people first. We must put aside our differences and...'

'Do what, Gaius?' Sage interjected. 'We've done all that can be done. I've trained our target-shooters, we have scouts patrolling the area, and we have roadblocks at all ingress points to slow any potential attack. What more can we do?'

'What can we do besides havin' someone drive up to LunaTec and knock on their front door?' Garan said with a shrug.

'No. We can handle this!' Sage spat.

Abril shot Garan a pained look. But it was Niklas who responded.

'See that you do,' he said.

Sage scowled at him, then continued, 'at a guess, we have two days. With Orian's intel, we can prepare, and if there are raiders out there who want to take a stab at Hope, we'll be ready and waiting.'

The room fell silent while the council members contemplated what had just transpired.

Eventually, Gaius sat forward, wiped a hand over his craggy face and asked, 'what say the council?'

From reading the atmosphere in the room, Orian could tell a cloud of doubt still overshadowed some council members. But having lost the argument, they didn't press the issue.

And with no further objections, Gaius declared. 'Council dismissed.'

The council members rose from their chairs, put their breathers on, and filed out the front door, leaving Gaius, Sage and Orian in uncomfortable silence.

Orian gathered her things as Gaius shuffled indirectly towards her, collecting cups. It was such a small room; they couldn't avoid each other any longer.

'Hello Gaius,' she said politely.

Gaius opened his mouth, but his stuttering hindered his speech. Failing to get the first word out, he gave up and averted his eyes. Sage stood next to him like a defensive hound protecting his master.

'Would you give us a moment, please, Sage?' Orian asked in a gentle voice. 'This is something Gaius and I need to talk about alone. If he can forgive himself and relax.'

Sage gave Gaius a puzzled look, but the older man just returned a sad, conceded nod.

A tear rolled down Gaius's face as he glanced up. A pained smile appeared momentarily, then he turned away.

'I'll be outside,' Sage said, leaving the two alone, closing the door as he went.

After an awkward pause, Orian approached her old friend. 'I missed you too, Gaius,' she said softly.

'This isn't the time,' Gaius stammered. 'I'm sorry, I–' again, Gaius opened his mouth, but the words failed to form.

Orian gently placed a hand on his arm to settle him. He was a trembling, much more fragile version of the Gaius she once knew, but it was him all the same.

What happened to him? she wondered.

'Gaius,' she said, her voice soft and reassuring, 'it's okay, it's me.' She gazed into his warm brown eyes, and familiarity reflected back.

Eventually, he spoke, wiping away the tears running down his cheeks. 'I never expected to see you again.'

'You never expected to see me? Gaius, I wrote to you, but when my letters returned, I thought you were dead. *They told me* you were dead.'

He dropped his gaze, his expression revealing it was news to him.

She continued, 'I couldn't live with the grief, so I did the only reasonable thing I could do; move on. I didn't leave you, and I never remarried,' Orian reassured, caressing his arm. 'I want you to know that.'

'I'm sorry, life...' Gaius paused, 'was complicated. Were you happy?'

'As happy as one could be, considering the situation. I committed to my work. That was my life. What about you?' she asked. 'Were you happy?'

Orian allowed him the time to gather the courage to answer. 'I went looking. But I couldn't... Then Rika—she was the one who cared for me after... You would have loved her. She was kind, beautiful and strong, like you.'

'Where is she now?'

'She passed in 01 from the sickness.'

'I'm so sorry, Gaius.'

He slumped into the nearest chair with a sigh, taking a sip from his mug and staring despondently at the ceiling.

'What's passed is past. Everything happens for a reason.' He shrugged and took a few deep breaths. To Orian, it was plain to see he was fighting to curb the stuttering that had been mincing his words. 'Neither of us can change that.' He sipped the rest of his water in contemplation. 'Now, I have this village to look after, and they look to me for leadership...'

'From where I stand, you have a good lot of people helping you,' she said, shooting a glance at the door.

'You think so, do you? Even after that...?'

'They just need a little order, that's all. Their hearts are in the right place.'

'What we need is you, Orian,' Gaius said.

It took her by surprise. 'Me? How do you mean?'

'The way you...' he struggled for the words, 'fixed that. None of us can do that. I can't.'

'They're your people, Gaius. They respect you. I just showed them how silly they were being.'

'But we need that. I need that,' he paused again, taking a deep breath. 'I want you to be our Speaker, Orian. I need you to guide us like you did today. Can you do that?'

'I don't know Gaius. I'm only a newcomer.'

'You are just what we need. Please?'

'What about someone else? Abril perhaps? I don't want to step on anyone's toes.'

'I don't think so. You saw for yourself none of us can do it. Besides, you were always good at your job. This is you.'

She stopped to think, allowing the silence to hang. Even now, after all this time, he knew her better than she knew herself.

'For you, Gaius, anything. But only if you go easier on yourself. Promise you'll do that, and I'll be your Speaker—if the others agree to it, of course.'

'Yes, yes, of course. Thank you.'

With that, his weary face crinkled to a smile she recognised, showing a glint of actual happiness.

She smiled back. 'It's good seeing you again, Gaius. I am glad you are well,' she said, stemming tears welling in her own eyes. Putting on her breather, she opened the door to find Sage standing on the step, about to knock. He caught Orian by surprise.

'Oh,' he said, 'I was just going to see if you were still coming.' He peered through the gap at Gaius, then at Orian, and back at Gaius again.

'What just happened?' he asked.

'It wouldn't be prudent of me to answer that,' Orian said, 'but let's just say a very heavy weight has been lifted.' She shot an affectionate, knowing glance at Gaius, whose head rested in his hands. 'Although you might want to give him a few decs, he has a lot to process.'

08 – Hope Besieged

Slabs of concrete and piles of rubble littered the road, while smoke haze choked the air from the fires burning all around. A mound of piled up debris surrounding a hole in the middle of the road provided cover for the twelve of us. Chilton, Balsam and Nelles took point on the edge of the pit and returned fire.

The ground shook when a mortar exploded on the other side of the mound.

'It's not going to be long before they get their aim right,' I yell over the rain of dirt and gunfire. 'Contact HQ.'

Vassell, the comms operator, removed his pack, wound the handle and passed over the handset.

'This is Colonel Sempro, requesting air support.'

Another mortar exploded, dropping Chilton where he lay.

A voice on the other end of the line, broken by static, replied, 'negative on air support, Colonel.'

'Damnit, the place is crawling with Ced's. We're pinned.'

The voice in the handset came back. 'Mission's scrubbed. Do not enter zone. Repeat, DO NOT enter the zone,'

'Too late,' I yelled into the mouthpiece, 'we're surrounded, cannot retreat. Need extraction.'

'Negatory, Colonel. Location is hot. Have to ride it out.'

'FRAK!' I threw the handset back into its hard leather holster, then grabbed the paper map from my breast pocket. Folded so the local area came out on top, I searched for a safe exit. 'There's a river beyond these buildings. We're going for it. You five,' I pointed at the soldiers furthermost from the retreat point, 'cover us while we make a break for that building.'

Slugs ricocheted off concrete, showering us with chunks and dust as we ran for shelter. A mortar exploded and its concussion wave threw me forward.

Clambering out of the dirt, I turned to find the five mangled bodies of my squad lying motionless in the hole where we'd just left them. Fear plastered the faces of my four remaining soldiers. Together, we shuffled our way through the remnants of the building and moved into the next.

A loud droning whistle of falling objects came from high above. We scrambled for cover. The first exploded to my left in the rubble outside, the second blew in multiple floors from above, then a third detonated on the right, sweeping me up and propelling me like a rag doll into a concrete pylon.

Gaius jolted awake in a cold sweat to the piercing screams of unknown objects raining into the centre of Hope. It took all his grit to steady the shakes paralysing him, muster the strength to sit up in his wingback chair and pull on his boots to stand. Forcing his arthritic joints over to his coat and breather hanging by the door, he put them on before snatching it open.

The scene reminded him of a recurring nightmare. Several shacks burned like beacons in the night as bits of debris rained down on the street and buildings surrounding him. Gunfire reverberated from an unseen location nearby. There was no sign of the enemy.

'Not again,' he cried before retreating inside.

Garan emerged from the shadow and came to his side, helping him into a nearby chair while the whistling of another incoming fireball became louder, its high-pitched shriek piercing the night.

'Gaius,' Garan shouted over the noise of the projectile hitting the main street, its force shaking the little hut. 'Are you okay?'

But Gaius just put his arms over his head and sunk deeper into the chair. 'I can't do it,' he wailed, quivering uncontrollably. 'Not again. I can't do it.'

Alerted by the sudden attack, Sage leapt out of bed and shrugged on his heavy coat, boots and breather. Then, grabbing his rifle, he plunged into the fray. Outside his front door, the street resembled a war zone. Sections of the village were ablaze, with patches of the ground at his feet burning as though fuelled by nothing. He braced himself and sprinted for the community hall. As he approached the mound, an explosion from behind blew him off his feet, tossing him face-first to the dirt. He rolled around on the cold ground extinguishing his coat, his ears ringing with a deafened muffle as he scrambled to stand, shake off the dizziness and dive through the door.

It had only been a day since the twenty-nine newcomers arrived from Gotthard. While some of them had already found accommodations around the village, ten remained camped out on the floor of the community hall. Orian was among them, and she met Sage at the door, her eyes wild with fear.

'Are we under attack?' she cried.

'Can't talk now,' Sage called back over the noise. 'Get your people out of here. Follow the others to the evac point.'

She hesitated.

'Go!' he shouted as he ran past her, dodging people scurrying around in the dim light. His shins collided with a cot. 'Argh,' he cried. Ignoring the pain in his shins, he scrambled to the storeroom and lifted the floorboard. Once he had sounded the alarm, he took off into the shadows again, this time darting between the fires, buildings and scrambling people, towards Gaius's hut.

The door was already ajar when Sage arrived. Out of the corner of his eye, he caught Jaxson sprinting up from behind. Like Sage, he still wore his bedclothes under his coat. 'I came as fast as I could,' he said, fastening his pistol belt around his waist.

'I've only just arrived myself,' Sage said.

Jaxson took point by the door, waiting nervously outside while Sage went in.

As he scanned the room, dread washed over him. Abril and her son sat on the bed, hugging each other while Garan leant over the dining table with his back to the door. His head turned around at Sage's sudden appearance.

'Sage!' Garan exclaimed, his startled expression replaced with relief. 'Thank the Progenitors you're here. I can't settle him.'

Garan stepped aside to reveal Gaius sitting on a chair at the table, rocking back and forth, gripping his head.

Sage rushed to Gaius's side, removed his breather and dropped it on the table.

Garan placed his hand on Gaius's shoulder, attempting to comfort him but with little success, and spoke to Sage. 'I think he's havin' another one of his episodes.'

'Gaius,' Sage said, trying to remain calm, 'we have to go, right now.'

A long-rifle barked in the distance.

Gaius flinched and clenched his hands tighter around his head. 'They're coming again. The damn Ced's are coming again.'

Garan gave Sage a puzzled look. 'He keeps sayin' that. Why's he sayin' that?'

'He's probably referring to the Cedreau, but why he's saying that, I haven't got a clue,' Sage replied.

'Yes, the Ced's, the Ced's are coming.' Gaius leaned further forward, hugging the back of his head, dropping his elbows to his knees.

'Sir. Gaius Sempro,' Sage pleaded, pulling back a chair and placing it beside the stricken administrator to sit down. He dropped the urgency in his voice. 'Gaius, listen to me,' he said, speaking into the older man's ear. 'We need you. *Hope* needs you.'

'You don't need me, son,' Gaius whimpered, half the words inaudible by his stutter, 'I'm just a tired old fool. Leave me, save yourselves.'

'We can't do that, Gaius. You know that.'

'Come on, Gaius,' Garan added, 'me and Abril aren't goin' without you, and if we're not goin', Rodi's too young to go by himself. You saved our lives, so what kind of people would we be if we left you here?'

'Same here,' Sage added.

Gaius lifted his head. 'You crazy fools...' three rifle shots interrupted him, forcing him to bury his head again.

Jaxson propped his head around the door. 'Come on, guys, we've gotta get moving,' he said with desperation in his voice.

Sage glanced up at him and shrugged. 'In a moment,' he mouthed, waving for a little more time. Jaxson changed position to take cover behind the door, keeping watch of the street through the crack. 'It's getting worse out there.'

Sage sighed, turning to Garan with a pained expression. 'We have to go, now. But we can't leave him here.'

'I'll drag the old cod if I have to,' Garan grunted, 'but with me bunged leg, I don't think I'll get far. Not out there.'

Sage turned back to Gaius. 'Hey, old man, you remember that museum I tendered the plans for? Well, I'm thinking of adding a Gaius Sempro memorial hall. It'll be wonderful. It'll feature everything about you and will have a three meta tall statue of you with your pants down.'

Gaius raised his head and shot him a dirty look. 'You will do no such thing.'

'Well, if you're just going to sit there and die, how are you going to stop me?'

'You play a cruel game, Sage Solon,' Gaius said, lifting his head and glancing a rueful smile at the younger man, who smiled back. 'You're a good man,' he added, resting a hand on Sage's shoulder. 'Cheeky, but a good man.'

'Are we good now?' Sage asked, but Gaius shook his head. 'I don't know. My legs won't move.'

Abril stepped forward to join the men at the table. 'Maybe I can help,' she said, kneeling at Gaius's side. She cupped his hands in hers and spoke to him in a calming voice. 'Gaius, I need you to listen to my voice. Close your eyes and ignore the noises outside. It's just you and me.'

He nodded and closed his eyes.

'Okay,' she continued, 'I need you to take a nice, deep breath. Can you do that?'

Gaius nodded again, following her instructions. Abril guided him to take two more deep breaths before his shoulders relaxed, and he opened his eyes.

'How do you feel?' she asked.

'Better,' he replied, seeming calmer.

'Good, now I've got you. Come with me, and we will walk together.'

'Now, can we please get out of here?' Sage pleaded.

'I think so,' Abril said, helping Gaius from his seat.

With his newfound courage and Abril and Garan on either side, Gaius stood, straightened, put on his breather, and moved towards the door.

One by one, they exited the hut. Rodi took his mother's free hand, while Gaius and Garan shuffled along as fast as their disabilities would allow.

Safety may have only been a short distance away, but with the warzone raging all around them, it felt much further. Driven by the urge to escape, they put their heads down, did their best to avoid the flaming shacks and raining debris, and shuffled on. At least Gaius was still moving.

Sage and Jaxson followed close behind, scurrying along opposite footpaths with weapons drawn, protecting the vulnerable from the rear. The fires flanking either side cast eerie, shifting shadows while plumes of choking black smoke obscured their vision.

The dancing silhouettes made movement detection difficult. Still, the two younger men remained vigilant. Sage trained his rifle on anything that moved, covering the gaps between the huts in front of Jaxson, as he did the same for Sage.

Materialising like a ghost from out of the smoke, a man-shaped silhouette emerged. Sage aimed, and without slowing, pulled the trigger twice, actioning its lever and reloading after both shots. Adrenaline invigorated him again.

Jaxson hurdled the slumping body sprawling on the pavement in front of him, leaving Sage to plough into another darkened figure. They spilled out onto the cold road with a grunt, and on his back, Sage caught the glint of steel. Like a wild animal, his opponent leapt at him, his outstretched knife hungry for the taste of Sage's flesh. His training kicking in, Sage rolled away, avoiding the menacing blade as it sailed past his exposed chest and grazed the compacted gravel instead.

On the other side of the street, Jaxson regained his footing, lifted his pistol, and squeezed the trigger. But the solitary shot sailed past its target as, from the shadows behind him, an enormous figure emerged, tackled him and drove him headlong into the side of a burning hut.

The man grappled Jaxson hard around the middle in a crushing embrace. Jaxson howled, scrabbling at the raider's mask, tearing it off and punching him in the face. Blood burst from the big man's nose, forcing him to release Jaxson and giving him an opening to deliver an uppercut to the gut.

'Argh,' Sage cried, lifting his rifle to block a body-weight strike from his attacker, the raider's forearm landing on the exposed metal of Sage's slender shield. Sage's eyes widened as the blade hung only a finger's width above his heart. The raider thrust his bodyweight down onto Sage again, this time almost dropping the knife on his chest. Sage and the raider wrestled in a frantic tussle, Sage leveraging his rifle to fend off the blade. The raider shifted his weight, recoiled his hand, punched Sage once, then twice in the face, knocking off his mask and exposing him to the choking air. Dust mixed with the metallic taste of blood in his mouth, and he spat, spraying it onto his opponent's faceplate. It was the distraction he needed. Raising his knee into the man's chest, Sage wedged a gap between them, wrapped his rifle strap around his enemy's knife-hand, and thrust upwards with his leg, pushing the assailant away.

Sage glared into the whites of his enemy's eyes, savouring the expression of surprise as he took control. A sudden strike with the rifle butt into the man's jaw allowed Sage to break free. Manoeuvring his weight, Sage clambered to his feet, forced his thrashing opponent to his knees. Then looping the strap around the man's neck, Sage twisted. With his one free hand, the raider flailed, gurgling with howls of pain while the strap tightened around his throat. Relentlessly, Sage kept twisting, crushing the man's windpipe. The raider's feet kicked and scrabbled at the ground as Sage held him tight. In a final jarring crunch, Sage jerked the rifle, the raider's neck snapped, and his body fell limp.

Across the street, Jaxson's battle continued, his opponent rounding back for another attack. Sage watched helplessly as his friend dodged an eclipsing right hook, the raider's massive fist sailing past Jaxson's face and clipping his ear. Jaxson ducked, sidestepped, and delivered a jab to the large man's kidneys before overbalancing and falling to his knees.

In desperation, Sage tried to untangle his weapon from the dead raider's body. There was something peculiar about him, but Sage didn't have time to investigate. He tried to free the strap, but it wouldn't budge.

'Sage, RUN!' Jaxson yelled with a pained gasp, giving Sage just enough warning to glance up and catch movement in his peripheral vision. Two more raiders carrying rifles had materialised from the shadows behind and were rushing towards him.

Caught in indecision, Sage hesitated, glancing at his tangled rifle, then at Jaxson. Part of him wanted desperately to retrieve his prized weapon and go to his friend, the other part knew he needed to run. Jaxson fought on, his foe laying into him while he lay sprawled on the ground. The two raiders closed in. Unable to pull his rifle free, Sage grabbed the stock, tilted the barrel upwards and fired. The lead raider dropped where Sage's slug had felled them. The other kept coming. Sage snatched up his mask, and like a tightly wound spring, leapt to his feet, and charged at the raider, bowling them over.

'Run,' Jaxson implored. 'Save Hope.'

Sage glanced at the carnage, then at Jaxson. There was no other choice; he ran.

Gunfire intensified, and another whistling fireball exploded somewhere behind. Darting through the debris-lined streets to the edge of the village, Sage headed towards the place where he knew Hope's residents had congregated in safety. Two guards held open the doors to the underground bunker just long enough for him to slip through.

Once inside, he removed his mask, and the shelter erupted in applause. Doctor Colyar was busy with the village apothecarist, Ferne, tending to those in need when he arrived. When she saw Sage, with his face bloodied and beaten, she dropped what she was doing to see to him.

'Sage,' she cried, directing him to the nearest chair and pulling a handful of soft antiseptic swabs from her medkit to dab his bleeding nose. 'What in the Progenitor's names happened to you?'

He winced. 'I'll be fine. Are Gaius and the others safe? Did they make it?'

'Yes, they arrived about a dec before you.'

'That's a relief.'

'What about Jaxson? Where's he?' she asked, handing him a wad of tissues to hold against his nose.

His face turned sombre. 'We were ambushed,' Sage replied. 'He didn't make it.'

'Oh,' she said, sitting beside him. She held the back of a gloved hand to her mouth in shock, and Sage could see tears beginning to well in her eyes.

'I know how you feel,' he said, placing a hand on her shoulder in comfort. It was all he could do to stop himself from joining her. 'But we have to focus on our work right now. It's what he would have wanted.'

'You're right,' she sniffled. Wiping away the tears, she went back to tending to Sage's face.

'Do you know if we got everyone else out?' he asked.

'I think so...'

'Colyar?' said a voice. Sage and Lexi both looked up to see Cristal standing over them. Her face held the expression as though she had seen a ghost.

'Lexi Colyar? Is that really you?' she asked again.

This time, the expression that flashed on the doctor's face was not one of fondness.

'Yes?' Lexi replied in a curt tone.

'But you're supposed to be—'

'Dead?' Lexi finished the question for her. 'Yes, well, I understand why you would think that. That's to be expected when you get gunned down by your superior officer and left for dead.'

Sage's eyes widened.

'Sincerest apologies, Lexi. There was no telling he was going to do that,' Cristal said. Her voice showed genuine remorse.

'But you still went with him, and you didn't even bother to stop and check on us,' she said, seeming to be doing everything she could to maintain her calm.

'He didn't give us much choice.'

'Where is he, anyway? Is he here?'

'No.'

'Ah, I see. And Staff?'

'He's around. Look, Lexi, that incident was truly regrettable—'

'Save it,' the doctor snapped. 'That doesn't help the others. I've had a few cycles to get over it. I suggest you do the same.'

'Please, you must believe that. Personally, it is a relief you are okay,'

'Do me a favour, Cristal, don't talk to me.'

Cristal shrugged, then nodded acknowledgement to Sage before leaving without saying another word.

'What was that all about?' Sage asked, still holding the tissues to his nose. He'd never seen this side of Lexi before.

'Ancient history. I don't wish to discuss it, sorry.'

'Did it have anything to do with that day we met?'

'Sage, please don't.'

'Fair enough. So, you knew her, then?'

'Cristal Spriggs? Yes, I knew her,' she said as though sucking on something bitter. 'We worked together for a time, but I don't know her now. Whatever you do, Sage, don't trust her.'

'Ahh,' Sage replied, 'she's our attaché to LunaTec.'

'I see. Just be careful, then. I may have been shot in the front, but she stabbed me in the back.'

As Lexi finished up with Sage, Abril came over and threw her arms around him. 'Sage!' she cried with relief, 'I'm so glad you made it.'

Sage flinched at her touch. 'Ow,' he moaned.

'Oh, I'm sorry,' she said, pulling back. 'We thought... where's Jaxson?' She glanced around the room for the man often referred to as Sage's shadow. But Sage just shook his head.

Abril gasped and cupped her hands to her face.

'I have to go,' Lexi said then, gathering her medkit. 'I think Sage will live. But come find me if you have any issues.'

Sage raised a hand in gratitude.

'Thanks, Lexi,' Abril said.

The doctor placed a gentle, acknowledging hand on Abril's shoulder as she left.

For the first time since its construction, Sage was able to see the inside of LunaTec's new bunker for himself. It was a sterile, white-painted concrete room with high, curved rendered ceilings. Its only light source was the large industrial sodium lamps suspended from the ceiling.

'Why does it feel like we're prisoners in this bunker?' Abril asked, discreetly eyeing the guards wearing LunaTec security uniforms patrolling the crowd. 'I must admit, it was much better in the cave.'

'We wouldn't fit there anymore,' Sage replied, 'and besides, since LunaTec... commandeered the mountain, they've built us this place instead. At least it's something.'

'But do they have to guard us like that? I get the sense we're nothing but a herd of animals to them.'

'They're doing their job; they're protecting Hope.'

'Hope is burning, Sage,' she said in a curt tone. 'They should be out there with our people defending our homes.'

'And do what, die too and leave us defenceless? Hope is the people and not just the buildings. We can rebuild. They're here making sure we're safe, that's the main thing.' He stopped to survey the room. 'Where's Gaius?' he asked.

Abril looked around for him, too. 'I don't know. He was just over there.'

'Xisnys Kacir, what happened to you, Sage?' Garan cursed after having picked his way through the crowd and stopping in their circle of conversation.

Abril interrupted, 'Garan, stop being so lewd.'

'Well...' Garan said, lifting his hand toward Sage.

Abril glared at her husband.

Garan continued. 'I thought you'd want to know, Gaius is sittin' amon'st the stores in the dark.'

'What's he doing there?' Sage asked.

'I don't think he knows, but he could use your help.'

'Okay, thanks, Garan.' He let out a pained groan as he stood and ambled over to where Garan had directed him.

Gaius had retreated to a darkened corner, staring with a blank expression at a spot on the floor. When Sage, Abril and Garan approached him, he didn't move.

'How are you doing, Gaius?' Abril asked gently.

He stammered an inaudible reply.

'Gaius,' Sage said, 'is everything okay?'

'Ahh,' he mumbled, scratching his head, visibly distraught.

'You know, you should be proud of yourself,' Sage said, trying to ease him. 'You did yourself and everyone else here a service tonight.'

Gaius struggled to form the words, 'how so?'

'Well, you're here, aren't you?' Sage said.

'You really would have stayed? For me?'

'Yes,' Sage replied, glancing at Abril, and she nodded. 'Well, if it came down to it, I probably would have knocked you out and dragged your unconscious arse here, no offence, sir, but no question we would have stood by you and made sure you got out of there in one piece. Anyone in this shelter would have done the same.'

'You obviously don't understand then how much you mean to us,' Abril added. 'You saw the reception we received when we arrived. I can guarantee most of that was for you. Now, if you think differently, ask anyone.'

'Go stand on a box and say a few words. See what reaction you get,' Sage said.

Gaius looked at the boxes lined up against the wall. 'I can't do that.'

'You're more than a leader to these people. Just by you and Rika being here, most of the people in this room owe their lives to you,' Sage said, patting his chest, 'including me. I don't think you realise just what kind of positive influence you have on these people. And I bet, if you stand up there, the spirits of this room will brighten tenfold. So don't tell me you're scared to address the people who see *you* as Hope.'

Gaius spoke in a low voice. 'If I must,' he conceded, 'what shall I say?'

'Make it up like you always do,' Sage said before dragging out a small wooden box filled with ammunition into the main area.

Gaius scowled at it. 'Charming. Thanks.'

Sage stepped up and raised his voice over the crowd. 'Attention everyone,' he announced, 'quiet, please.'

The room hushed, and all eyes turned to Sage.

'Gaius would like to say a few words.' He stepped down to allow Gaius to take his place, and the people responded with welcoming applause.

With his legs quivering, Gaius steadied himself on the box, using Sage and Abril's shoulders for support. Then, taking a breath, he addressed the bunker, speaking in a clear and resounding voice, punctuated only with the minimalist of stutters.

'My family and friends of Hope.' The instant he started talking, Gaius's shoulders set into their natural posture, his head held high, and he exuded the charisma typical of the enigmatic man Sage knew Gaius to be. 'I know you're scared. So am I. Hope is under attack. We don't know why or by whom. But we are still here, and we will find out. I want you to know we are all in this together. Right now, trained professionals are looking after us, and they are doing everything they can to ensure Hope survives this. Be kind to yourselves, remain here, get comfortable, help out the person next to you, and once it's safe, we'll let you know. Until then, please stay safe.' Gaius gripped Sage's shoulder a little firmer to let him know he'd finished, and Sage helped him down.

As soon as Gaius's foot touched the floor, the room became lively with an ovation, lifting everyone's spirits.

Then Sage stood on the makeshift podium. 'Thank you, everyone,' he said. 'You heard Gaius. It's safe here in the bunker. We'll get you home as soon as we can.' He dabbed at a fresh drop of blood escaping from his nose with a tissue, pocketed it and stepped down.

Gaius clapped him on the shoulder. 'Thank you, son,' he said, with a warm fondness, 'I needed that.'

'So that means you're feeling better?'

'Not quite, but I'll be fine. TEDD is a fickle thing.'

Sage knew the old man suffered from Traumatic Emotional Distress Disorder; it was a mental health condition that afflicted a number of Hope's residents, but it was something rarely brought up in conversation.

Gaius continued, 'enough about me. You, my boy, have come a long way. How you acted back there is to be commended.'

'Thank you, sir, but I'm not done yet.'

'Well, if you'll excuse me, these old bones are. I'm going to retire over there with some nice calming tei. You want a cup?'

'No, thanks, Gaius. You rest. I still have work to do.'

Gaius nodded, patting him with a show of support on the shoulder before disappearing with Abril into the admiring crowd.

Alone, Sage bent over to move the box back against the wall. As he did, his pained body reminded him of Jaxson and his team outside. He couldn't bear the thought of being inside, safe in the bunker while others put their lives on the line, fighting and most likely dying without him. He wondered if he could make it across the room to the security door before anyone noticed, then grabbed his mask and made a beeline for it. Behind him, he overheard the sound of two women giggling. 'Go on,' one of them said, barely audible over the hubbub of the room. 'He's right there. Now's your chance.'

'I can't,' the other voice said.

'Well, if you're not going to...'

Two attractive women intercepted his path. One gazed up at him with flirtatious eyes, while the other held back.

'Hi Sage,' the flirty one with blonde hair said.

'Hello Anja, Jaylyn,' he replied, more fixated on the door than the women. 'I'm sorry, but I...' was all he could say when the shy brunette stepped forward, cupped his round baby-faced jaw between her hands and pressed her lips against his.

At first, he resisted, not sure what to do, but then his knees weakened, his mind went blank, and he surrendered to the kiss, pulling her closer.

When she finished, she let her hands drop and stepped back. 'Thank you for saving us,' she said, blushing and considering him with gentle affection.

'Um,' he stammered, feeling flushed himself, 'you're welcome?'

Still trying to comprehend what had happened, he hesitated. Why hadn't he noticed her before? He waited for his vision to clear, forgetting for a moment what he was doing before he got waylaid. Then it all came flooding back.

'I'm sorry, ladies,' he said, 'but I have to go.' And he continued his way through the crowd.

'Be careful out there,' he heard Jaylyn shout after him. At least for the moment, he was smiling.

By the time he approached the guards at the heavy door, his tension had returned.

'I need out,' he said.

'No can do. We have orders to stay here until we get the all-clear.'

'And who do you think will give that all-clear?'

The guard eyed Sage up and down, recognising the red coat.

'Yes, sir,' he said, reaching for the button on the large comms box on the wall. He spoke into it and when a static-y voice replied, 'scopes-a-clear,' the guard turned the wheel on the door to open it, the metal hinges groaning with a slow creak.

Sage caught the sound of Orian calling his name as the heavy door slowly closed behind him.

He almost made it to the steep-cut stairs in the rock face when a slug whistled past, thudding into a nearby tree.

That was too close, he thought as he started the climb.

It took only a dec for Sage to reach the overlook. There, one of the part-time overseers, Dany stood with a pair of distance looking-glasses surveying the area, while Ossie, the comms operator, listened for reports from the defence teams.

Dany and Ossie were rugged-up in dark, heavy coats, thick pants and breathing masks, but Dany's breather was self-styled and hand-painted to match her bubbly personality.

She handed Sage the scuffed up looking-glasses, and he studied the landscape to see what was happening below.

'What's the situation?' he asked.

Dany responded, 'sir, we've lost comms with nine target-shooters, all from the river side of the village where the first fireballs landed.'

'Anything else?' Sage asked.

'No, sir. Will Gaius be joining us?'

'No, Administrator Sempro is busy overseeing the shelter tonight.'

'Is everyone cosy?'

'As cosy as can be,' Sage replied.

The gunfire exchange continued, with fireballs landing in the village's surrounding area, burning the trees and the hiding places of the target-shooters.

'Sir, they're well-armed for raiders,' Dany observed.

'You're telling me. Can you see them? Do we know who we're up against?'

'No, sir. They're like spectres. They came out of nowhere. Our scouts didn't see them—we lost comms with them before they even fired the first shot.'

'Dammit, this must be the mob Orian warned us about.'

'She did?' Dany questioned.

'Don't ask,' he grimaced, trying to focus the glasses for a better view.

The comms on Ossie's table crackled to life.

'Shooter eighteen. Enemies advancing on my position, low ammo reserves. Out.'

'Shooter fifteen. Taking on enemy for eighteen. Low ammo reserves. Out.'

'Shooter eight. Been shot, can't move from the waist down. Limited view on eighteen. Out.'

A fireball hurtled through the air.

'Shooter twelve. They have reinfor—' Twelve's comm dropped out.

'Bring back twelve,' Sage cried to Ossie.

'Twelve's gone, sir, I can't do anyth—' he ceased talking when a burst of fresh shooting started on the other side of the river.

'Oh, may the Progenitors save us. They have reinforcements. There must be another thirty or *more* out there,' Sage said with frustration. 'Orian said there were about thirty raiders, not twice that.'

The comms crackled. 'Shooter fifteen. Enemies have turned around toward fresh fire. Remaining two rounds for their backs. Out.'

'Shooter eighteen. Someone is attacking the enemy. Out.'

'Maybe the Progenitors are looking out for us after all, Sage,' Dany said.

The shots thinned out, the time between them getting longer until there was silence. Now only the winds pushed the night along.

What now? Sage thought.

After several long moments, the comms unit crackled. 'This is Admiral Artimus Wyrm to the defending force. I demand to talk to a representative of this installation. Out.'

Sage looked at his companions in confusion. They shrugged.

A few midecs later, the comms unit crackled again. 'I repeat, this is Admiral Artimus Wyrm to the defending force. I demand to talk to a representative of this installation. Do you hear me? Reply back. Out.'

Without Gaius, Sage had no choice but to take command. As the vice-administrator of Hope, it was his duty to protect his people, so either he would surrender Hope or die tonight. He didn't care much for those options.

Sage thought aloud, 'what does this guy want?'

'Defending installation, I'm waiting for a response. Out.'

From the overlook, Sage had a good view of the village. The invaders were rounding up the remaining target-shooters, hiding in the tundra, escorting them to the hall and stripping them of their coats. Armed soldiers stood behind them with their weapons drawn.

With hesitation, Sage asked, 'Ossie, put me on comms with this admiral.'

The comms operator handed him the wireframe headset to the portable unit and pressed the button, allowing Sage to talk.

'Come in, Admiral...' he glanced to Ossie, fishing for the name.

'Artimus Wyrm, I think he said it was,' Ossie responded.

'Admiral Wyrm, this is Sage Solon, Vice-Administrator of Hope. State your intention. Out.'

'Mister Solon,' the gravelly voice came back through the static. 'Do you have authority to speak for your installation? I'm not interested in speaking to middlemen. Out.'

Not this again, Sage thought.

He sighed and pressed the button on the radio again. 'Yes. Now state your intention. What are your demands? Out.'

'Demands? Oh, you think that's me? No, Mister Solon, they're not my men. If they were, your people would already be dead. I'm not here to kill you or your people, but I can't say the same about them. Out.'

Sage considered the action in the main street where eight of the invaders, all dressed in dirty, patch-work clothing, were terrorising his people, lining them up with their hands tied behind their backs.

'No, he won't execute them, surely,' Sage said to nobody in particular. 'I can help your people, though.' The gravelly voice continued. 'Looks like you've not got much time to decide. I'll be waiting for you behind your brick building. Hurry if you want your friends to live. Out.'

The radio went dead, and Sage knew if he were to find out what this man wanted and whether he would kill his people, he would have to go down there. As Sage prepared to leave, Dany stepped around the comms table.

Sage handed the headset back to Ossie.

'Sir,' she said, with concern in her voice, 'you can't go down there by yourself. We don't know what his intentions are. Let me go with you.'

Sage took few steady breaths to calm himself. 'No, sorry, but I can't risk anyone else's lives tonight.'

'Understood, sir.'

And without further delay, Sage was sliding down the slope.

The path to the verge behind the community hall was dark; Sage could easily make the short distance without being seen. Every midec delay could cost him the lives of his friends. That was not something he wanted to risk. As he came nearer, he caught movement of a solitary figure dressed in dark fatigues stepping out from the shadows to intercept him.

'That'll be close enough,' the figure hissed, levelling a pistol at Sage's chest. Sage raised his hands in supplication, and from where he stood, he could see the execution line-up becoming more organised. The lone man stepped forward to pat him down. 'What? No weapon?'

'What do you want?' Sage pleaded.

The man responded, 'so what will it be, Mister Solon? Do you want my help or not?'

'You must be Artimus?' Sage's eyes darted from the stranger to the scene in the main street and back to the stranger again. Sage couldn't be sure, but by his size, he knew he'd lose out in a fight between them. 'Do I have a choice?'

'By the looks of it, you now have about a dec to decide.'

The armed raiders in the main street were still abusing the target-shooters; their warm ursus coats now lay in a pile. One figure among the group caught Sage's eye. Compared to the others, this hostage wore bedclothes, and his brown coat lay on top of the pile with the target-shooters'. It was Jaxson, and it appeared he wasn't making it easy on his captors. He spat at a raider and received a swift rifle butt to the head for his trouble, dropping him face-first into the gravel. The aggressors aimed their rifles, preparing to shoot. Sage's heart pounded in his throat.

'Yes,' he said, bowing his head in agreement.

'Are you sure?' Artimus asked.

In defeat, Sage replied, 'yes. Please help them.'

The man in dark fatigues raised a wireless radio to his breather, and simply uttered two words; 'Do it.' The eight raiders in the main street fell all at once, like sacks of grain being dropped. Then the sound of target-rifles echoed through the night.

The hostages looked around at their dead captors with apparent confusion.

'That's it,' Artimus said. 'It's done.'

What have I bargained Hope for? Sage thought.

Footsteps in the dark caught both Artimus' and Sage's attention. With lightning-fast reflexes, Artimus pointed the pistol at the source of the noise.

Dany emerged from the dead foliage, picking her path with caution, rifle in hand. She dropped it the moment she looked up and saw the pistol pointing at her.

'What's this?' Artimus asked, glaring at Sage, then back at Dany. Sage couldn't tell if the man was angry or not.

'I'm sorry,' Dany whimpered. 'I thought it looked like you needed help. Sir,' she pleaded to Artimus, 'please don't kill me.'

'Your man is doing fine now. But you can give me that,' Artimus growled, pointing at the rifle on the ground with his pistol.

Keeping a careful eye on the man holding a pistol at her, Dany picked up the weapon by its leather strap and passed it over to him.

'Right then,' Artimus said, looping the rifle strap over his shoulder. 'If you have no more people hiding in the bushes, I'd like to get out of this cold, and we can discuss the terms of our arrangement.'

Artimus ushered the two Hope residents around the corner of the council hall. There, Sage found Jaxson scrambling on his back for a knife to cut his binds.

Sage rushed over. 'Here, let me help you,' he said, relieved to see Jaxson alive. 'Man, you look awful.'

Jaxson squinted up at him between swollen purple eyes. 'Thanks, but damn, you don't look so hot yourself. Compared to the way I feel, it looks like you came from a beauty pageant.'

Sage chuckled. 'Thanks, man.'

'What just happened?' Jaxson asked while Sage cut his bindings.

'I'm about to find out, but this big guy in the camo,' he pointed an elbow at Artimus, 'just saved all our arses.' He passed the knife to Jaxson. 'I've got to talk to him now and find out what his help has cost us. I'll leave you to release the others.'

'Shall I fetch Gaius?'

'No, best he stays where he is until we know what we're up against. Don't even go there.'

Jaxson nodded.

Four armed soldiers wearing green and black uniforms jogged along the main street, saluted to Artimus, and continued on their way.

'If you don't mind, Mister Solon, you were going to show me the inside of this splendid hall and have a little chat.'

09 – HomeGuard

Two soldiers clad in green and black guarded the community hall's entrance, which now showed signs of a struggle. Slug holes peppered its external walls, and the doorjamb around the entrance was splintered like someone had kicked it in. Inside, a few more armed soldiers stood with rifles, and the bodies of two raiders lay dead in a heap on the floor.

The doors closed behind Sage and Dany as they followed Artimus inside and removed their breathers.

'How about we get some lights on in here,' Artimus said, motioning to Dany.

As she rushed off under guard of one of Artimus's soldiers to turn up the lamps, the red twisted and knotted skin covering the entire right side of the admiral's face became clearly visible. It gave Sage the impression it had been melted and did nothing to quell his concerns about the man. Instead of hiding it, the admiral wore the scars like a badge of honour. His right eye lacked pigmentation compared to the blue on his left, and he tilted his head a little, presumably so his good eye could see Sage better.

'So,' Sage began, albeit nervously, remembering how the last negotiations held in this room concluded. 'I don't suppose you just happened here by accident. Am I supposed to thank you or...?'

Artimus ignored him. 'What is this place?' he asked, strutting back and forth, considering the hall.

'This is Hope,' Sage replied, watching him. 'We're just a village. We used to be a refugee camp but then LunaTec...'

'Village?' Artimus scoffed, 'and why does a village of refugees have a squad of trained target-shooters?'

'After tonight, I would think that'd be obvious.'

'This happens a lot, then?'

'Often enough to warrant our defences. Ever since I've been here, at least, I've made sure Hope has a formal line of defence.'

'And how's that working out for you?'

'My defenders are trained well enough to take things seriously.'

At that moment, one of the admiral's soldiers entered the hall carrying a target-shooter rifle and handed it to him. 'Sir, this was found wrapped around the neck of a dead raider.'

Artimus examined the rifle's polished timber stock, embossed leather strap, and actioned the lever until all the rounds had been ejected. 'Interesting,' he said, glancing into the scope. 'Precision lens. This is a nice rifle. It's well looked after. Simple refugees, you say?'

'Yes,' Sage said flatly.

'Not soldiers?'

'No, just well trained to defend the families here.'

'What about you, *Vice-Administrator* Solon? Are you a soldier then?'

'Do I *look* like a soldier?'

'I don't know, you tell me?'

'What can I say, Admiral? I'm well read.'

'You take me for a fool? Books can't teach you how to shoot long distance in these conditions. Your people know strategy and show skill. They may lack experience, but I can recognise professional training when I see it.'

Sage crossed his arms. 'We're all just simple refugees,' he insisted.

'Then care to explain this?' Artimus said, brandishing the rifle.

'That's mine. I've had it for a while.'

Artimus gave a wry smile. 'That, my friend, is a Cedreau Special Ops target-shooter rifle. A *professional's* weapon. If you're *just* a simple refugee, as you say, unless you stole it, you shouldn't have a weapon like this, much less know how to use it.'

'We all did what we had to do before the war. In Hope, we don't dwell on history that's best left forgotten.'

'Then, you won't mind me holding onto this?'

Sage scowled, 'I said, that's mine, I want it back.'

'Not anymore.'

'Tell me, Admiral, how do you suppose I protect my people without a weapon?'

'You just leave that to me,' Artimus replied, smiling again, causing the scarring on his face to crinkle in a manner that made Sage feel uneasy.

'Ahh,' Sage said, 'I can't allow that. While I'm grateful for your help tonight, the defence of Hope is my responsibility.'

Artimus pulled over a chair and sat down, laying the rifle in his lap, close enough for Sage to see it but out of his reach, then gestured for Sage to join him.

Sage hesitated, but then took a seat at a comfortable distance.

'You seem like a smart man, Mister Solon,' Artimus probed, 'what's your take on those raiders tonight?'

'What raiders?' Sage replied.

Artimus raised an eyebrow, and Sage continued. 'We've had raider attacks before, but nothing like this. They may have *looked* the part, but they weren't raiders.' Sage glanced at the pair of dead bodies on the floor, and it occurred to him what was odd about the raider that had attacked him earlier. It was their clothes. They were torn and stained with what looked like mud and sweat, as he would expect, but as Sage examined the bodies more, the stains were fake. It was as if they were wearing an outfit made to look like raider garb.

'They're too neat and clean,' he said. 'That one's clothes still has fold marks.'

'Clever. How long did it take you to figure that out?'

'Long enough. You knew?'

'Suspected. I've been following that mob for a tendawn now. Like raiders, they've pillaged every wanderer, encampment and caravan they've come across. But this lot, they've been growing in number. I've never come across a mob larger than ten or twelve. There was over forty here tonight. When I heard wind of a planned attack on a large camp—that's what they called this place, I followed them. Unlike real raiders, though, these seemed less interested in looting and pillaging and more in burning this place to the ground.'

'Why? Why would they do that?'

'You tell me? If this is just a refugee village, as you say, what attracted them here?'

'If you have the answer to that, I'd like to hear it. As I keep saying, we're just simple refugees.'

'Well, this simple refugee village just kicked their arses,' Artimus said. 'That will not go down well. How long do you think that lot will wait until they try again?'

'With respect, Admiral, before tonight, we were more than capable of handling our own. Raiders or no, *if* they come back, we'll be ready?'

'Ready, you say? Like tonight?'

'Excuse me?'

'It's a simple question, Mister Solon. What happened tonight? How did you fail?'

Sage stammered, taken aback by the gall of this man to ask such a thing. 'Not that it's any business of yours, but they outnumbered us. They came in hard and fast, armed with heavy artillery.'

'Yet you had the home ground advantage, the element of surprise and clear military training. So, HOW. DID. YOU. FAIL?'

Sage's words caught in his throat.

'I'll tell you how,' Artimus said, leaning in with his good eye glaring at Sage to emphasise his point. 'You failed because you got complacent. You mistook having never lost as invincibility and underestimated your enemy. If it weren't for my intervention, that mistake would have killed you and lost you your precious village.'

'I... I,' Sage spluttered. But he knew Artimus was right. Jaxson and the rest of his target-shooter squad were midecs from execution. Had Artimus not shown up when he did, they would be where the dead false raiders now lay, and it would have been only a matter of time before Sage and the rest of Hope joined them.

How could I be so stupid? he thought.

'The fact of the matter is, you weren't prepared,' Artimus stated. 'But it's not because you weren't skilled enough. You never stood a chance.'

'I get it,' Sage stressed, 'what's your point?'

'I want you to surrender defence of Hope to me.'

Despite the admiral's straight face, Sage was looking for a sign the man may be kidding. 'You want me to do what? You're playing with me, right?'

'Do I look like a man who "plays"?'

Sage considered the admiral's stern expression. That glare could have turned water to stone. 'I can't do that.'

'You can. And you will,' Artimus declared. 'Your time playing soldier is over. It's time for you to hand over defence of Hope to more capable parties. It's time to hand over defence of Hope to me.'

Sage brushed a hand through his scruffy blonde hair, processing what Artimus had said. One thing was clear, it was his own arrogance that had almost cost them. A flood of what–ifs swirled through his mind.

What if Orian hadn't warned us?

What if I'd been better prepared?

What if Artimus hadn't come at all?

At that last thought, he shuddered to think what would have happened. Perhaps it was time he stepped aside and let someone more capable take over.

'Even if I agree with you,' Sage said, half trying to convince himself it was the right choice to make, 'not one of us has the authority to commit to any such demand. I must raise it with the Council.'

'Then assemble the Council, and we will discuss it.'

'We?'

'Yes, Mister Solon, we,' Artimus said with a level tone. 'You need me. And if I am to assume defensive command in this place, I must do so as a leader on its Council.'

'Why is it whenever a stranger comes here offering to make us a deal, I feel we're getting bent over a barrel?' Sage retorted.

Twenty decs later, the four remaining council members with Cristal and Orian filed into the community hall. Weary from their ordeal, they sluggishly took seats at the assembled table and prepared to bring their late-night meeting to order.

The instant Orian set eyes on Artimus, already seated at the table, she stopped dead in her tracks. He reclined in his chair, considering her with a sardonic grin.

'You have got to be kidding me,' she said with exasperation.

'What, is something wrong?' Sage asked.

'Only him,' she replied, pointing at Artimus.

'The admiral? You know him?'

'*Rear*-admiral, oh, yes,' Orian said with a callous tone. 'I know him, more than I would like.'

'Seems to be the night for reunions,' Sage joked, but she wasn't laughing.

'What's he doing here?'

'Same thing as you, I guess.'

'The fact he's here can't be good.'

'Why?' Sage said with confusion. 'He's the one who saved us. He's the reason we're still alive.'

'That'd be right,' she muttered under her breath. 'He's up to something. He's got to be up to something.'

Sage watched her with a considered expression. She stopped speaking and took her place at the table.

After all the members had taken their seats, Gaius cleared his throat. 'Before we begin, I want to commend everyone on a job well done this night. At last count, we had twelve casualties and only a few injuries. All things considered, we fared well. I give my deepest condolences to the families of those we lost.'

'If it wasn't for the ineptitude of our defence, we wouldn't have lost anyone,' Niklas piped up, shooting a snide glance in Sage's direction. 'No thanks to the stranger, we're lucky we're not all in a raider cage tonight. Who is this man anyway, and what happened to his face?'

'This is Admiral Artimus Wyrm,' Sage said. 'He helped our people.' He was about to say more but Gaius cut him off, speaking in his usual calm manner. 'Yes, it may be true he came to our defence, but I would not call our own performance inept, Niklas.'

'Still, does this mean Sage owes Orian and Abril an apology?' Niklas snickered.

'What for?' Sage growled.

'What did you say? Orian's convoy was a caravan of sitting water-aves? You personally assured us we had nothing to worry about.'

'Back off, Niklas,' Sage snapped.

'This is not the time for accusations and "I told you so's",' Abril interrupted. 'As much as I'm disappointed it came to this. The loss of life, especially, is a devastating blow to our community, but it's *not* Sage's fault. I think Sage and his team should be commended, not berated. Even with Orian's prior warning, none of us could have seen this coming.'

'Ah hem,' Artimus interrupted.

'Mister Wyrm, have you something to say?' Gaius said, motioning to Artimus to join the conversation.

Artimus stood and leaned over the table. 'It's *Admiral*, and warning or no, it wouldn't have made a difference.'

Niklas began to object. 'But Sage—'

'Has done an exemplary job,' Artimus cut him off. 'Credit where credit's due, your man, Sage is skilled. He has trained your people well, and it showed in how they fought tonight. But that wasn't enough. He could not have prepared you for this, and that is a statement of fact. I am an admiral. I recognise a military operation when I see one. After all, I have commanded my fair share. What went down here tonight was a tactical strike.'

'Last I checked, raiders don't do "tactical strikes",' Niklas protested.

'Very observant, Mister...'

'Martell, Niklas Mar—'

'Mister Martell, those were not raiders. I don't know who they were, but they were not raiders. As I said to your man, Sage, I've been following that mob for a tendawn now. I've watched them attack small targets, including Ms Gracyn's convoy, but that was just practice.'

From the expression on Orian's face, Sage interjected, 'wait, you witnessed the attack on Orian's convoy? And you didn't help?'

'My directive was to circumvent this attack. Had I assisted with the convoy, it would have given away my position, and I would have lost the element of surprise. This attack would still have happened, but I would not have been able to guarantee your safety.'

'Then why weren't we warned?' Sage accused.

'Same reason. Their actual target was this place. I don't know what their motivation was or what you have here that interested them, but everything they have done leading up to now was preparation for this strike. I had to ensure I did not fail. If there are any more out there, they will be angry, and I'd bet they'll be back. And if they do, you best be ready. The question you need to ask yourselves is, can you handle it, or will you need my help again?'

Gaius replied, 'Admiral, we are grateful for your help but if you're expecting repayment, we can't.'

'Administrator, you won't have to.'

'I beg your pardon?' Gaius stammered.

'You don't have to repay me because I'm taking over defensive control of this place.'

The room erupted into an audible murmur as all the council members gasped in disbelief.

'Excuse me, Mister Wyrm, but I'm a little hard of hearing. You'll be doing what?' Gaius said.

Artimus raised his voice, not so Gaius could hear, but to drive his point. 'I'm assuming defensive control of Hope. A police force or militia, if you will.'

'But we're not a military camp. We're barely a town!' Gaius protested.

'Absolutely not!' Niklas shouted. 'I refuse to agree to hand over control of Hope's defences to a bunch of army thugs.'

'You may not have had a choice had things turned out differently tonight. Had I not been here, what would you have done then?'

'I don't know,' Niklas protested. 'I'm sure we would have come up with something.'

Artimus sniggered.

'What are you planning to do anyway, Admiral? How are you any different to them?' Niklas gestured at the bodies now pulled up against the wall and covered in a sheet.

'I don't plan on massacring everyone, if that's what you're asking,' Artimus replied with a smirk. 'Are you familiar with HomeGuard?' he then asked the room but directed the question more at Gaius and Sage.

Niklas shook his head, and the others, aside from Orian and Sage, wore equally blank expressions.

'HomeGuard?' Sage replied, 'leading up to the war, they were some kind of militarised police force, weren't they?'

'We were more than that,' Artimus said. 'We preserved order, maintained peace and kept people safe. Our duty was to uphold civility and protect with honour, but when the war started, we were disbanded, forced to merge with the military and fight. Now the war is over, civility and order must be restored, and for reasons you witnessed tonight, I am re-establishing HomeGuard.'

'But what has that got to do with us? Why Hope?' Gaius asked.

'Because, my friend, why not? It makes no difference to me whether you accept my terms or not. I can leave here tonight and think nothing more of it, but how will *you* defend yourself?'

The audible murmur returned as the council members discussed Artimus's comments while Sage sat in quiet contemplation.

'This place, Hope,' the admiral continued, 'will be the new HomeGuard base of operations. Under my leadership, HomeGuard will assume defensive control, and you will have the peace you so desperately need. You asked me about repayment. That is my price.'

'If that's the price, what is the cost?' Gaius objected. 'Hope is a democracy, not a police state. We have no intention of surrendering our freedom to a militia.'

'Without my intervention tonight, there would be no Hope, and those freedoms you hold so dear would not have saved you. You lost, and you only have yourselves to blame. The only reason you and your people are still alive is because I saved you. HomeGuard saved you. Now what I offer you is more than fair compensation for the help I rendered to you tonight. To keep your people safe, you need more than just a rag-tag bunch of armed refugees wearing animal pelts. You need me.'

'This is an outrage,' Niklas protested. 'First LunaTec takes our caves, and now this scar-faced army fanatic wants to control our defences. What next?'

'Niklas,' Sage responded in a calm and considered voice. 'I didn't like it either. But the admiral has a point. I can't protect you any longer. I did my best, and failed. We lost twelve good people tonight. Each one of them was family or a close friend to all of us. I can't allow that to happen again. I've spoken to Artimus, and I think his offer is reasonable. If this is the price we must pay to ensure our loved ones are safe in these tough times, I'll gladly pay it.'

'I know I'm only a newcomer here,' Orian said, speaking up for the first time since the meeting began, 'but you can't be seriously considering handing over Hope to a man you only just met? How do we know he didn't set this all up?'

Artimus sat back in his chair, crossed his burly arms, and scowled at her. 'Your man, Sage of all people, should know what it takes to train a squad. Why would I do that if I were only going to gun them down? That's a terrible waste of resources. No, Ms Gracyn, those were not my men out there. Whatever you think of me, subversion is not my style.'

Gaius rested his elbows on the table. He looked tired, and it showed in his voice. 'This message is for the both of you. You're both new here, so you deserve the benefit of the doubt. In Hope, we have but one rule; what's passed is past. We don't dwell on history. If you want to live here, all we ask is that you leave your baggage behind. We don't ask questions about where you came from or what you did. All that matters is what you do here and now. If both of you can agree to those terms, you are as welcome here as anyone else. On the matter of our defence, if Sage thinks Mister Wyrm can defend Hope and protect us from attacks like this, then I say let him. I, for one, prefer to see Sage take on other duties.'

'I agree,' Abril said.

'And me,' Garan agreed.

Gaius then turned to the others, 'Sage, Niklas, what say you?'

'I say yes,' Sage replied.

'I guess I don't have much of a choice,' Niklas replied. 'My answer is yes, as well.'

'Cristal, Orian, do either of you have anything to add?'

Orian crossed her arms. Despite her apparent misgivings, she didn't object. As for Cristal, she shook her head. 'LunaTec has no objections,' she replied.

'Then that's that. Mister Wyrm, you have yourself an accord. We will entrust the defence of Hope to you. We will adjourn until the morrow. Council dismissed.'

As the council members rose from their seats, Sage had the distinct impression he'd been cheated again. The one thing he had devoted himself to since arriving in Hope now was the responsibility of somebody else. For a moment, he sat in his chair and stared at the tabletop, feeling sorry for himself.

'Cheer up,' Artimus said, slapping him on the back. 'You're not convinced this deal is fair?'

'How did you guess?'

'Well, from where I'm standing, you're getting the best deal of all. You've just bought yourself an army. What can be better than that?'

10 – Orders

The door to Elihus's office made a pleasant click as it closed. *Silence, at last*, he thought, strolling across the room, past the side of his ornate, dark polished timber desk. Peering through the slender, reinforced window beyond his office's dull reflection, he watched a pair of aves fly over the moors in the distance.

Elihus's office was his castle, containing his prized collection of pre-war artefacts, artwork and stone busts. Among the peculiar arrangement of objects on the bench behind his desk were a nondescript wooden ticker-tape box and a boxy black tonagraph machine.

The late afternoon sun cut through his glass of aged spirits and ice, casting a multicolour projection over the papers covering his desk. Elihus removed his jacket and hung it up inside the closet beside the window, picked up the glass from the red-stained leather coaster and relaxed in his enormous, red-stained cushioned leather swivel chair.

He closed his eyes and inhaled the fine spicy aromas wafting from his glass, relishing the chilled amber liquor on his tongue.

BURRZ, BURRZ!

Elihus jolted, coughing and spluttering. He spat the savoured liquid back into the glass and wiped his chin with a hand.

BURRZ, BURRZ! the tonagraph's obnoxious buzz sounded again, a distant memory from before the war when orders came to him from a faceless voice.

Until now, the black box behind his desk had spent the last four cycles sitting idle, occupying space. Now, he turned and hesitated, staring at it just to make sure it wasn't his imagination.

After the third buzz, he reached forward and picked up the elongated corded receiver and put it to his ear, pressing the button on the box to connect the call. 'Hello?'

'Name?' asked a stern male voice.

'Elihus Kinton. Sir, is that you?'

After a delay, the line distorted with static, the voice asked. 'Designation?'

'Patriarch,' Elihus replied. He couldn't recall the delay being so off-putting. 'Sir, I thought you were—'

'Code and verification?' The voice asked, not waiting for the delay or Elihus to answer before the next question cut him off.

'Project Hildr, verification Epsilon 10082003. Sir, does this mean you have returned?'

'Is your facility operational?' the voice asked, ignoring Elihus's question.

'Yes, sir. It is.'

'Status report.'

Elihus leaned forward and placed his glass on the bench. 'Well, sir,' he began, 'we took heavy casualties during the war but have maintained a sufficient number of assets. Thanks to the refugee camps and shelters, we have managed to acquire a new cohort. They are currently undergoing preliminary training with the primary assets. They will be assessed and commence their proper training soon.'

The delay was excruciating. After a moment, the voice responded. 'The mission is key. No compromises. Have the new assets assessed as a matter of priority. They will be ready in ten cycles.'

'Rest assured sir, the new assets will be trained and ready, sir.'

'See it is so. Are your primary assets mission ready?'

'Some of them are, yes.'

'Good.'

'Shall I prepare them?'

'Soon. First, you will go to Hope. Are you familiar?'

'Yes, sir, I am familiar with Hope, although it's nothing more than an overgrown refugee camp run by a blithering idiot.'

'Irrelevant. Hope is establishing a provisional government. Your mission is to contact their leader, Gaius Sempro. Establish yourself as a confidant and infiltrate. He must trust you and see you as a worthy associate. I care not how you do this. You will establish an inextricable link between Garret Gord and Hope. You have ten days. Confirm.'

'Ahh, yes sir, but are you sure you don't want me to send an asset?'

'No. This mission requires your expertise. Do not disappoint.'

'Absolutely, sir, orders confirmed. I will not disappoint—'

The line went dead.

∞

Chairperson Orian Gracyn stood tall and elegant in her tailored blue cloak behind the podium of the council hall, her braided grey hair resting on her left shoulder in the folds of her hood.

Seated around the table were the Hope council members and LunaTec attaché, all dressed in their council finery. A gallery of Hope's residents watched on from rows of chairs seated along the walls, eager to hear Orian's next announcement.

'The motion to form a provisional government has passed,' she declared. 'Let the records show that at four thirty-three on this morn, the three hundred and eighteenth day of New Calendar five, the decision to elect the first standing provisional government of Hope has passed. Formal elections will take place in the new hall on the first day of New Calendar six in twelve days' time. Hopefully, it's completed by then.' Orian tapped her wooden cube-shaped gavel on the sounding block to the people's jubilant applause.

'And it shall be confirmed,' she concluded. 'Gaius Sempro, Sage Solon and Artimus Wyrm be nominated for candidacy to the position of Virtuous Surprime. We welcome luck to the three candidates. May the Progenitors guide us toward selecting thon most suitable. Council dismissed.' She tapped the gavel once more, gathered her notes, and prepared to leave.

She touched Gaius on the shoulder and was about to step away when she happened to glance up and see a white-bearded stranger pushing his way through the exiting crowd. Once he'd shouldered his way clear, he strode towards the podium with the air of a pompous bureaucrat not seen since before the war.

From his neat, tailored suit complete with flared sleeves, brown and black striped waistcoat, and black briefcase, it was clear he had not come to Hope for refuge. This man had business in mind.

Gaius stood, but discreetly remained behind with Orian to watch the unusual visitor.

The man approached them, standing far enough away, presumably to observe them both. 'I'm looking for the leader of Hope, Gaius Sempro. I presume I will find him here?' the man asked, eyeing up Gaius.

Gaius blinked at him.

Orian watched on with interest, stepping away from the podium while Jaxson loitered in the background.

Outside, visible through the closing doors, the congregation gathered around a polished green sedan car with a driver seated behind the wheel.

'Nice car,' Gaius said. 'Yours?'

'She's a beauty, is she not?' the man replied with a smug expression. 'You do not see many like that anymore.'

'Not here in Hope, no,' Gaius said with a flat tone, getting better at overcoming his stutters. 'What can we do for you...?'

'Kinton, Elihus Kinton is my name,' he said, flashing a set of bright white teeth to match his suit and beard. He extended his hand to Gaius and took two steps closer.

Gaius hesitated, scrutinising the man just out of arm's reach. When he didn't take the last step in, Elihus did.

'Gaius Sempro,' the administrator replied, taking the stranger's hand with apprehension.

'Gaius Sempro, and you are the leader of this town, yes?'

'Not a town yet, but yes?' Gaius replied.

'Do you have a moment to talk? I have something I would like to discuss with you.'

Gaius floundered, his eyes darting in Orian's direction in a silent plea for help.

'Excuse me, Mr Kinton,' she interceded, stepping up to the table, hoping to take the pressure off Gaius. 'Orian Gracyn, Council Speaker. Administrator Sempro is rather busy at the moment. But if you could tell me what this matter is about, I may be able to assist you.'

'Ah,' Elihus said, dismissing her, 'I didn't come all this way to talk to a woman. No, I need to speak with Administrator Sempro myself.'

Orian tightened her jaw.

'No,' Gaius said, his voice stern with sudden anger. 'I will not speak with someone who does not respect my council.'

Elihus bowed his head in subjugation. 'Forgive me,' he recanted. 'I overstepped my bounds. I meant no disrespect, Ms. What I meant to say is I require your expertise. Ms Gracyn is welcome to join if she so pleases.'

Gaius relaxed a little. 'I suppose I could spare some time. What is this about?'

Emboldened by Gaius's concession, Elihus motioned to a chair in front of him. 'Do you mind?' he asked.

Gaius nodded, gesturing for the man to sit.

Elihus placed his briefcase on the table with the Councillors taking chairs across from him.

'Rumour has it you are looking at establishing a provisional government,' Elihus began. 'I believe I can help. In my old life, before the war, I, myself, was a government minister. I know a thing or two about effective working governments. I would like to offer my services and expertise.'

'I wouldn't put much stock in rumour, Mr Kinton,' Orian scoffed.

'So, it isn't true?'

'Now I recognise you,' Orian said. 'You were education minister for the Skoyca Government Alliance. Wasn't your portfolio being investigated for corruption?'

'That was unfounded!' Elihus retorted.

Orian scoffed again, 'Allegedly.'

'Now look who's indulging in rumour.'

'An internal investigation into your behaviour is not rumour, Mr Kinton.'

'And neither is a meeting where you make a declaration to form a provisional government, as you did just five decs ago.'

'I think he's got you there,' Gaius laughed.

She shot Gaius a disapproving look. 'Whose side are you on, anyway?'

'You political types do amuse me,' Gaius mocked.

'Says the man who would be Surprime.'

'That wasn't my idea, Orian.'

Elihus grinned, clearly enjoying the banter he'd caused.

Orian turned to him. 'No, I think we can do well not to take advice from you. But thank you for the offer, Mr Kinton.'

'And what credentials do you have?' Gaius asked, to Orian's dissatisfaction.

'I'm glad you asked,' Elihus began, opening his briefcase and placing a beige folder on the table. 'You want to establish a government but know not how. Right here is my four-point plan on making that so.' He tapped the folder.

Orian didn't buy into it, 'so what, you can weasel your way to a parliamentary position? What's in this for you?'

'No, as a matter of fact, all I seek is an advisory role. To see Hope blossom into the thriving economy it's meant to be.'

Orian gave a strangled laugh. 'Why do you care what happens here? Do you even live here?'

'No, but I can see your potential. A strong and stable government is as beneficial to me as it is to you.'

'Oh, no. Not another businessman selling empty promises.'

'Not a businessman, Ms Gracyn, but I do have a requirement to utilise your services from time to time. A partnership between us would be of mutual benefit to us both, wouldn't you agree?'

'Come on, Orian, give the man a chance,' Gaius implored, his stutter returning. 'Elihus is correct. We need to do this right. None of us have enough experience in doing that. I don't, and you were a speaker. That helps, but it is not nearly enough. We need all the help we can get.'

Orian huffed, conceding she wasn't going to win this argument. 'Gaius, you beautiful, soft old fool. Okay, I'll hear him out, but I need you to be less cavalier about this.'

'Noted.' Then Gaius turned to Elihus. 'So, you said you were education minister?'

'And before that, I was Grace-General of the Grales Province education department. For ten cycles, I served as a guiding representative of educational excellence in our glorious city. I established forty educational institutions throughout my career and drove a program of reform that reshaped the learning curriculum. They found my method to be seventy-five percent more effective. Less truancy and more students graduated to paid employment. My process works, and I am offering it to you.'

'Um, we don't even have a school,' Gaius objected.

'That can be arranged. Our youth's education is paramount, Mister Sempro. Not to be neglected, especially in times such as these, for right now, it is imperative our children grow from this horrific event with a future firmly in mind. The only way we can give them that future is through quality education, discipline and order.'

'That all sounds wonderful, Mr Kinton,' Orian said, 'but how do you suppose we do that? We haven't formed the government yet.'

'That's where I come in, my good lady,' Elihus said with a sly grin.

Orian cringed.

'You have twelve days, do you not?' Elihus asked.

Both Orian and Gaius agreed with a nod.

'Establishing an education curriculum or a stable government, the principles are essentially the same. In ten days, I can set down my plan, get you everything you need to lay the foundations. Perhaps you could begin with a school, a hospital, get the essentials right. Establish your portfolios, draft a declaration; a code of practice or constitution, if you will, assign your ministers and set them to task. In no time, Hope will be a living, breathing, working, learning machine ready for every challenge this new world has in store for it. What do you say?'

'That reeks of political rhetoric, Mister Kinton,' Orian said in a cynical tone.

'That sounds good, Mister Kinton. We do need a plan,' Gaius mused, rubbing his chin.

'Ahh,' Orian stepped in before Gaius could entrust Hope's fate to this man. 'I think we need to put it to the Council. Maybe they'll be able to, ahem, make a wise decision about what we should do.'

'Yes, yes, of course,' Gaius agreed.

Orian relaxed.

'If that is what you need to do, then please do,' Elihus said. 'But time is of the essence, is it not? You must not delay. I will take my leave now and allow you and your wise Council to consider my proposal. I will remain here in Hope and will send around my assistant shortly to give you my contact details should you need me. Please do send for me once you have made your decision. Until then, Gaius, madam, wonderful day to you both.' Then Elihus gathered his papers, shoved them in his briefcase, and left, taking his fancy green car with him.

After more than two cendecs travelling the windy, rutted, unsealed road between Hope and Garret Gord, Elihus eased himself down into his red leather chair with an audible sigh of relief. His ears now rang in the silence, only interrupted by the resounding clink of an ice cube rolling in the fresh glass of rich, aged amber liquid.

It had been ten days since he last sat in his comfortable office. But having succeeded in convincing the council to appoint him as the new provisional Educational Minister, he almost cringed at the thought of having to make this trip on a more regular basis.

Now that the seed has been planted, all I need to do was water it, and it will grow. He mused.

At least, it meant being able to get the resources he needed to keep Garret Gord running.

He set down his briefcase on the counter behind his chair and noticed the black-stained timber box had a strip of ticker-tape paper curled up, sticking out of its side. It had been so long, he'd almost forgotten the reason that box was even there.

Elihus tore off the length of paper, staggered with punched holes, and read the encrypted message. He gazed up at the ceiling for a moment, trying to recall the decryption key, which only he and his superior knew.

His eyes widened, re-reading the text just to be sure.

He then picked up the receiver of his tonagraph, and waited until the deep husky voice at the other end answered. 'Name?'

'Elihus Kinton.'

'Designation?'

'Patriarch.'

'Code and verification?'

'Project Hildr, verification Epsilon 10082003.'

'Mister Kinton. Begin message.'

Elihus trembled with excitement as he clutched the handset with one hand and the strip of paper in the other. 'Orders acquired and acknowledged,' he said. 'Dispatching asset.'

After an excruciating delay, the voice replied. 'Confirmed.'

The line went dead.

11 – Predator and Prey
NC06

Ice crunches in the dark, trampled by something unseen moving out there, like someone is rolling a barrel around in the scrub, followed by aggressive snorts.

'Boarts,' Sera whispers, stirring on the branch beside me.

The moon emerges from behind patchy cloud cover. As though summoned by the light, eight pairs of beady yellow eyes glow from the bushes, making the foliage appear alive.

Nervously, I cling tighter to the rope tethering me to this branch, hoping the knot holds.

Sera continues, 'you may get to see your first one tonight if they come closer. What can you tell me about them?'

'They're nocturnal, vicious and built like four-legged fortresses with razor-sharp tusks and will eat anything,' I recall from my textbooks. 'Bone plating covers their upper face and body, making them difficult to kill. Weak points for knives are under their jaw, neck and inner groin. Pistols will only annoy, and rifles might kill if you aim for the eyes or if you're lucky.'

The first boart shows itself, a stocky creature that matches what I'd just described, with seven others following close behind. The sounder approaches the base of our tree, stopping to sniff the air. At this distance, the white of their tusks pointing up beyond their snouts gleam menacingly in the intermittent moonlight. Except for one—it has a broken tusk. *I'll call that one Chompers.*

'Tell me about their predators,' Sera queries. She sounds oddly distracted, as though asking out of obligation rather than actual interest.

'They don't have any, except us,' I reply. 'They are territorial apex predators that like to dance and play dress-up.'

'That's good, Jayne,' she says absentmindedly.

That response was definitely not what I was expecting. Sera's apparent mood has me troubled. Perhaps she got a bad night's sleep or isn't feeling well. Right now, though, I'm more concerned about the freaky glowing yellow eyes watching us.

The pack's assumed leader, let's call them Bully, snorts a few times as Chompers swaggers forward, tilts its head, and charges the tree. They impact the tree with the force of a battering ram, sending vibrations through the trunk and me.

Maybe Chompers broke their tusk doing this?

Bully seems unimpressed, and they appear to disagree, snorting and grunting at Chompers, concluding with Bully head-butting their subordinate.

Chompers faces the tree again and rams it two more times before turning away from the group and us, disappearing into the night. The others remain behind, watching and waiting, I can only guess, for us to come down.

I don't think so, my hairy, armoured friends.

By the morn, the boart pack has moved on, their trail leading off in a different direction to the one Sera pushes me along.

This is our ninth camping trip together, every time providing new experiences, and every time the temperature is warmer, and the weather is better. The air this morn is clear, and we stow our masks in our packs to enjoy the freedom of breathing and talking without them. It's a shame, though, because this time, Sera doesn't seem talkative, and when she does, her usual smile is missing.

Today's hike finishes on the side of a mountain, and we find shelter in a shallow cave just big enough for two.

Without saying much, Sera props herself on a chair-height boulder, removes her pack and pulls out a petite bottle filled with a light blue liquid. She sets it down on a flat surface and cranks a handle in its wooden base, causing light to emanate from the bottle and bathe the cave in a cool blue hue.

As the first bright star emerges in the twilight sky, we make ourselves as comfortable as we're going to get. Sera breaks open her dinner rations and nibbles while gazing up at that distant star, seemingly becoming lost in that other world shining above the horizon.

'Do you want to talk about it?' I ask after watching her for a while.

She doesn't respond.

'Sera?'

'Hey? What?'

'What's going on?'

'What do you mean?'

'You were quiet yesterday. Today you've barely said anything, and we've been moving so fast, we almost ran here. Is something wrong?'

'We will be staying here again on the morrow.' Is all she says.

'Are you sure you don't want to talk?'

She disappears into her thoughts again and continues nibbling her rations until the light in the bottle fades.

∞

Orian Gracyn stood proud in her speaker robes on the top step of the new town hall, taking her position at the podium. Behind her, the building's new whitewashed facade almost gleamed in the clear morn sunlight. Its two large, solid timber doors remained closed, tied together by their doorknobs with a ceremonial blue cloth.

At the foot of the three steps, a considerable crowd had gathered. Election day had finally come, and most of Hope's residents had turned out to cheer on their favourite candidate. By day's end, one of them would become the first Virtuous Surprime of Hope. As Orian delivered her introduction, the three candidates sat at the head of the crowd, awaiting to deliver their speeches.

'Gracious people of Hope. It is with great honour I stand before you on this first day of New Calendar six to celebrate not one but three momentous events in our humble history,' Orian announced in her strong, Speaker's voice. 'First, the Progenitors have gifted us with this fine, warm weather. Even the wind is kind enough to be elsewhere, at least for the moment. Second, we will elect our first Virtuous Surprime, who will carry Hope forth into a new era of growth and prosperity. Soon you will hear from the three candidates. Listen well, for you will then cast your vote to decide which of them will lead us forward. May fortune favour the candidates. And finally, we will open the new *TOWN* hall.'

The watching crowd applauded and cheered.

As they settled, Orian resumed, 'I'm sure over the last few days you have all had a chance to speak to the three candidates. They will now deliver their closing speeches and explain to you how Hope will flourish under their leadership. So, without further ado, please welcome Gaius Sempro to the doors.'

The crowd applauded again while Gaius stepped forward, and with the aid of an elegant, newly crafted dark timber cane, hobbled up the steps. He looked smart in his tailored ensemble of dark-grey shirt, waistcoat and double-breasted jacket with its deep blue lapels and tie accentuating the grey flecks in the dark hair at his temples. The gathered crowd fell silent, waiting with patience as he removed a folded piece of paper from the inside of his jacket, unfolded it, and took his position behind the podium. Gaius stood as tall as his pain would allow, taking a few breaths, giving himself time to form the words in his mind to subdue any stutter.

'Ahem. My dear Hope. Look what we have achieved,' he began, speaking each word with care. He took another deep breath to centre himself, only just controlling the impediment threatening to paralyse his tongue, and focused on the texture of the paper in his fingers. After a pause, he raised his hand at the brand-new council hall, looking up at it with pride. 'Behind me stands a building I never thought we'd build, in a town I never dreamed would ever be, from the beginnings of a refugee camp that never should have existed. If my wife Rika were here today, she would be proud. She always had big ambitions for Hope.' Gaius paused to process the memory, bowing his head in solemn reflection, as did those who sympathised with him. 'She had such grand vision for this place; our place. I only wish she could be here to see it realised. I stand before you not as a candidate for Surprime, but as your friend and confidant. Should you see it fit to vote for me, I will humbly accept and vow to continue Rika's legacy. Thank you.' Gaius lifted his head to thunderous applause. As he stepped down from the podium to take his seat back at the head of the crowd, people reached forward to touch him on the shoulder and wish him luck. Even Sage, seated beside him, congratulated him on a speech well delivered.

'I only hope I can do as well,' Sage said, patting Gaius on the back.

'Please welcome Sage Solon to the doors,' Orian announced, beckoning Sage to the podium. Sage stood, and with hands raised in the air, jogged up the steps to the crowd's enthusiastic applause. Like Gaius, he too was dressed in a new double-breasted black waistcoat and tailored shirt, only he still wore his distinctive red coat over the top, as if people didn't already know who he was. The instant he stepped forward to the podium, his mind went blank. They expected him to say something as moving as Gaius, but he froze, his rehearsed speech eroded by several hundred sets of eyes glaring at him. He was more used to delivering information, not speaking just so people could listen to him talk.

'So, um, yeah. Hi everyone,' Sage began, wringing his clammy palms together.

Not a great start. He cringed inwardly.

'Ah um Sage Solon, um, candidate Surprime. Um.' He stopped for a moment to lick his lips, trying to get moisture back into his dry mouth so he could form the words.

Is this how Gaius felt? he pondered.

That gave him an idea. 'Isn't this building wonderful?' he said, gesturing at the new building in a feeble attempt to imitate Gaius. 'It was my idea. Well, um, actually no, it wasn't. But I complained about the other one so much we had to build it.' That earned him a smattering of awkward laughter from the crowd. Sage stammered on. 'Um,' clearing his throat again, he took a breath and attempted to compose himself. 'Most of you will know I spent quite a bit of time studying under Gaius as his protégé. I never imagined I'd be running against him for anything. Hi Gaius.' Sage broke his speech to wave to the old man, who gave him a confused wave back, then continued. 'Um, well, ah, he taught me a lot, and I think I can do well for this town. All I want is what you want, a safe place to call home. Hope is home. I've seen it grow, and I would like to see that it continues to grow stronger and better. I've served you the best I can. Well, I think so anyway. I have listened to all your stories, and I think I can help. I want to make Hope our home, not just for my beautiful wife, Jaylyn and our little one due within days...' he gazed lovingly into the crowd at his wife, seated in the second row, '...but for you, the people. So please vote for me, Sage Solon. Thank you.' He gave a slight bow as the crowd applauded, not as vigorous as they did for Gaius, but it was still applause. It lightened his heart to think some in the audience considered that pitiful performance worthy of praise. He bounded back down the steps and took his place next to Gaius. 'Well, that was embarrassing,' he muttered under his breath to no one in particular.

Niklas, who sat behind him, leaned forward and patted him on the back. 'Nice work, putz.'

Beside Niklas sat Jaylyn, heavily pregnant and beaming with adoration. 'Don't mind him, my love,' she said, leaning over the best she could to give her husband a gentle rub on the shoulder. 'You did great.'

'And finally,' Orian announced, this time with less enthusiasm, 'Artimus Wyrm.'

Artimus shot a smirk at his contenders before stepping forward and marching up the steps.

Unlike Gaius and Sage, he wore the meticulous grey dress uniform of a military admiral, pressed and complete with ornate brass buttons, medals and polished black boots so shiny he could see his reflection in them. His appearance earned him a cool reception of claps from the crowd.

'Thank you, Chairperson and the people of Hope,' Artimus said in a gruff, authoritative voice. He placed his hands on the edge of the podium, and standing with his head held high as though commanding an army to war, ignored the nervous chatter in the crowd and continued his speech. 'Since I arrived that fateful night back in 03, I have made a significant difference to Hope's security. Raiders have stopped attacking, and it's clear they fear my strength and the power I have vested here.

Under my leadership, Hope will prosper. I will see the continual development of industrial infrastructure.

Under my leadership, Hope will be strong. I will determine that all citizens enter civil service for a minimum term of one cycle and conscription when required to ensure our town is suitably defended.

Under my leadership, Hope will be just. I will fight to combat crime, crush our enemies and see that punishment is duly dispensed.

Under my leadership, I will bring order to Hope.' A single person somewhere in the back gave three awkward claps. 'This is my pledge to you, good people of Hope.'

He returned to his place next to Sage.

'Oh kay,' Orian said with sarcasm, unsure how to follow that. 'You have heard the closing remarks from our three candidates. Show them how much you support them with your vote. I now invite all three candidates back to the doors for the ceremonial cutting of the cloth.'

To boisterous applause, Gaius, Sage and Artimus ascended the steps once more to join Orian. As they did, assistants handed them each a pair of decorated scissors.

'But before we do the official opening,' Orian proclaimed, 'we have a little surprise for you all. We have been hiding something special behind these wooden panels. Something LunaTec has been developing. A building such as this *deserves* something extraordinary.' She lifted her hands to the two people standing on either side of the stairs. 'Please open them!'

And with the wave of her hands, they opened the wooden shutters, exposing windows. The crowd cheered, elated at the sight of glass.

'This building is not just for the council; it is for you, the people,' Orian continued. 'A place that firmly marks Hope on the map as a town. So today, we witness a new beginning for Hope. As we cut this cloth, we say goodbye to the old, refugee village Hope, and welcome in the new, Town of Hope.'

The three candidates, along with Orian, stepped forward, and each cut a piece of the ribbon, allowing it to flutter to the ground. 'And with that,' Orian proclaimed, arms outstretched, 'I now declare the town hall of Hope, open!'

The crowd erupted into raucous applause, louder than they had done before, celebrating their town's new beginnings. Once the officials had entered the hall, they all lined up to see the new building and finally cast their vote.

Beyond the double doors was a spacious main hall, its high ceilings held up by six timber columns spaced evenly throughout. Windows dotted all the external walls, their protective shutters latched open to allow the bright, warm sun to shine through. At the rear of the hall was a single door that led through to other offices, and an open pair of double doors, exiting into a second, grander Ministerial Chamber still under construction. A makeshift barricade of chairs blocked its entrance but allowed visitors to safely observe the work in progress.

Throughout the day, the residents of Hope streamed through the hall to cast their ballots and perhaps grab a bite to eat from the table set up with a spread of food, kahwah and tei, provided for everyone to enjoy.

As people came and went, the three candidates mingled with them, chatting and answering questions while Orian and the two vote counters waited, overseeing events.

Finally, when the long day came to an end, and the last person slipped their ballot into the box, Orian ordered the doors and shutters to be closed, and the oil heaters turned up. She flicked on the switch to the electric lights for the first time with a sense of pride and satisfaction.

Relishing in the silence compared to the busy day, the candidates and officials retired to their respective tables, set up for them at the rear of the room, while Orian upended the ballot box for the counting to begin.

Other council members, acting as adjudicators, gathered around to observe the count; Abril for Sage, Garan for Gaius, and Niklas for Artimus. Niklas watched on with a sour expression. 'This can't be right,' he complained, referring to the paltry pile of votes for Artimus.

Orian took the opportunity to visit the refreshment table, poured herself a cup of kahwah, grabbed a bite to eat from the leftovers, and was about to return to her chair when Artimus cornered her.

'So,' he said, reaching past a collection of mugs to pick one closest to her. 'You disapprove?'

Orian sighed. 'What do you think, Artimus?' she replied in a curt tone. After such a long day, she was far too tired and disinterested in talking to him. 'If you think forced conscription will win you this election, then good for you. Who am I to judge?'

'What is your problem, Orian?' he demanded, moving to block her from walking away. 'You've been less than civil to me ever since I arrived here. After what I did, the least you could do is be grateful.'

'Grateful, Artimus?' she scowled. 'Is that what you think?' She set down her cup and crossed her arms beneath her breasts. 'I don't owe you anything. And neither do any of these people. You think you can come in here and scare off some raiders, and suddenly, you're some kind of a hero? You think they should build a statue for you? Well, if half the people here knew you like I do, after what you did, they wouldn't build a statue for you, they'd build an effigy to burn. You'd be lucky to not be thrown on the pyre yourself. So, stop it with the arrogant, self-officiating nonsense. It's not impressing anyone.'

'Some things never change,' he said simply.

'And what's that supposed to mean? You know what, I don't care. I have no idea how you convinced the council to allow you to entertain this little power-play fantasy of yours, but I'm not buying it.'

'Speak for yourself, Orian,' he chided. 'How long were you here before you got appointed as Council Speaker, huh?'

'Where are you going with this?'

'Oh, I think you know. Tell me, Orian, how is it you came by that position? Or did you try some positions on Gaius first?'

Orian slapped him.

Artimus flinched, but he didn't attempt to stop her. 'Don't think I'm not aware of your relationship with him,' he pressed. 'That's a little convenient, don't you think?'

'How dare you!' she yelled. 'For your information, our *relationship* is nothing but professional. Yes, we *were* married. Not that it's any business of yours. Gaius and I...' she stammered. 'There's nothing. Go ask him yourself.'

Artimus smirked.

'Artimus, if you're going to be that way, go crawl back into whatever hole you came out of. Just keep out of my way.' She was about to push past him when Gaius crossed the room to see what the commotion was all about.

'Is everything alright?' he asked, reaching for a clean cup while looking at Orian, trapped between the wall and the wall of a man.

'Perfectly fine thanks, Gaius,' Artimus replied, turning his shoulder to address him. 'Orian and I were just having a little chat. We were just reminiscing on the good ol' days. It's funny, we've known each other all this time, and yet she's never once mentioned you.'

'I see,' Gaius said, holding out his hand to Orian to help her out of the corner. 'What's passed is past. We don't dig up old wounds, you know that.'

Orian took Gaius's hand with relief, grateful he'd noticed her predicament and come to her aid. Since Artimus arrived, she'd done her utmost best to maintain a professional distance between them. Artimus, it seemed, had other ideas. Whatever the reason may be for this little game of his, she could only guess. It made her uncomfortable nonetheless. Perhaps that was the point.

'Like it or not,' Artimus said as she pushed past him. 'Sometimes old wounds have a habit of reopening.'

'Not if you don't dig at them,' Gaius said flatly. 'If you excuse me, too much kahwah, I think,' he said, returning the unused cup to the table and escorted Orian away.

'Thank you for that,' she said, smiling at him. 'After the day I've had, I don't need that.'

'Whatever he's trying to brew between you, it isn't worth it.'

'I know.'

'I really do need to, you know,' he said, and she realised she was holding his arm. She let go when he glanced down at it, and with a knowing grin, he took his cane and hobbled through the door leading into the hallway.

Orian visited the counting table to watch the progress, hoping it would distract her from the interaction with Artimus, which still stewed in her mind. There, the three adjudicators and vote counters had their eyes fixed on the shuffling ballot papers. With only a handful of votes left to count, the mound of slips for Gaius towered over the other two. Seeing the small pile for Artimus lifted her spirits. She chuckled inwardly and turned around to face the room. Sage swung on his chair behind his table, chatting with his wife and Jaxson. Gaius's table was still vacant.

It's been fifteen decs. He hasn't returned yet, and where's Artimus? Orian thought.

A cold draft wafted into the room as the door to the hallway opened, and Artimus's bulky frame came through.

'Where's Gaius?' she asked him.

'How should I know?' Artimus shrugged. 'I didn't hold his hand. Maybe he left?'

'Out of my way,' she said, pushing past him and into the darkened hallway. The air felt much cooler in there.

No windows should be open at this end, she thought.

The lights in the hallway weren't on either.

Who puts the light switch halfway along a corridor?

Her hand touched the switch, lighting the passage just as her foot kicked something, and it clattered across the timber floor.

'What the...?' she said, bending over to pick it up.

Gaius's cane. But what's that doing here?

'Gaius!' she called. 'Are you up here?'

Cautiously, she approached the end of the hallway, glanced down towards the bathrooms on her left, and touched the closed door to the storage room in front. On her right, the door to the corner office swung ajar, tapping on its latch in the wind.

That's odd, she thought, grabbing the handle to push it open a little further. A blast of cold outside air bit at her exposed face, and she noticed the open window.

She flicked on the light and was about to enter the room when she glanced down at the floor. There, lying slumped against the wall by the door, was Gaius, a knife handle protruding from his chest. He gazed up at her, mouth open as though trying to speak, but before he could get the words out, the fire in his eyes extinguished, and he fell limp.

Immediately, she rushed to him, kneeling beside to clutch his ashen face between her hands. 'Gaius?' she called, shaking him.

Tears streamed down her cheeks, and she let out a loud, agonised scream. 'HELP!' she cried out in desperation. 'SOMEONE, PLEASE HELP!'

Within midecs, Sage and Jaxson were there.

Sage took one look at the horrific scene and rushed in.

'Gaius!' he exclaimed, stepping around and kneeling beside him, careful to avoid the seeping pool of blood on the floor. He checked Gaius's neck for a pulse.

'I'll get the Doc,' Jaxson said before rushing off.

Sage bowed his head. He was no stranger to death, he'd seen enough of it, but to have this happen to Gaius, of all people, it was unthinkable.

Orian let out a strangled cry. 'Gaius, no,' she wailed, shaking uncontrollably and clutching his head to her chest. Sage reached over to console her, as much for his sake as for hers. It was enough to help him draw the courage to look upon the face of his dearest old friend. Gaius's eyes and mouth were still open, and he lay slumped against the wall with his neat new shirt and jacket drenched in his life, his natural, caramel-toned skin drained of its colour.

By the time Jaxson returned with the doctor, several people had huddled by the door, curious to see what was going on. Among them was Garan, with Abril trying to poke her head through the crowd, but Orian's back blocked her view. Upon noticing Abril, Sage gestured to Garan to escort her away.

Carrying her medkit, Lexi pushed her way through the crowd and into the room, followed by two nurses bearing a stretcher. Sage moved aside to let her in. She took one look at Gaius and choked back tears of her own, swallowing them down in an apparent attempt to stifle her urge to cry.

Jaxson opted to shuffle the crowd of gawkers away, closing the door behind him on his way out and allowing the doctor to work in peace.

With a stony expression, Lexi moved closer to examine Gaius, while Orian and Sage watched on in silence. Orian held Gaius's still warm hand in hers as though to comfort him.

'There's nothing I can do,' Lexi eventually said, her stony expression fading into sadness and voice wavering on the verge of tears. 'Even if I were here when it happened, I still wouldn't have been able to help him.'

'It's not your fault, Lexi. You've done what you can,' Sage said.

She nodded. 'That isn't much, Sage. One thing's for sure. Whoever did this knew what they were doing.'

'How can you tell?' he asked.

'The knife has sliced through his aorta. Gaius bled out in no time. The only concession here is, it was quick. But the knife's so big, my guess is they had no choice but to leave it.'

'Who would do such a thing?' Sage said in disbelief. 'Everyone loved Gaius. This doesn't make any sense.'

Everyone looked at him as though he'd just said what they all had been thinking. Sage couldn't help but look at his old friend, lying there like that and want to tear the world apart. He wanted to scream and curse, but he also wanted to find out who did this and tear them apart instead.

'Can you get it out?' he asked, breaking the silence.

'The knife? The doctor asked. 'I don't know. He's impaled pretty good.'

'If I'm going to find who did this, I'll need it. Besides, we can't leave him like this.'

'I can try,' she said. 'Give me a few decs, but you might not want to see this.'

Sage helped Orian to her feet, and the two left the room, closing the door behind, allowing the doctor to extract the knife from Gaius's prone body.

Overcome with grief, Orian collapsed into Sage's arms.

He held her in a firm embrace, trying to comfort her but also to conceal the fact that he was fighting to maintain his own composure.

'I don't understand it,' she sobbed into his chest. 'I only just found him again. How could someone do this to Gaius?'

'I wish I knew,' Sage replied, further words escaping him. All he could do was stand there and hold her.

When the door eventually opened, Lexi handed him the cloth-wrapped knife. 'Find the person who did this, Sage,' she said, wiping her face with the sleeve of her coat. Her tone almost sounded like a challenge. 'Gaius deserved better than this.'

Within the room, the two nurses were busy lifting Gaius's body onto the stretcher. Before they could cover him, Orian rushed in, kneeling at Gaius's side again, leaning forward and placing a tender kiss on his cheek. 'I never stopped loving you, Gaius,' she whispered into his ear and laying her head on his shoulder.

Sage gave her a moment to say her goodbyes before stepping in and resting a gentle hand on her back.

New tears streamed down her face. 'Goodbye, my dear old friend,' she cried, sitting up and allowing the nurses to drape the sheet over Gaius's head.

Sage felt numb. As the full force of his grief took hold, the realisation finally dawned on him. Gaius; his friend, his mentor and the closest person he had to a father, was gone.

Orian clambered to her feet to join him, and they stood in silence, watching the doctor and her nurses carry Gaius's shrouded body from the room. They proceeded down the hall towards where Abril and Garan were waiting. Abril stopped them for just a moment to lift the cloth, and when she saw Gaius's face underneath, she shrieked, turned to her husband and sobbed into his chest. 'Gaius,' she wailed, her words muffled by Garan's body. He held her tight to stop her collapsing and allowed the procession to continue on their solemn way.

Sage returned to the room, gazing despondently at the puddle of blood on the floor. Anger replaced grief as he clutched the cloth-bound knife in his hands; wanting to destroy the very thing that ended Gaius's life. 'Lexi's right,' he said, wringing the wrapped parcel tight. 'We have to find who did this, and we have to...' he trailed off.

Orian sniffled. 'Can I see that for a dec?' she asked.

Sage unwrapped it. The large, reverse-barbed blade glistened red with Gaius's blood.

'I've seen that before,' Orian said, inspecting it.

It was beautiful, despite its use. Engraved images of delicate feathers adorned its ornate, milky green and white handle. The intricate etchings of winged creatures bearing talons and pointed beaks on its blade had become red rivulets of coagulated blood.

'Artimus,' she growled, 'he did this.'

Sage looked at her, astonished. 'Artimus? Why?'

'That's his knife. I'd recognise it anywhere.'

Filled with a resounding rage, Sage bolted from the room, with Jaxson following in close pursuit. They passed through the construction zone, picking up a roll of adhesive tape along the way. As they entered the main hall, Artimus waited, reclining in a chair with his feet up on a table, seeming oblivious to the commotion going on around him.

'I was wondering when...' he said as Sage and Jaxson charged towards him. They didn't bother with the niceties. They grabbed him, yanking his feet off the table, and restrained his arms behind his back. 'Hey!' he yelled. 'What are you doing? Get your hands off me!'

'Artimus Wyrm,' Sage growled. 'We detain you for the murder of Gaius Sempro.'

'What!?' Artimus retorted, struggling against their restraints. But with a few choice manoeuvres from the two strong men, they managed to overpower him and forcibly march him to the small storage closet down the hallway, taping his wrists and ankles to a sturdy wooden chair.

'You don't have the right!' Artimus protested while Sage tore off another piece of tape.

'Try me, just try me, Artimus,' Sage scowled, and slammed the door, closing out Artimus's cries of protest, leaving him alone in the small, dark room.

Orian, her face still wet from her tears, and whose emotional state had shifted from grief to anger, spun to Sage with a fiery determination in her eyes. 'What are we going to do with him?' she demanded.

Sage sighed. 'Beats me. He's supposed to be the crime prevention around here. But if he did this, we can't trust him or his HomeGuard. We're on our own. That means we will have to handle this our way.'

Orian braced herself, took a deep breath and after a moment, wrenched open the door to the storage cupboard.

'I didn't do it!' Artimus bellowed.

'Then explain this... ' Orian lurched forward with the bloody knife and stabbed it into the wooden armrest of Artimus's chair, the blade just missing his bound hand.

Artimus's eyes widened at the sight of the knife. 'I... where did you get that?' he demanded.

'Are you really going to do this, Artimus?' Orian spat. 'Where do you think?'

'No, I mean how'd... '

'I was hoping you were going to tell us that.'

'I don't know what you're talking about, Orian.' He struggled with his bonds. 'Get these off me, now!'

'Not until you confess.'

'Confess to what?'

'You killed Gaius.'

'Oh, for frak's sake. I DIDN'T KILL GAIUS!'

'Then how did your knife get in his chest? Tell me that, Artimus?' Orian, with her face bright red with anger, was livid. 'Don't you dare tell me you don't recognise it.'

'What do you want me to say? Yes, I *had* a knife that looks like this, but that was a long time ago, and a long time ago I lost it to a frozen river attempting to get ice. I haven't seen it since. That's not my knife. It can't be.'

Orian leaned forward and looked him square in the eyes. 'I don't believe you.'

'Aghhhh!' Artimus raged through clenched teeth, pulling at his bindings. 'If this is some kind of retribution, Orian, I will... '

'You'll do what? Kill me like you did Gaius?'

'Orian, if I wanted you dead, I wouldn't need to do it in a darkened hallway. You and I both know you have no provocation for leaving me here.'

'No? Then how is it that out of all the people in this hall, you don't seem to care that Gaius is dead? What are you really doing here, *Rear* Admiral Wyrm?'

'Grrr, you and your Progenitor-forsaken conspiracy theories! Come on, Orian,' he objected. 'So, we weren't friends. That's no reason for me to want to kill him.'

'But you aren't exactly winning this election either.'

'Oh my...' Artimus retorted. 'So you think I killed Gaius to win, is that it?'

'I wouldn't put it past you, *Rear* Admiral. Wyrm by name, worm by nature.'

'It's ADMIRAL!'

'In who's army? Yours? Only you seem to care about rank at a time like this. I mean, look at you. You're a pathetic fool, clinging onto a deluded notion of a time when you believed you had actual power. Is that why you—?'

'This has nothing to do with that, and you know it,' he raged. 'This is petty. How many times must I tell you, I didn't kill Gaius? Either someone found my knife and is trying to frame me, or IT'S NOT MY KNIFE. And if that's the case, we have bigger problems.'

'Bigger? Than Gaius being MURDERED! Either you confess now, or we start that bonfire and forget the effigy!'

'Orian, I'm well aware of what you think of me, and it's easy to see me as the enemy. I'm going to ignore this emotional outburst. You're angry and want vengeance, I get it. This knife is not mine. Even so, you can't prove it. The fact is, whoever killed Gaius is still out there, somewhere.'

She stepped back, folding her arms.

'I'm telling you,' he continued, in a more serious tone. 'These people are dangerous. You can't go looking for them. I don't care if you believe me or not. I didn't kill Gaius, but I can find the person who did. The longer you leave me here restrained, the more time you are giving them to get away. LISTEN to me, please. Get me out of here and let me do my job!'

'It's awfully convenient, Artimus, but I'm not convinced.'

She removed the knife from the chair and closed Artimus in the dark once more.

Outside, Sage was pacing along the hallway, his eyes fixated on the floorboards. 'What if he's right?'

'He's not. He's just trying to worm his way out of it. It's what he does.'

'What is your gripe with him?'

'This is not the time, Sage. Right now—'

'Yes, I'm aware of that, but if Artimus is right about one thing, it's that we have no actual evidence against him. We can't prove that's his knife any more than we can prove he wanted Gaius dead. We will have to let him go.'

'Then what, he takes his revenge out on the rest of us?'

'I don't think so,' Sage said calmly.

'You don't know him. You don't know what he's capable of,' Orian yelled. This was not the calm and collected Orian he knew. This was an irrational, paranoid version of Orian he had never thought he'd ever see. Given the circumstances, he could sympathise.

'I understand,' he said, trying to calm her, 'but that's no reason to accuse him, Orian.' He grabbed her by the shoulders and held her in a soft embrace, but she just cried again. 'We have to find the killer,' she sobbed, placing her arms around Sage's waist and burying her head in his chest. 'We just have to, and we're running out of time.'

'Yes, I know.' He wasn't sure how to respond further, so he let her hug him for a while longer. 'We have the Council,' he said after she let go. 'Let them decide what to do with Artimus.'

Sage and Orian, arms linked, emerged from the hallway to find the Councillors gathered in the main hall along with a few other members of the Hope community. The vote counters had ceased counting ballots and pushed the table against a wall out of the way. Even Elihus Kinton was there, seated by the food table with a steaming cup in his hand, looking sombre. Abril, still inconsolable, leaned into Garan's shoulder as he tried to comfort her.

As Sage and Orian stepped into the light, the room fell silent, gazing at them with nervous expressions, awaiting news of what was going on.

Sage let go of Orian and stepped forward, clearing his throat to address the crowd.

'Friends, family, humble people of Hope,' he said in the calmest voice he could muster. 'I'm not sure how to say this, so I'll just come right out and say it. Gaius has been murdered.' A chorus of gasps echoed throughout the hall as people came to terms with the news. Sage stifled the grief welling in him and carried on. 'We're still investigating, but he was killed this even using this knife.' He exposed the handle and raised the knife aloft so the people could see it. 'We're still looking for the killer. This will come as a shock to many of you, as Gaius was a very well-loved and respected member of our community. He will be dearly missed. But once we find who did this, we will bring them to justice. If anyone has any information or has seen anything suspicious in or around this building, please come forward. We would appreciate the help.'

'Rumour has it you already have a suspect,' Niklas called out from the back. 'Is it true you have detained Artimus Wyrm?'

Sage nodded. 'Yes, we have Artimus in custody. He is a suspect at the moment and is currently being detained.'

'Why Artimus?' Niklas called out again as though trying to incite a more significant reaction from the group.

'Without going into details, we have reason to believe the murder weapon may be linked to him. That's all I can say for now.'

'I knew it,' Niklas shouted. 'From the moment he arrived, I knew we couldn't trust him.'

'Niklas, please,' Sage said, attempting to quell the murmur rising in the room. 'That's a matter for private discussion. I need to see all council members in a closed session. Thank you.'

Sage led Orian, Abril, Garan, Niklas and Elihus down the hall to one of the other vacant offices, flicked on the light and closed the door.

The moment the door closed, Sage turned to Niklas with dismay. 'What was that?' he demanded. 'We don't need more trouble right now. We need to be discreet. Yes, we have Artimus in custody, but our evidence against him is sketchy. I need you to help decide what we should do next, not lose your head and incite a mob.'

'I'm only saying what's on everyone's mind,' Niklas said.

'Only because you put it there,' Sage snapped.

'I think what Niklas is tryin' to say is we need to find the killer,' Garan intervened. 'If not Artimus, then we need to let him go.'

'Yes,' Sage agreed, 'but it's complicated. As our law enforcement, Artimus and his HomeGuard are empowered to lead the investigation. But, if we're wrong, and he did kill Gaius, we will not only have let the killer walk free but also control the investigation.'

'Hmm, I see,' Garan replied.

Elihus stepped forward. 'The murder weapon, may I see it?'

Sage hesitated, but then handed it to him.

The old, bearded man unwrapped it from its cloth sheath and held it to eye height so he could examine the etched blade gleaming red under the electric lights. 'Impressive,' he said. 'Who would leave such a blade behind after doing such a terrible thing? And you suspect Admiral Wyrm, why?'

'We have our reasons,' Sage replied.

'Then do tell us, my good boy.'

'We believe he has a knife like this. But he claims to have lost it.'

'Maybe he did, maybe he didn't,' Elihus said.

'Still,' Garan added. 'We can't hold a man on a maybe. Unless we can prove it, we have to let him go.'

'No,' Abril shouted. 'Gaius must be avenged.'

'We can't have vigilante justice,' Sage protested. 'But if he didn't do it...?'

'I think you have your decision, Sage,' Garan said, his voice strained from his own grief, but level with wise logic, 'none more than me, would like to see Gaius avenged, but as much as we would like to see the killer found, and brunged to swift justice, an easy scapegoat does not a fair trial make. Let Artimus go. Let him use his resources to find the killer, and when he does, put them on trial. Make them answer for what they've done. It's the only way.'

'I hate to say it, but I agree with Garan,' Niklas said, taking the knife from Elihus and handing it back to Sage. 'He'll be needing this. May the Progenitors guide him and bring Gaius's murderer to justice.'

Sage opened the door to the storage cupboard. Artimus blinked at him as his eyes adjusted to the light. Without a word, Sage pulled a small knife from his belt.

'What are you going to do with that butter knife?' Artimus asked, a little strained.

Sage ignored him, bent forward, and without saying a word, cut the tape binding his hands and feet.

'So, I guess this means I'm free to go?' Artimus asked, ripping the adhesive tape from his hairy wrists without flinching.

'You'll be needing this,' Sage said, handing Artimus the cloth-bound, blood-stained knife. 'But if I find you have so much as deceived us about anything that happened this even, I will have your head on a pike faster than you can say "lying scumbag".'

'Alright,' Artimus said, 'I have work to do then.'

The sun breached the horizon, welcoming the morning with a warm glow, contrary to the mood of the town.

Artimus stood in the open doorway of the hall, his thick grey military coat flapping in the frigid wind, waiting to see the man called Hunter. He finished his tei, savouring the warm feeling sliding down his throat, when a cold pistol muzzle rested against his temple. 'Hunter?' Artimus asked, unflinching.

The muzzle lifted, and Artimus turned. 'Is that the same pistol? It looks bigger than last time.'

Hunter secured the hand canon in a formed metal holster on his scale armour protecting his thighs. 'You called?'

'With all that armour on, how do you sneak around like that?' Artimus asked, admiring Hunter's breastplate etched with a faint image of an ursus fighting a giant serpent. Lamellar plating covered every part of his body, exposing only his leathery face.

'Sneaking is for thieves and murderers,' Hunter replied in his deep, gruff voice.

'We had a problem with a Surprime candidate, and we need you to find the person responsible,' Artimus said, leading Hunter through to the back office. The beast-like man moved as though unhindered by his armour.

Hunter knelt and inspected the fresh stain in the timber, allowing Artimus to get a better look at the short-barrelled rifle strapped to his back. Hunter's gaze shifted to the window. He stood to inspect its frame before opening it and the shutter, then with only a brief hesitation, vaulted through the open window. Like a predatory animal tracking its prey, the large armoured man charged towards the trees bordering Hope and disappeared.

The hunt had begun.

12 – Boulder-dash

Ajee stepped off the gangplank onto the main deck of the Fenix for the first time, and tilting her pale face to the glorious sun, she revelled in her newfound freedom. Before being escorted under guard to the bridge, she took a moment to glance up toward the foredeck. There, adorned in a regal, red leather coat with pointed tails, was the infamous Captain Branton Nash. As she ascended the stairs to the helm, he turned from the wheel and strutted away towards the railing. Ajee didn't care for his arrogance. Instead, she brushed it off and stopped at the wheel to run a hand over its smooth timber surface, breathing in the brief history of the ship, envisioning the orders bellowed from this very spot.

'Impressive, isn't it?' Branton said, acknowledging her presence without looking at her.

She bottled her excitement and settled for a simple reply. 'Yes, Captain.'

The young captain turned to face her with a stern expression. 'I know who you are and how you came here,' he said, his short tousled brown hair blowing in the wind. 'But I don't trust you. Not yet, anyway. Just because I gave you a second chance, doesn't mean we're friends. I selected you for my crew because you have the skills I need. That's all. Because of your history, you need to prove your loyalty and that you can be trusted.'

'How do you suppose I do that?' Ajee replied.

'We'll see,' Branton said, 'for now, you're allowed free roam of the ship, except command and operational areas. These areas are off-limits unless escorted. Is that clear?'

'Yes, Captain,' Ajee said, 'it's just nice to see the other side of those bars.'

Branton smiled. 'Now, find a spare bunk and stow your gear. We sail at high tide.'

It's freezing cold in this cave. Even the rising sun doesn't warm the air, forcing me to set down the book, pull my coat tighter and jog on the spot. Sera told me not to light a fire. I don't know why, but I really could use the warmth about now.

Enticed by the golden light bathing the rocks outside, I take my book and bask in the sun.

Sera left yesterday morn with only a few rations and a day's worth of water. With no word of where she was going or why. I can only hope it isn't far.

I shove a piece of bland protein slice into my mouth, pick up my book and jump back into the imaginary world of Ajee Yond.

Just as it's getting exciting, a cascade of tumbling rocks pulls me from Ajee's adventures and, dropping the book, I roll into the cave to hide.

'Jayne,' echoes an urgent whisper, and a Sera-shaped silhouette enters the cave's mouth.

'Sera!' I exclaim, leaping toward her in excitement.

'Shush, quiet! We have to go this midec.'

'Okay, just let me grab—'

'No!' she snaps. 'There's no time. If it is not in your pack, leave it.'

Sera steps into the light. Dark stains cover her face and clothing, and her unexpected appearance causes me to hesitate. 'Is that your blood?' I ask with concern. 'Are you okay?'

'Forget about me,' she says in a panicked voice. 'Please, Jayne. We must go.' She picks up my pack and thrusts it into my arms, grabs my hand and pulls me from the cave.

Outside, the terrain is steep and covered in slippery shale, dotted with sparse vegetation. Sera studies the slope, then glances down. 'He's quicker than I thought,' she mutters and scrambles towards the peak.

'Oh, my book!' I yell, pausing on the rocky slope.

'Leave it,' she shouts back, not even turning to reply.

'*But*... I'm not leaving without it.'

Sera ignores my pleas and continues to climb. With great reluctance, I turn away too. The last thing I see before following her is my precious book, sitting on the landing where I'd dropped it.

'Is there someone chasing us?' I call out to Sera, but she doesn't reply. Instead, she pushes on, higher and higher, keeping close to the recesses and scaling the slope like a nimble genet.

I scrabble up behind, trying to catch Sera before glancing down to see the reason for our haste. There, only a few metas below, a lone figure pauses at the cave's entrance where we'd just left, glances in, picks up my book, then continues their ascent.

'Sera,' I ask again, nervously. 'Who's that?'

'Just keep going.'

Our climb pushes us up into patchy clouds, and we rest for a moment at the summit to catch our breath.

On the other side is a very steep embankment. While Sera tries to figure out a safe way down, I get a good glimpse at our pursuant. Garbed in an outfit of sturdy, overlapping plates, with a stout rifle slung over his back, the stranger closes in like an armour-clad juggernaut.

'How on Jorth are they making this climb in all that armour?'

'I don't know,' Sera replies. 'But that's not our concern right now.' She points to a small flat ledge, about one hundred metas below, where a single L-shaped tree juts out from the embankment. 'We must get down there.'

I've never heard Sera talk like that before.

'Ahh,' I say with extreme unease. 'How?'

'Trust me,' she says, then charges down the slope.

Between the armoured man and that steep decline, I can only hope Sera knows what she's doing.

I launch myself after her. With my feet carrying me on their own, somehow between the rush of adrenaline and the urge not to fall, I stay upright.

Ahead, Sera reaches the flat ground and collides with the tree in a sickening stop.

'SER–RA!' I yell as I hurtle towards her.

Bracing for impact, I squeeze my eyes shut.

Please catch me, Sera.

THUMP!

The force of the collision strips the wind from my lungs. The world spins, and I tumble around and around. I expect to hit solid ground, and for that to be it, but there is no pain. When I think it's over, I open my eyes. Sprawled on the ledge in front of the odd–shaped tree, Sera holds me tight in her arms.

She caught me!

I want to cry, but for some reason, I laugh instead.

'Are you okay, Jayne?' Sera asks, laughing too.

'I–I think so,' I reply, gripping her tighter to be sure she's actually there.

'Good, we must keep moving.'

Clouds drift overhead, and I watch them in dazed confusion while I wait for the spinning to stop. 'O–Okay. In a midec.'

'We don't have time, Jayne,' Sera insists. 'We must get up and take this tree down.'

While I shake off the dizziness, Sera sifts through the surrounding shale, finds two fist–sized chunks, and pushes one into my hand.

'Do as I do,' she says, using the axe–head shaped rock to chip away at the base of the tree. Despite my confusion, I follow Sera's actions.

'What are we doing?' I ask after the first few strikes. 'Wouldn't your knife be better for this?'

'Just help,' she snaps.

After several decs of frantic pummelling, splinters of timber start flying and the two of us chip away at the tree, desperately hoping we finish whatever it is we're doing before that person catches up.

Sera drops the rock. 'Keep going,' she shouts as she pulls and swings on the tree. It groans and cracks, then with one last pull, bends beyond breaking point and falls to our feet.

Sera kicks off branches, leaving a few of the bigger ones, then with its slight bend pointing upwards at the front, drags it into position at the edge of the drop–off.

Behind us, the stranger has reached the peak and yells out something lost to the wind.

'Get on, hold tight,' Sera yells.

A branch explodes in front of Sera's face.

Her scream and the thunderous echo of a gunshot make me leap behind Sera in terror, gripping her tight around the waist.

With a sick feeling rising in my stomach, the tree tips over the precipice.

Our makeshift toboggan careens down the mountainside at an exhilarating speed, flying over dirty snow and compacted dust like we're riding a wooden missile.

The ride descends, hitting rocks and other branches in violent shudders along the way, causing the vehicle to disintegrate.

Surrounding us, the landscape zooms by in a blur. Small rocks become larger, the density of dead trees, thicker. With no means of steering, a boulder set in our path becomes a deadly hazard.

'LET GO!' Sera yells, slapping away my hands. 'JUMP!'

She pushes me off, and the world tumbles again.

At such a speed, I surrender to momentum, curl into a ball, and try to keep my limbs from flailing. Something with claws and sharp edges arrests my fall, ripping at my clothing and face. The world continues to spin even after I stop tumbling, making my protein slice revisit and add its colour to the drab mountainside.

'Jaa-yne.' I hear a muffled cry.

I must have passed out again.

Glancing around in disorientation for the source, I'm thankful a pillow of fresh snow, twigs and an assortment of other organic matter cushioned my landing. I can't say the same for the toboggan—it lies shattered to pieces around a boulder.

'Jaa-yne.' Sera's pained voice calls again from just beyond the boulder.

'I'm coming, Sera,' I yell out, dragging myself to stand and making the descent towards her voice. Over difficult terrain, it takes several decs to reach her. There, by a wall of boulders, she lies clutching at a blood-soaked patch in her side where a stick protrudes.

Amity reaches out her hand, her face contorted with intense pain.

A wave of panic washes over me. I shut my eyes and take a deep breath to steady myself.

It's not Amity. It can't be.

When I open them again, Sera is lying there, reaching out.

'I've smashed my knee,' she gasps, 'and I seem to be nursing this stick.' Even in her state, Sera maintains her odd sense of humour.

Seeing her like that sends a prickly sensation all throughout my body. It's as if I can feel her pain.

'No, it's okay,' I say, trying to lighten the mood. 'You just won't be dancing anytime soon.'

'Leave me,' she says, trying to keep a composed face while cupping the wound at her side. 'It is me he's after, anyway.'

'What are you talking about? Don't you dare talk like that!' I tell her off. 'I'll get you home.'

'We will both die today if you help me.'

'I have never heard you speak like that before, and I don't want to hear it again. I'm going to find help. And don't you even think of moving. That'll just make it worse.'

I've never spoken to anyone like that before, let alone Sera.

'All right. You must hurry. We have a good lead, but this,' she says, gesturing at the stick, 'will slow us considerably. Where's your pack?'

'Oh no,' I say, feeling at my back, 'it must have come off in the fall.'

Thankfully, having fared better than she has, Sera's pack lies with torn straps at her feet.

'At least we have yours.' I retrieve it, and dig around inside for useful items. 'Hey, Sera,' I ask, turning everything out on the ground, 'where's your knife? I can only find its sheath and medkit.'

'I don't have it anymore,' she says with a pained expression.

'You lost it?'

'Something like that,' she winces. 'Please, Jayne, enough with the questions.'

'Okay, I'll find something else, then.'

Despite Sera having trained me in basic first-aid, it's very different having to do it in real life. It's even harder with limited medical supplies on someone you know. My hands shake uncontrollably as I administer an injection of painkillers and dress her wounds, but I don't dare touch the stick or try to remove it. Instead, I pack bandages around it to stem the bleeding and stabilise her leg with a stick splint. 'Sera,' I ask, trying to keep her conscious. 'Where'd you go?'

'Hope,' she mumbles, and I wonder if it's the name of a place or she cut herself short in some kind of delirium-induced dream-speak.

'And why is that person after us?'

At that point, the painkillers take full effect, and she looks right through me, muttering something about orders.

While I do my best to make Sera comfortable, somewhere off in the distance, contrasting colours and unnaturally sharp lines stand out amongst the sparse trees, and I stand to get a better view. Further down the slope, there appear to be buildings.

'There's something I want to check out down there,' I say, not sure if Sera heard me. 'Could be a town. I'll see if I can find help. Will you be okay here?'

'Mmmm, alright. Not like 'm goin' anywhere,' she moans. 'Than' you, Jayne. Good work,' she adds, raising a hand to touch my face. Her hand drops, and she's out cold.

From the condensation steaming from her nose and the gentle rise and fall of her chest, she's still alive.

But for how long?

'Just stay with me, please, Sera. I'll be back soon.' Then, placing Sera's pack under her head for comfort and concealing her with heaped leaves and branches, I run off to find help.

The terrain flattens out, and I enter a forest of various-sized boulders scattered against a three meta high staggered stone wall. It would appear the wall was erected to protect a small community of about thirty buildings nestled beyond it. Debris piled up behind the break wall shows the area is prone to frequent avalanches, but by its depth, it has seen a few and now it is only just doing the job. A section at its centre has already broken away, leaving a sizeable gap, and a hump created by cycles of piled up snow and debris.

Buildings might mean people. Could anyone still be here?

Conflicted by the need to help Sera, and the voice telling me not to trust anyone, I go with my instinct and enter, passing through the gap in the wall and emerging into a snow-covered clearing.

Sizeable boulders rest in the open space among an assortment of stone people, some missing heads or limbs, standing on platforms also made of stone.

'What happened here?' I say aloud in wonder.

At the other end of the space, a stone man, undamaged and larger than life, stands on a plinth facing the buildings, holding his right hand high as though taking an oath. A metal plaque at his feet reads;

In commemoration of Mayor Raydon Osman, forever to watch over Curio and protect us from the Progenitor Codan and his boulders.

Beyond Mayor Osman, perpendicular to the clearing, is a single main street lined on either side with simple, mixed construction buildings in various states of disrepair. An enormous boulder rests in the middle of the first house on my left. The next has no glass windows intact on the ground floor, allowing dirt to pile up inside as deep as the tables are high.

Curiosity urges me to explore this relic of a town that seems oddly frozen in time.

Some houses are barely standing, with their contents destroyed; nothing of interest remains. The rest, still with their windows to protect them from the extremities, are mostly intact. I peek in to find tables set as though ready for dinner, but only dust-covered bones remain of the meals.

Through all the dust and debris, it gives me a glimpse of how people might have lived before the war. Had Sera been with me, she would have loved this place. That thought kills my excitement, and I go back to my search.

Desperate to find help, I rush from house to house, checking doors and peering in windows to see if I can find any sign of life. Failing that, anything useful. By the time I reach the end of the street, one thing's clear; the town's deserted.

There, at the far edge of town, the ground dips away to one last house nestled in a hollow by a narrow, frozen river. A smeary window looks into a large room and sitting in the middle of which is a vehicle similar in size and shape to the one Sera and I recovered. Other objects adorn the walls and tables surrounding it.

This's promising. I'm bound to find something useful here.

I grab the handle in the centre of the big door to the room; it lifts open, almost striking me under the chin.

At least it's unlocked.

Like all the other houses, a thick coating of dust covers everything, and it appears the occupants had just up and left, leaving their car in pieces. The front is open with tools littering the engine bay, and the wheels are missing. It's not going anywhere.

After rummaging around the room, I find a backpack, a small water canteen, and a cupboard stacked with sealed cylinders of food. Taking down the first one, a metallic object resembling a tiny knife drops past my face, clattering to the floor, followed by a folded piece of paper that flutters away.

Who puts knives up high like that?

I take as much as the bag will hold.

As I search the rest of the room, I find more tools and other equipment. Most of it I don't recognise, but along a wall is a sealed box of blankets and hanging above it is an old wooden sled. It isn't long enough for Sera to lie on, but with a bit of ingenuity, I fashion a cot on the flat surface using some lengths of timber, rope and blankets.

Before leaving, I search the rest of the house. It offers little of anything useful—perhaps the occupants took all the useful stuff. It's times like these, I wish I'd brought my fire bracelet. In the kitchen, I rush to the tap, hoping to fill the canteen with fresh water. Moments after turning it on, it emits a reverberating hammering noise, then a gurgle, and a thick, murky brown substance belches from the tap. With little time to lose, I abandon the search and return to the car-room, grab the sled, and drag it back to Sera.

To my relief, she's still alive, but unconscious. Her face has lost its colour, her pulse is weak and rapid, and she's shivering.

This isn't good. I have to get her home, fast.

'Sera,' I whisper, giving her a gentle shake. 'Wake up, we have to go.'

She groans, 'Jayne, is that you?'

'Yes, Sera, I'm back. I found a place called Curio. There was nobody there, but I found this,' I say, positioning the sled beside her to check its length. 'I also found what looks like food, but I don't know how to open it.' I hold up a cylinder for her to see.

Sera replies with a pained chuckle. 'That's pet food,' she winces. 'Did you bring a can opener?'

'A what? Never mind,' I say, tossing the bag of armoured food into the sled. 'Hopefully, this can get you home. I can help you on, but you're much bigger than me.'

She manages a weak smile. 'You are stubborn, Miss Jayne Doe. You should have left me.'

'The thought never crossed my mind,' I reply, reaching out to help Sera shuffle onto the cot. From the pained expression on her face, this is going to be no easy task.

Careful not to hurt her further, I rest the sled against a rock to steady it. She throws her good leg over, and I pull her onto it with all my strength.

With Sera in place, I secure her with rope. Then with a few cautious tugs, I start the sled moving across the hill, manoeuvring it in line with the hole in the break wall.

Just as we are about to commence our descent, a tree explodes right in front of us, showering us in bark. Instinctively, I drop to the ground as the loud crack of a gunshot echoes around the valley.

A rumbling emanates from the mountain above. At first, small rocks dance around my feet. Then, shale covering the ground starts to slide underfoot towards Curio. In no time, debris from above, carried by the dislodged soil, forms into a rolling torrent, rapidly gathering in mass and momentum.

'Avalanche!' I yell, as a massive cloud of rolling death descends upon us.

Sera's voice quivers. 'Whatever you're doing, you better do it faster.'

'I'm working on it,' I yell back, struggling to control the sled. 'This thing doesn't steer. If we get the direction wrong, we crash.'

'Jayne!'

It's tough going, dragging the heavy sled through loose shale. Despite the looming danger, it makes our descent excruciatingly slow. But, as soon as the skis touch snow, it speeds up unexpectedly, cleaning me off my feet, and I land on top of Sera, just missing the stick poking out of her side.

Once again, we ride an uncontrolled transport towards an unknown destination.

Please let our stop be more comfortable this time.

Smaller rocks pass us and bounce over the break wall, showering parts of the town in destructive hail. Powerless to escape, death gains on us, pushing us forward. Our ride sails through the gap in the break wall, over the hump, past the crushed building and down the main street of Curio.

With the force of a million Codans, the roaring avalanche pounds into the wall. I take one last glance behind. There, the statue of Mayor Raydon Osman, with his hand raised as though waving us farewell, stands defiant amongst the raining debris just as a massive boulder clears the wall and annihilates him.

Now that's irony. Thank you, Mayor Osman, at least for helping us.

A deafening roar reverberates throughout the deserted town as the avalanche breaches the break wall and ploughs through the park of petrified-stone people.

Like a rolling blanket of doom, the brown cloud gains upon us, pelting us with falling rocks and consuming the abandoned buildings as we pass.

Our sled, following the road's gradual decline, carries us with no sign of slowing.

With a rough bump, we leave the icy road and careen on a collision course with the lone house by the river.

Gritting my teeth, I grip the sled tighter and lean my weight to one side, attempting to correct our course.

The house draws nearer.

Just when we might collide, I throw my weight into the sled once more.

As though Mayor Osman willed it, we miss the edge of the house by metas, and veer away towards the frozen river, leaving Curio and the hungry brown cloud behind.

The instant our sled's wooden skis take to the icy surface, our ride smoothens, and we speed across it like a rocket.

Our ride slows to a stop at a bend in the river about a hundred metas from town. Shaken and dizzy from the thrill, I relish in the calm and take a moment to check on Sera.

'Did you see that?' I ask, slowly climbing off her.

Sera gives me a weak smile in response. Her face is paler, and beads of perspiration now pepper her brow.

'How are you doing?'

'Been better,' she replies through chattering teeth.

I reach for her bag, pull a shiny blanket from the medkit and wrap it around her. 'This is the best I can do.'

'Done good,' she says, touching my hand. 'Find any water?'

'No. But I did find this,' I say, holding up the small water bottle.

'That fine,' she says, and I can tell she's fighting to get the words out. 'Find fresh snow.'

'Will it be safe to drink?'

'Better than nothing.'

'Okay,' I concede, taking the bottle. Thankfully, rafts of fresh snow are piled up alongside the riverbank. I don't know how clean it is, but I collect up the whitest I can find to fill the bottle. Sera instructs me to lay the bottle between her feet where heat from the sun and the thermal material of her blanket can melt it.

Until now, dehydration has been the least of my worries. At least the stranger is no longer tailing us.

Behind, the town of Curio is no longer visible. It's what lies ahead that concerns me now. Even if I can get Sera home, the distance is still several days by foot. I doubt in her condition she'll make it alive. While I try not to think about it, I attempt to break into one of the cans of armoured food. Without a 'can opener,' it proves impossible, and I discard the excess weight on the ice. With such a long distance to traverse by nightfall, I stretch my weary limbs, and continue the cold, long walk down the windy river toward home, dragging the sled behind.

Judging by the angle of the sun, it's about noonday, and I stop once more to check on Sera. I try to give her some of the melted ice, but she refuses to drink, muttering something about me needing it more to get us home. Perhaps it's the fever-delirium talking. Whatever the reason, I'm too exhausted to argue. After that, she drifts in and out of consciousness, and as the cendecs go by, her condition noticeably deteriorates.

Night falls, the temperature drops; shivering, starving, and exhausted, every step drags as though gravity's increased. My vision plays tricks on me in the low light, and I see strange things in the shadows—monstrous things.

As I round another bend, the frozen river meanders ever on, passing beneath a shadowy cave that looks like a good place to stop. Sera's pulse is very weak now, her skin is icy, and I'm afraid she won't last the night.

In the darkness, it's hard to see the ground, but I sweep my foot around to clear a space to sleep. Our rations and water have run out. Without a knife, trapping equipment or my fire bracelet, the only thing I can do is lie on the ice. And without a groundsheet, the cold penetrates through my clothes, sapping precious heat from my body. After what feels like a cendec shivering, I hop into the sled and snuggle up beside Sera. Despite the exhaustion, sleep doesn't come easy.

Howling wind whips squalls of ice all around—whiting out my surroundings like an oppressive, claustrophobic veil. There are no trees here, no buildings, no structures of any kind, just white. A fleeting glance behind, and a dark shadow darts from the corner of my vision. I break into a run. A voice inside urges me to find a downward slope. If only I can make it there and get a good run up, maybe I can fly. It isn't far. Besides everything else still shrouded by the blizzard, the long, gradual slope is clear. The shadow creature stands behind me now, not even bothering to hide anymore. Its shapeless form snarls, baring sharp, dagger-like teeth, dripping with saliva. It's now or never. I take my position at the top of the hill and start running, gaining speed with every step. So too does the shadow creature behind. Faster now, I just need to go faster. With the shadow monster clawing at my heels, I reach full speed, hit the bottom of the hill, and leap with all my strength to propel myself into the air. Just metas from the ground, I soar like an ave while the shadow monster roars below...

Something in the distance rumbles, and it permeates my dream, startling me awake. As I open my eyes, beams of early morning light cut through the thick grey mist, giving colour to the world. The brighter light reveals the structure overhead is a bridge and not a cave. At least it provided shelter and cut out some of the icy cold wind.

Beside me, Sera remains asleep. Her breath is barely noticeable, and I watch for the gentle rise and fall of her chest to confirm she's still alive. It's subtle, but it's enough to relieve my anxiety for now.

Without trying to wake her, I drag my aching body out of the sled.

'I'll be right back, Sera,' I whisper, knowing she won't respond. 'Just going to check that out.' It takes every scrap of energy to clamber up the embankment to the road above.

The rumbling sound grows louder.

Unable to go any further, my legs give out, and I drop like a bag of sand to the ground.

Semi-conscious, I lie in the middle of the road waiting for the inevitable. At this point, it wouldn't matter if they are friend or enemy. With Sera so near to death and me unable to even stand in my present condition, I doubt things could get much worse.

Brakes squeal, and the approaching truck halts at the opposite end of the bridge. The vibration of its engine is almost soothing through the ground. Doors slam, and multiple sets of boots crunch across the compacted gravel toward me. One stops to lean over, revealing green and black military fatigues.

'Hi there,' a female voice says. Her face is so blurry I can't make out her features. 'Sir, it's a girl,' she yells to someone else.

A male voice replies, 'check under the bridge.'

A detachment jogs off down the slope. Moments later, a muffled voice calls out from beneath the bridge. 'Sir, there's a woman down here. She's injured pretty bad.'

'Bring her up,' the same man says, his voice getting louder as he comes closer. 'They could be the two we're searching for.'

He takes a knee, and with a softened tone, asks, 'girl, what's your name?'

I don't want to answer him, but something makes me speak. 'Jayne.'

'Who's the woman under the bridge, Jayne?'

Even if I wanted to answer him, my mouth won't form the words.

'Is she Seraphin MonLantry?' he asks.

Surprised to hear a stranger say her name, I nod in reply.

'Good. You two aren't easy to find,' he says, smiling. At least, I think he's smiling. 'I'm Captain Fenton. We're here to take you home.'

Fenton and his soldiers carry us to their truck. They set me down on one of the hard wooden benches while they slide Sera, lying unconscious on a stretcher, into the centre aisle.

I don't remember Captain Fenton and his soldiers hopping on board, or the truck moving away, but the next time I open my eyes, I'm covered in a blanket, and a largish, masculine woman sits beside me, holding up a bag of clear fluid. She fiddles with a tube coming out of the back of my hand.

In panic, I react to rip it out, but she gently grabs my hand and holds it firm.

'It's okay,' she says in a calm voice. 'It's just saline. You were badly dehydrated, so I had to give you this to help you feel better. Do you feel better?'

I blink a few times to clear my vision. That's when I notice the white cross patches on her uniform. 'Yes,' I mutter, but my attention drifts back to the stretcher.

'What about Sera? Will she be alright?'

The woman sighs. 'She's a different story. Is she your mother?'

'No.' I reply sullenly. 'She's my guardian.'

'Oh, well, your guardian is quite sick and is going to need a bit more care. You've done a fantastic job dressing her wounds, though. I only hope where we're going, they have what she needs.'

'Lieutenant Dagley,' Captain Fenton interjects, 'that's not for us to judge. Our orders are to find them and bring them home, that's all.'

'Sir, Hope is closer and has the best hospital facilities anywhere around. I can't understand why we shouldn't be taking them there?'

'I know, but those aren't our orders,' Fenton says in a no-argument tone. 'Just do what you can.'

'Yes, sir.'

'What's Hope?' I ask Fenton, after Dagley returns to tending to Sera.

He gives me a puzzled expression. 'You don't know?'

'No.'

'Then where have you been?'

'Camping.'

'I see. Well, Hope is a town just over that mountain range,' he says, pointing through the rectangular window at the rear. 'It's where we come from. And lucky for you we did. I'm not sure you and your guardian would have made it much further.'

'Are you the army?'

'No,' he chuckles, 'what gives you that impression?'

'Your uniforms and this truck.'

'Well, we're not the army. We're HomeGuard. We protect the people of Hope.'

'But we're not from Hope. Why are you helping us?'

'Because, my young friend, as I said to Dagley here, we have orders to take you to a place called Garret Gord. And we're following those orders.'

'But I've never been to Hope.'

'And I've never been to this Garret Gord. Strange, I thought nothing was out here. How is it that two lovely ladies like yourselves ended up getting this far away?'

I shrug. 'I don't know. We got caught in an avalanche.'

'My goodness. That must've been terrifying.'

'Yes, Sera got hurt and... is Hope a nice place?'

'Yes, it is,' the captain says, smiling warmly. I'm relieved he decided not to probe further. 'Maybe you can visit sometime.'

'I'd like that.'

He pats me on the shoulder in a show of support. With his military uniform, short greying hair and tough appearance, Captain Fenton may seem gruff, but he's doing what he can to help us. Despite his attempts to distract me, each time everything goes quiet, my attention drifts back to *her*.

'Seraphin's in excellent hands,' Fenton says, after watching me for a while. 'We'll take good care of her, I promise. You see, Dagley here, she's the best medical officer I know. I don't think Seraphin could be in better hands.'

'Aw shucks, Captain,' Dagley says, glancing up.

'Don't let it go to your head, Lieutenant,' he mocks, then turns to me. 'Now you, miss Jayne. Just sit back, relax and enjoy the ride. You let us take care of her.'

Relax? that's funny. In this cold, bone-shaker of a truck with Sera like that? *How can I possibly relax?*

'Say, you hungry? You look hungry,' the captain says, again pulling me from my despondency. From a box stowed beneath the seat, he passes me a green canvas bag and opens it so I can select from its contents.

'No, thanks. I'm not hungry,' I murmur.

'You sure? Because, if you don't want anything, mind if I do?'

I give him a confused nod and watch as he removes a pouch from the bag, bends it in the middle, and after a few decs the smell of hot stew wafts through the truck.

'You thought it was some dull protein bar, didn't you?' he says, with a smug grin. I glare at him in surprise.

'I'll let you in on a secret,' he says, pulling out a fork. 'In HomeGuard, we don't eat boring rations.' He's about to take a mouthful when my stomach rumbles, and I snatch the steaming pouch from his hands.

'Ohh, it's hot,' I say, burning my mouth on a forkful. They're the tastiest rations I've ever eaten.

He chuckles, 'yeah, be careful. But I'm glad you changed your mind. I'd already eaten.'

'Out of the truck,' a voice yells from outside.

I must've dozed off again.

This time, when I open my eyes, the truck's rear doors are open, and Captain Fenton is facing down ten soldiers wearing Garrett Gord browns, greys and whites, all with their rifles drawn.

'I said, out of the truck!' The lead guard bellows, motioning with his rifle.

'I heard you the first time,' Fenton shouts back. 'We have two wounded on board with orders to bring them here.'

The guard brushes off the captain's retort with an indignant poke of his weapon. 'Hands where we can see them.'

'Alright, alright,' the captain replies, complying with raised hands.

'Dagley,' I ask, still groggy from sleep. 'What's going on?'

'We've arrived. But it seems your guards aren't being too hospitable,' she says.

'Dagley,' Captain Fenton calls back, climbing out of the truck. 'Go with the stretcher and young Jayne to medical. Make sure they make it there.'

'Eye, sir,' Dagley says.

A guard pushes past Fenton and mounts the rear step to peer inside. Dagley is busy preparing Sera while I lie on the bench, watching with disbelief as the guards outside taunt Fenton and his team.

'Sir,' the man shouts to his superior after having seen us. 'They have MonLantry and the girl. They're wounded.'

Another guard steps forward, takes one look, but doesn't seem to notice or care who we are. 'Take them to medical,' he barks back, 'the rest of you, leave your weapons and get out of the truck.'

Two guards climb up, collect Sera on the stretcher and carry her away, while another steps forward for me.

Dagley stands and blocks their way. 'I'll take the girl,' she says, staring down the comparatively small armed guard with vehemence. 'If you intend for them both to live, I must go with them,' she protests.

The guard turns to his superior officer for confirmation.

'The medic can go,' he says in a stern tone, 'but the others stay here.'

'It would seem your guys aren't too keen on us being here,' Dagley says with a worried expression, placing the pouch of liquid in my lap.

'This is not how I was expecting our return home to go,' I reply.

'Don't worry,' she says, scooping me up into her arms and carrying me from the truck. 'You and Seraphin are home now. Captain and the others can take care of themselves. I'm sure this is just some kind of misunderstanding.'

We follow the stretcher holding Sera to medical, and I peer over Dagley's shoulder at Fenton to give him a wave.

He gives a nervous wave in return before the guards line him and his team up alongside the truck.

I've never seen a HomeGuard truck before. Except for its colours and the lettering *HG-CA20* painted in white on its doors, it's very similar to the others at the Gord.

It's the last thing I see before we disappear inside.

13 – Aftermath

'Aside from mild dehydration, the girl's completely fine,' says a woman's voice from behind a privacy curtain.

'We needed to monitor her condition closely,' says another, and I recognise this voice as Dagley's. 'That's why I suggested keeping her overnight.'

'Thank you, Lieutenant Dagley,' the first replies. 'Is that what you said your name was? But you'll soon learn here, these girls, they're trained to be tough. Take Seraphin, for example. I've patched her up and sent her on her way more times than I can recall.'

'So, this is common, then?'

'Oh my, yes.'

'Sounds like the HomeGuard cadets,' Dagley chuckles.

The other doctor continues with a more serious tone, and I strain to hear what she's saying. 'Seraphin's more of a concern. She's stable for now, but the stick punctured her spleen, and she had gone into septic shock.'

'I noticed that, too. That's why I administered *Deplacillin*. Isn't she responding?'

'Not as well as I would have hoped. She requires surgery again.'

'In that case, I'd like to assist if you can use my help.'

'Thank you, Lieutenant. I'll consider it.'

'I assure you, I'm a skilled surgeon with five cycles experience working in field hospitals patching up cases just like this.'

'I'll bring it up with the Patriarch. In the meantime, please check on Jayne. She should be just about ready for discharge.'

'As you wish, Doctor. Oh, and speaking of young Jayne, I commend her field first-aid skills. If it weren't for her, I doubt Seraphin would have made it. May I ask who instructed her?'

'Why Seraphin did, of course.'

'Of course, she did.'

The curtain sweeps open, and the two doctors peek their heads into my private little area.

Since being brought in the day before, they've confined me to this bed. Occasionally, Dagley and the other doctor, a blonde-haired woman about the same age as Sera, come to check on me, holding conversations like these by my bedside when they think I'm not listening.

When Sera's not being taken away for treatment, she remains unconscious in the bed beside me, but they keep the curtains drawn so I can't see. Every time I ask about her, they give me vague answers like; 'she'll be fine' and 'don't worry, Seraphin's a fighter.'

The longer I stay here, the more I learn about her condition. It does nothing for my anxiety.

'Mornin',' Dagley says, giving me her usual warm smile. Despite that, she's still wearing her HomeGuard uniform. From the dark circles around her eyes, it doesn't look like she's slept. 'And how's patient Jayne doing this day?'

'Okay,' I reply, trying to sound less well than I am.

'Well, I hope so,' she says, removing the needle from the back of my hand. 'We need to make room for other patients.'

I glance around the room in confusion.

What other patients? Aside from Sera and myself, the entire medical wing is empty.

'But can't I stay here with Sera?'

'Afraid not,' the other doctor says. 'She needs more time. You, on the other hand, don't. You're well enough to go.'

'Doctor Davi and I will take good care of her. I promise,' Dagley adds.

'But that means... I've never been home alone before.' Just thinking about that churns my stomach.

Dagley places a comforting hand on my shoulder. 'You're a brave girl. I'm sure you can handle yourself for a little while.'

I'm not convinced. 'When will she be coming home?'

'She needs to stay here for a few days more,' Doctor Davi says, sitting on the edge of the bed. 'But you can come and visit her whenever you want. How about that?'

Glancing between the two doctors, I know they mean well, but the prospect of living in that empty apartment without Sera even for just a few days is terrifying. Sera taught me to be strong, but I've never had to do anything on my own before.

'Okay,' I concede.

'Where is that fraken woman?' a man's voice booms from outside the room and the two doctors visibly stiffen.

'Who's that?' Dagley whispers to Davi.

'The Patriarch,' Davi replies, standing and rushing to greet a wiry, white-haired old man. Although I'd never met him before, from this man's appearance, dressed all in white, it confirms he is indeed the Patriarch.

'Who's this girl?' he stabs a pointed finger in my direction.

'That's Jayne, sir,' Davi replies. 'Seraphin MonLantry's daughter.'

'And MonLantry? Where is she?' he barks.

'Being prepped for surgery again, sir.'

'Surgery? Again? Whatever for?'

'Complications from a ruptured spleen. If all goes well, we should have her right in a few days.'

The old man grumbles something under his breath and changes the subject. 'And who's that?' he asks, noticing Dagley.

'Lieutenant Dagley, sir. The HomeGuard medic who brought them in. She—'

'Enough,' he snarls. 'Just advise me the instant she awakens. I must have words.' He then turns on his heel and strides away.

'He's a basket of sunshine, isn't he?' Dagley says with a sour expression.

Doctor Davi finally takes a breath. 'That's the Patriarch for you.'

'That's Elihus Kinton,' Dagley says. 'Wait a dec. *Elihus Kinton* is the Patriarch?'

'Yes, you know him?'

'Doesn't everybody?'

It's strange being in our apartment alone. Sera is usually busy in the kitchen cooking up something scrumptious or helping with my studies, but without her, it feels cavernous and vacant.

After a long hot shower, my appetite returns. At least Sera taught me a few simple recipes, and I manage to prepare a half-decent meal of chopped up vegetables and meat scavenged from the icebox.

As I sit on the couch to eat, in the silence, thoughts whirl like leaves caught in a storm —

Why was Sera in Hope?

Why were we being chased by a strangely armoured man?

Who called Fenton, and why did he rescue us?

So many questions.

I turn on the visiontube to find something watchable in the hope it will drown out the thoughts.

The moving pictures act as somewhat of a distraction, but my vagrant mind, being the incorrigible nuisance it is, keeps replaying the memory of Sera lying with that stick in her side. In frustration, I flick the VT off, set my empty plate aside and opt for some fresh air instead.

Outside the apartment, the hallway is dark and empty as usual, lit only by minimalistic overhead strip-lights that allow you to see where you're going and not much more. Loitering towards the stairs, another apartment door opens, and a crack of light crosses my path. From within, the face of a girl of similar age framed by long dark hair peeks out through the gap. Something about those sorrowfully shy, pale blue eyes makes me hesitate.

I'm about to say hello when a voice from inside the apartment bellows, 'close the door, you useless wretch!'

The girl's gaze drops with despondence, then she slowly turns and closes the door.

That poor girl.

Ascending the three flights of stairs to the surface, the pale-eyed girl behind the door replaces all other thoughts.

Who was that?

Why haven't I met any other girls before?

Maybe there are others, and will I meet her again?

So many more questions.

Absently, I press down on the lengthy handle of the heavy metal door. Its rubber seal squeaks, and its massive hinges groan as it swings outward, revealing bright daylight and a slight, cool breeze.

The warmth of the afternoon sun turns on and off as small fluffy grey and white clouds drift across the skyline. With the sun behind setting the stage for a shadow puppet show, they morph into unique shapes; a tomadai turns into a dragon that eats a mountain with a tree on it.

Outside, a few people, mostly guards clad in their brown, grey and white uniforms, scurry here and there. As I round a corner heading towards the occupied truck bays, an extra truck sits on the compacted ground where a few more people wearing grubby overalls busily prepare paint cans and stencils.

'Heya,' I say to one of them as I approach to see what they're doing.

He glances up in my direction, and with a disinterested flick of his head, continues what he's doing.

'Whatcha doin'?' I ask.

'Work. What does it look like?' he grumbles. 'Now rack off.'

It could just be any truck he's painting, but the faint lettering of *HG-CA20* on its side says it's not.

That's Captain Fenton's truck.

'Where's Captain Fenton?' I ask the man.

'Who's Captain Fenton,' he replies in a not too polite manner.

'Isn't that his truck?'

'I said rack off!' the man barks, stamping his foot as though shooing off a pest. I poke my tongue out at him before hurrying back to the apartment.

For some reason, they've commandeered Captain Fenton's truck, and he's nowhere to be seen. The thought fills me with dread as I wonder what's become of him.

Between that and Sera still in medical, all of a sudden, the world feels very small.

Over the next several days, I spend as much time in medical as Doctor Davi will allow, watching over Sera. She lies unconscious in the bed connected to beeping and bleeping monitors and medical equipment by an assortment of coloured wires and tubes. In this state, she looks so serene yet so frail it makes me nervous just seeing her like that.

Occasionally, Dagley brings me food and tells funny stories while she keeps me company.

When I'm not sitting sentry by Sera's bed, I'm lounging on the couch at home, watching mindless shows on the visiontube to pass the time.

One night, the sound of something sliding into the mail chute wakens me, and in my sleep inertia state, I lumber over to the front door to see what it is. A small card in the mailbox reads:

Jayne Doe, report to medical. End.

Without hesitation, I rush out the door.

Buzzing fluorescent lighting illuminates the path I'd taken many times, past the main office, through the unused sections of the medical wing. The dim lighting provides just enough of a glow to create silhouettes of the beds and equipment occupying the gloomy rooms. At the far end of the ward is the sterile white-walled room where Sera is being kept; a single point of light surrounded by undressed beds divided by drawn-back green curtains.

Only Doctor Davi, wearing her usual white coat and holding a metal clipboard greets me.

'Hi, doctor. Where's Dagley?' I ask.

The doctor gives me a peculiar look. 'Dagley? Who's that?' she replies, with an awkward expression.

'You know, Doctor Dagley? Is she around?'

'I'm sorry,' the doctor says. 'I don't know anyone by that name. But Seraphin's awake if you... '

'Sera!' I exclaim, momentarily pushing aside my concern for Dagley. That can wait. Darting into the room, I almost jump on top of Sera in excitement.

Propped up, her head rests on one of the many pillows surrounding her. 'Oh, careful there,' she says with a weak smile, her eyes following my movements. 'You don't want to put me back in surgery, do you?'

'Sorry. I'm just relieved to see you awake. You're looking better. You have more colour in your face since the last time I saw you,' I say, a little disappointed to see she's still not well.

Sera places a weakened hand on mine. 'I heard you saved me,' she says with pride.

I give an uneasy nod.

'You came just in time,' Doctor Davi says. 'I was about to talk to Seraphin about her condition. You may as well listen in too.'

'Okay,' I reply, sitting on the edge of the bed.

Davi continues, talking to Sera. 'Your injuries were quite extensive. Thanks to young Jayne here, we were able to stave off the worst of it. We've cleaned and patched up the penetration wound in your side. But you were extremely lucky. After the stick ruptured your spleen, you went into septic shock. We've put you on a strong course of antibiotics to treat the infection and will need to keep you in for a few more days to monitor your progress, but so far, you're doing well.'

'And the leg?' I ask.

The doctor pales a little, and replies in a more sombre tone. 'I took a photo-scan. You have a compound fracture to the left tibia and a shattered patella. I've done what I can to stabilise and repair the damage to the ligaments, but I'm afraid you will require a complete knee reconstruction.

Even then, it may not fully heal. Seraphin, you will need rehabilitation and the use of a cane for the foreseeable future. I'm afraid you may never be as active again, so Jayne, you're going to be caring for her for a little while until she's back on her feet.'

'I am sorry, Jayne,' Sera says, with disappointment written all over her face. 'It appears that may be the end of our camping trips.'

My heart sinks, and my eyes well up. I turn away to wipe the tears, grit my teeth and try to not let her see how upset I am. 'I'm sure we'll be getting chased by boarts and raiders again... '

'It is okay, Jayne. I think you have proven yourself to be an avid survivalist. There is little more I can teach you.'

'But I enjoy going camping with you,' I protest.

'With your training about to begin, I am afraid there will not be much time for that. I can still help you with your studies, but we will be unable to go out for lengthy trips like we used to.'

Nodding, I clench my jaw to will the tears away.

'That's all I have for now,' the doctor concludes. 'I'll leave you two alone. Seraphin can call me if she needs. But don't be too long. She needs her rest.'

The doctor resets the clipboard on the end of the bed, leaving us in our little corner of the medical wing.

Sera pats the bed. 'Would you like to join me?'

That puts a grin on my face, and I climb up to nestle between her and the railing.

She smells of disinfectant wash, but her hug is warm and comforting, and I'm content to have her back.

'I am so unbelievably proud of you, Jayne,' she says, stroking my hair with affection. 'You really saved my life.'

'There's no way I was going to just leave you there,' I reply, contemplating my next question. 'Sera? What were you doing in Hope?'

She stops caressing my hair, and tilts her head down. 'Where did you get that I was in Hope?'

'Captain Fenton told me.'

'Who's Captain Fenton?'

'He and his team are the ones who rescued us. I wanted to introduce you to Doctor Dagley, but I can't find her. Or Captain Fenton. They both wish you well, by the way.'

'Rescued? Jayne, what have I told you about trusting strangers?'

'It wasn't so much about trust, Sera. I didn't have a choice. Besides, someone sent them to find us and bring us back here.'

'Here? As in Garret Gord? Is that what they told you?'

'Yes. Sera, I didn't tell them anything, I promise. They were already looking for us. I didn't even need to show them the way. We could have gone to Hope, but the captain insisted he had orders. We were in trouble, and I only did it to save you. There wasn't any other way. Did I do something wrong?'

'Hmm,' she sighs, and I sense her relax. 'No, Jayne, you did well. But the mission is key, remember that.'

'I don't understand.'

'You have grown up so fast, Jayne. Soon you will understand.' She hugs me as firm as her body will allow and kisses me on the forehead. 'I love you, Jayne. I hope you know that. You may not be my own flesh and blood, but you are everything I could have ever hoped for in a daughter.'

'Thank you, Sera.'

We lie in silence for a while, enjoying each other's company until she squeezes me again. 'So, are you going to tell me about the miraculous rescue, or am I going to make up that story myself?'

'I thought the doctor said you needed to rest?'

'Blah! Some rules are meant to be broken,' she smiles.

'Well, after the sled in Curio—'

'Seraphin MonLantry!' the Patriarch's voice echoes from the hallway outside.

Sera stiffens. 'I think you better get up,' she says, as he barges into the room.

'You again!' he growls at me, and I slide from the bed. 'Get out of here!'

'Jayne,' Sera whispers, 'it's ok. Go.'

Excerpt from Burn the Sky part 2 Chapter 1

Four long days had passed, and the town was still coming to terms with the tumultuous events surrounding the election, particularly Gaius's unexpected death. Despite their mood, the townspeople flocked to the steps of the town hall to witness the swearing-in of their new Surprime.

'And I give you Sage Solon, first Virtuous Surprime of Hope,' Orian announced, concluding her introductory speech and gesturing to the nervous-looking, sandy-haired man waiting at her side.

Sage adjusted the large lapels on his stately, long-flowing, deep-red robes. As he did, he glanced with affection at the beaming woman in the front row clutching their three-day-old daughter, then turned and kneeled before Orian, allowing her to drape a large golden chain of pressed metal discs over his shoulders.

Engraved in cursive script on the first disc was Sage's name, marking him as the position's official holder. The central amulet featured an image of cupped hands forming wings supporting the likeness of the new town hall, behind which emblazoned rays of a sunshine crest, depicting the emergence of Hope into a new dawn. Beneath that, a waving five-part ribbon read:

Hagalaz Othila ᚺᛉᛟᛖᛗ Peorth Ehwaz

In the old-tongue, it meant Rebirth, Heritage, Life, Traveller; four words that best represented Hope and its history.

Complete with political jewellery, he stepped up to the podium, looking the very picture of nobility, and he hated it.

He cleared his throat and prepared to recite his practised speech, pausing momentarily for the audience's subdued applause.

'Family, friends, good people of Hope,' he said with a painted smile, taking care to avoid a recurrence of his last disastrous speech but also conscious of the conditions under which he stood there. 'I am both honoured and saddened to accept the position of Virtuous Surprime. This, as you know, is a bittersweet day. Gaius should be the first name on this chain, not mine. He should be the one standing here, and it breaks my heart every time I think of why he isn't.' Sage allowed a wave of grief to wash over him, looking out at the gathered crowd to see he wasn't the only one stifling back tears. He gritted his teeth and continued. 'If you will allow me, before I begin with the formalities, I'd like to first say a few words in honour of Gaius.'

The crowd stilled while Sage extracted a piece of paper from inside his robes and placed it on the podium, smoothing it down with the palms of his hands. 'I think you all know my track record with speeches,' he said light-heartedly, hoping it would relieve some of the awkwardness. 'So, this time, I've asked Orian to help me. I think it's pretty well right.' He cleared his throat again and took a deep breath. 'Gaius was a great man,' he said, the words formed even without the aid of his notes. 'Hope would not be here without him. I look around at all of you gathered here today, and I can't see a single person whose life Gaius hasn't touched and made the better for it.

When I came to Hope in 02, I, like most of you, was a lost and desperate refugee, hungry, sick and in need of warm shelter. Gaius and Rika took me in, cared for me and gave me food and a home. They didn't care or even ask where I came from, they just accepted me as a person who needed their help. Because that's what they did. Gaius was more than a friend or mentor to me; he was like a father. He saw something in me I couldn't see in myself, and ever since, he had only ever striven to make me a better version of myself.

'He had a vision for Hope, too,' Sage continued. 'Both Rika and Gaius dreamed of making this place a town. A place where people could come and forget the world they've left behind and focus on something better. He always said, "what's passed is past. Everything happens for a reason," and while we may want to shut away from the horrific events of the past, they don't define us. Instead, like Gaius, they shape us and encourage us to learn, grow, move forward and become better versions of ourselves. I only wish to carry on this legacy so that I may not only provide a better place for my beautiful wife and new baby daughter, but for us all. It saddens me Gaius could not have been here to meet her. So, it is with that, I pledge to you, as Virtuous Surprime, I will make Hope a better version of itself. I will vow to carry on Gaius and Rika's vision and see their dream for Hope realised.' Sage wiped away the tears under each eye, and while he hesitated, it appeared there wasn't a dry eye in the crowd. The gathering gave him a delayed cheer, and it lightened his heart to know that even in their grief, he had given them something to cheer about.

As the cheers faded, Sage spoke again. 'Gentle people of Hope. In my first act as Surprime, I will dissolve the Council... '

And the applause melted into gasps and exchanges of confused glances.

'But,' he continued, raising his palms to the gathering to reassure them, 'in its place, I will establish a ministry of representatives who will help me govern the new Hope. Each one dedicated to seeing a part of that vision made real. Allow me to introduce your new Hope Peoples' Ministry.' Sage directed his arm toward the line-up of people standing in the wings, each stepping forward when he announced them.

'Treasurer, Abril Tope.

Minister for Defence, Artimus Wyrm.

Minister for Education, Elihus Kinton.

Minister for Property and Development, Indira Tryce.

Minister for Science and Research, Garan Tope.

Minister for Health, Alessandra MonBrelstaff.

Minister for Food and Resources, Niklas Martell.

And of course, our Speaker and Vice-Surprime, the wonderful, Ms Orian Gracyn.'

They all wore new, tailored robes similar to Sage but in black, with Orian, whose position was only lesser to Sage's, wore blue.

When the applause died down, Sage concluded his speech. 'I know that in the coming cycles, my ministry, your ministry, will do you all proud. It is all Gaius and Rika would have hoped for. That's why we call our home, Hope.'

The crowd erupted in glorious ovation, which continued as Sage said his thankyous and shook the hands of his ministry. While they dispersed, Sage descended the steps to join his young family at the foot, where those who remained flocked around him to shake his hand in congratulations.

When the last person had pressed their hand into Sage's, Jaylyn leaned in closer to whisper in his ear. 'When do I get to congratulate the Surprime?'

'Better make it later. My wife might see us,' he joked.

'Your speech was beautiful, my love,' she said, kissing him with affection on the cheek. She adjusted the cloth-wrapped bundle nestled in a sling against her chest. 'And I must say, those robes are really sexy on you.'

'What, these old rags,' he laughed, plucking at them. 'You really think so?'

'Seriously, I think Gaius would be proud,' she said, her eyes glistening with pride. 'Are you okay, though?'

'What do you mean?'

'Well, you know, after everything that's happened over the last few days, you look five cycles older... '

Sage choked out a chuckle. 'Thanks, and you're supposed to be on my side.'

'I'm proud of you, Sage Solon, first Virtuous Surprime of Hope.'

'Don't speak too soon. I've not done anything yet.' Sage smiled, trying not to let her comment trigger him. 'Thank you, my babe.' He kissed her on the lips, then gave his tiny daughter a kiss on the forehead. 'It's just a shame she missed him by a day. I was really looking forward to Gaius becoming a "grandfather".'

'Ohh!' Abril's familiar shrill voice came from behind as she made her way towards Sage and his family, her eyes beaming at the tiny bundle cradled around Jaylyn's body. 'I'd heard she'd come but hadn't had a chance to meet our newest resident yet.'

Jaylyn pulled the side of the sling over, exposing the fine, fuzzy blonde-hair of her daughter, and with the affection only a proud mother could give, smiled at Abril.

'The first child of the Surprime. She's adorable,' Abril said.

'With all the excitement, she's asleep at the moment. I think she just wanted to see her daddy get sworn in,' Jaylyn said.

Abril touched the bundle supported in the wrap, 'what's her name?'

'Averyx,' Sage replied. 'After my mother.'

'Averyx Solon, that's a beautiful name,' Abril said, smiling at the baby's adoring parents. She then looked down and crooned at the sleepy bundle, 'Hi there, Averyx. Aren't you a little cutie?'

'If you will excuse me,' Sage said, finding a moment to take his leave, 'there's something I have to do.' He kissed his wife again. 'It begins,' he said with a resigned look. 'Love you. I'll see you tonight.'

'You've got a good one there,' Sage over-heard Abril say, as he strode away. 'I always believed he would make a great father... '

Following the ceremony, Sage retreated to the quiet of the cemetery to visit Gaius's final resting place. Jaxson, dressed in a new black and red-piped formal uniform of the Surprime Guard, went with him, and together, they stood side by side at the large headstone. Engraved into the polished stone, emblazoned in gold were the words:

Here lies Gaius Sempro, husband to Rika, father of Hope.
May he forever find peace.
AP1894 – NC05

'I can only hope to do as well as you would have,' Sage said, wiping a tear from his eye. Beside him, Jaxson stifled back tears of his own.

'I failed him,' Jaxson despaired with a sullen expression.

'No, you didn't,' Sage said. 'You couldn't have known this was going to happen. None of us did.'

'Yes, but it was my job to protect him. I've never lost a charge under my watch, even the ones I didn't respect. But Gaius, he was more than just a charge to me. And I let him get killed.'

Sage patted his closest friend on the back. 'This is not your fault, Jaxson. Don't make it so.'

'Thanks, man,' Jaxson said as Sage pulled him into a manly embrace.

Footsteps crunched over the ground behind them, startling the two men. Jaxson unclipped his pistol and drew it as they separated and spun around.

'Gentlemen,' Orian said, holding her palms out by her sides and approaching with caution. 'It's just me.'

Sage relaxed, and Jaxson re-holstered his weapon, both trying to conceal what they had been doing.

'Apologies for the intrusion,' she said, moving closer to stand before Gaius's grave. 'I didn't mean to startle you.'

'It's fine, Orian,' Sage replied. 'We were just paying our respects.'

She smiled an affectionate, melancholy smile. 'That was a beautiful speech, by the way. Gaius would be proud.'

Sage bowed his head. 'Are you sure about that? You wrote it.'

'But it came from you. I just crafted it into something... intelligible.'

'Ha!' he laughed. 'I can just imagine my tombstone; "Here lies Sage Solon. He had a way with words..."!'

'Do you know how many speeches I've written for others over the cycles?'

He considered that for a moment.

Orian continued. 'It was just part of the job. But out of them all, yours would have to have been the most sincere.'

Sage sighed, his sadness and doubt returning. 'What am I doing, Orian? I'm not made for this.'

'Don't be silly,' she said, rubbing him on the arm. 'You seem to be doing just fine.'

'I've got my hands pretty full right now. Besides, I never asked for this. When I put my name forward, I only did it because *he* wanted me to.' Sage flicked a hand at Gaius's grave. 'Probably so he didn't have to, *the coward.*'

'I remember an impetuous young man who, only a few cycles ago, risked his own life to save a burgeoning village. While we sheltered in safety, this man braved a military attack and single-handedly negotiated a deal that saved all our lives. If there are two things I've learned over the cycles, first, you never get to choose the manner in which life decides to challenge you. Second, great people often do not seek out power. Circumstances push them into it.'

'*Great*? No, I don't think so. That was him.'

'I beg to differ,' she said. 'I've seen how you've risen to these recent challenges. How you've handled the investigation, the devotion you have shown to your family, and how you've balanced that with your new responsibilities as Surprime. Sage, you may not think you can ever measure up to Gaius, but you don't have to. We can't all be like him, and if you think that's what he wanted, you've completely missed the point. He wanted you to be a better version of yourself, not him. And from where I'm standing, you've done just that.'

To Sage, her words carried much wisdom and foresight, resonating something within him he knew to be true.

'She's right, brother,' Jaxson said. 'If it weren't for you, my brains would have been splattered all over the pavement. I can't think of a better person to lead us than you.'

'Thanks, man,' Sage said, slapping him on the back. All this emotional talk made him feel uncomfortable. He gazed at his feet with embarrassment, scuffing the ground with a shoe, contemplating what they had said. Eventually, he lifted his head to the cool afternoon breeze. 'You're right,' he said. 'You both are. And I'm grateful. Thank you.'

Orian smiled and gave a slight nod, while Jaxson seemed to be beaming with newfound energy. Sage felt a weight had been lifted, although, in his heart, he knew there was still a long way to go. But with these two at his side, no doubt he would be able to face whatever challenges came his way.

'Say Orian,' he said, as a thought came to him, 'if you don't mind me asking, what happened between you two?'

'Ah, you mean between Gaius and I? You really want to know?'
Sage nodded.

She sighed. 'Whatever happened to "what's passed is past"?'

'I'm sorry, you're right. It was improper for me to ask.'

'No, it's okay. It's probably time it was told, anyway. I did say I might tell you about it one of these days.' She gathered her thoughts. 'Well, we were seventeen when we met at our school graduation party. Within twenty decs of having met him, he proposed, which I thought was a bit presumptuous and odd, but I liked that. We became friends, after all, he seemed nice, was kind and handsome. After a few treys, he offered me his spare room, and I moved in. Not long after, he enlisted with the military, and after six cycles of only seeing him for short bursts here and there, I realised I was in love with him. So, I eventually accepted his proposal, and we married soon after.' Sage could tell from her wavering voice recalling this story was difficult. Wiping away a stray tear, she swallowed and continued. 'It was AP1943. Gaius was a colonel in the Aurora Liberation Army.'

'A colonel?' Sage said with surprise. 'No kidding.'

'Yes, and I was Parliamentary Speaker for the Skoyca provincial government when they called him to serve in a covert operation. I didn't know much of the details, but whatever happened, his entire squad were killed. It's a miracle he survived. His injuries were so severe, they didn't think he would make it. When I got the call, my world; the world we had built together, just imploded. We wrote to each other until his letters stopped coming and mine returned. A few days later, there was a knock at the door. They told me he'd died from complications. It devastated me. I didn't know what to do. I stayed in our house for a few treys after that. When it was clear he wasn't coming back, I left town to go live with my sister. That's when the bombs dropped and the rest's history.'

'I'm so sorry, Orian, I didn't know. Gaius never talked about this.'

'Well, so now you do.'

He allowed Orian's story to process for a moment. 'That does explain a lot,' he said.

She turned to face Sage, admiring him in his formal robes. 'He was very proud of you, you know, and would be thrilled to see you as Surprime.'

Sage smiled an awkward smile. 'Thank you, Orian. And thanks, old man,' he said, glancing at the headstone.

'Anyway, I came to find you. Artimus says the Hunter has returned.'

Shawline Publishing Group Pty Ltd
www.shawlinepublishing.com.au

SHAWLINE
PUBLISHING
GROUP

CPSIA information can be obtained
at www.ICGtesting.com
Printed in the USA
LVHW040327070721
691973LV00008B/661